A HOLE IN THE UNIVERSE

J.H WEAR

ISBN: 978-1-68046-905-9

Melange Books, LLC
White Bear Lake, MN 55110
www.melange-books.com

Cover Design by Ashley Redbird Designs

I remember watching the original TV series, Star Trek. It was great science fiction and many of the features on the show have since become reality, such as voice commands for a computer and teleportation (just particles as of today). The warp drive, and the ability to travel faster than light, has eluded us thus far.

One of the reasons many of us love Star Trek was the inspiration that humans are destined to someday reach the stars and come into contact with other sentient beings. It is the belief that all things are possible. It is what drives humans to explore and invent, and to study and experiment.

Thus, I dedicate this book to everyone who believes people will reach for the stars and succeed.

I want to give a special thanks to my cousin Doug, and to my neighbour, Rhonda, for their help in finding errors in the manuscript. If there are any remaining mistakes in A Hole In The Universe, that is entirely on myself.

[PART 1]

Jaret McLeod slowly achieved awareness from a deep slumber. He took in a deep breath, smelling the sharp tang of the antiseptic air. His eyes fluttered open. Blackness. He tried to blink. The dark remained as he attempted to lift his hands to his face. His wrists were halted in their movement by straps. He gave a short grunt of panic.

A warm hand rested on the back of his own.

"It's okay. You just woke up. You're in the infirmary."

He turned his head to the familiar voice of the ship's engine mechanic. "Tia, what happened? I can't see."

"Your eyes are bandaged. The doctor said you'll be able to see again after they're removed." She paused, letting him absorb the information. "There was an accident on the Gladiator. What do you remember?"

His brain began the process of recalling the horrifying event. The Gladiator was a mining ship, one of the many bare-bones ships used to mine the asteroids. It held a crew of seven in cramped quarters to pull pieces of blasted rock off an asteroid by high tension cables. From there, the rock was taken to the processing space station. The method involved pivoting the rock using cables and releasing it on course to the space station, where the rock would be broken into ore. The Gladiator was pulling a larger than average sized rock when a cable snapped, knocking their ship off course. Proximity alarms suddenly rang out, indicating a collision was imminent.

"Helmets!" a frantic voice shouted. Spacesuits were always worn inside the mining ships, but helmets were left off, kept within an arm's length in case of an emergency. The quick magnetic seal meant the helmet could be fully secured in seconds.

McLeod reached for his helmet. There was a thump on the side of the ship's hull. He frantically put on his helmet, just as white light and heat reached him. There was a searing pain on his face. He cried out as he was slammed into the wall behind him. Then nothing.

"I remember an explosion."

"Good, that means your memory is okay. You've been out for two days. You had a mild concussion, a cracked rib and some scarring on your face. Your helmet shield was shattered from an impact of shrapnel. Fortunately, Jeff managed to slap a patch on the ship's hull and kept air integrity."

McLeod took in the information. If his face shield had shattered, he would have died from the sudden vacuum if the spaceship's hull wasn't secured. "That was close."

"Very close."

"My face is itchy."

"That's why your hands are tied down. You have a burned face from the explosion, and you would be scratching at it."

"Oh." He licked his lips. "How about you? And the others. Anyone else hurt?"

"Eric died. Everyone else is okay."

"Jesus." He remembered where Eric was sitting in front of his console, right where the rock slammed into the ship that caused the explosion. "Poor guy. He was here only a few months."

"They'll be an inquiry, of course. Can I get you anything?"

"Scratch my face." He tried to grin, but the pain turned it into a grimace.

"You need to get some rest. I'll check on you later."

He heard her footsteps fade away and he fell asleep.

"Jaret, can you hear me?"

McLeod responded to the male voice dimly aware the question had been repeated several times previously. "Yeah, I can hear you."

"I'm Dr. Asher Burkhart. Do you understand you are in the infirmary because of an accident on board the spaceship Gladiator?"

"Yes."

"Good. You're lucky not to have suffered worse injuries. You had a concussion, so we kept you sedated while applying neuron repair drugs. However, you should now begin to feel more awake as the drugs wear off. You have a cracked rib, and that is healing nicely."

"My eyes and my face?"

"No worries about your eyes. We had to do a minor procedure on each eye, but you should have normal vision. The bandages are a precaution to help healing. I'm going to remove the bandages, but you'll need to wear dark glasses for another seventy-two hours. Your face suffered some burning, and you'll end up with a scar on your left side that will require cosmetic surgery to remove. Unfortunately, we don't do that type of work here. On a more positive note, there won't be any permanent damage to the rest of the skin."

"I can live with the scar. Thanks doc."

He felt a hand on his shoulder.

"You're one tough miner to have survived as well as you did."

———

A nurse helped McLeod out of the hospital bed and dress. He felt it was strange he needed help with his first few steps out of his room. He placed a hand on the shoulder of a medium height blonde until his legs found their strength and balance.

"Take your time. You haven't been out of bed for a week. The muscle memory will return soon enough."

McLeod, tall and used to physical work, felt embarrassed at depending on the nurse to stop himself from falling. He felt odd wearing the dark eyeglasses, not used to the reduced vision or how the frames sat on his ears. He took his hand off her shoulder and began to walk on his own, waving goodbye to the nurses at the medical station

He made his way across the laminated floor to the bank of elevators and waited for one of the four elevators to arrive. The medical station was located on the sixth level of the thirty-eight-level space station. The elevator doors opened, revealing a large car capable of holding twenty personnel at a time. The ceiling in the car was high for the occasions when it had to double as a freight elevator. He stepped in the nearly empty car, deciding to go to his room to wash up. Compared to the clean environment of the medical station, the elevator smelled of humanity.

The living quarters were located on the twenty-eighth and twenty-ninth floors. As the car travelled on its journey, more people stepped inside at stops on various levels. McLeod grimaced as he was jostled slightly in the elevator. His rib protested any movement and soon the car was full of workers leaving for the sleeping quarters from the decks below.

McLeod exited, walking down a narrow hallway with several other workers. He used his thumb to open the sliding door and stepped inside the efficient two room apartment. The bed folded up into the wall to provide space for a desk, two chairs and a combination of a sink, fridge, micro-oven and table. The other room contained a toilet and a shower.

He had hoped the shower would have a more positive effect. The shower head sent pulses of mist that, according to design engineers, was as effective as a regular shower. Users of the shower didn't believe their theory. After a few frustrating minutes of getting damp, McLeod dressed. He heated a plastic tube of high protein dinner, adding pepper to the paste. He slowly ate, trying to detect the flavour of beef, and washed it down with sugar and mineral enhanced water. McLeod looked around his room. *I'm not going to relax in here with these walls so damn close. I think I'll head to the cafeteria. At least it'll have lots of room.*

He went back to the elevator and hoped it wouldn't be too crowded. It was.

Fifteen decks later, the elevator doors opened to the noisy floor of a hundred voices. Most of the workers spoke English, or a variant of it. There was also a mixture of other languages and dialects competing to be heard. Still, English was the official language of space, and anyone wanting to work in space was required to have at least a conversational level in it.

The smell of bodies, machine oil and ions didn't bother him, having been used to it during his time spent on the space station. Still he longed for fresh, mountain air, or even the dry air of Mars. He sighed, bored that he didn't have anything to do, and no place of interest to go. He picked up a coffee and a pastry from a conveyor food belt and sat alone at a table, feeling frustrated. He knew the other crew members from the Gladiator were likely on other ships working. Tia Dermott, the engine mechanic on the Gladiator was working in the maintenance shop, helping to service the various mining ships that came in. He thought the petite woman was one of the best mechanics among the mining ships, although her skills were not yet fully appreciated by conservative mining corporations.

"Hey, Jaret. Are you in disguise or something?"

McLeod looked up at the lanky man, recognizing the navigator.

"Hey, Chuck. How's it going?"

"Same old grind." He sat at the table. "What's with the eyewear?"

"Doctor's orders. My eyes suffered some temporary damage from the explosion on the Gladiator."

"Shit, yeah, I heard about that. Bad stuff. I heard that one of the crew died. When do you get back on a ship?"

"Not soon enough. I've got to pass medical first." He used a finger to point at his eyes. "I also have a rib injury."

"I hope you get back in the saddle again soon." Chuck stood. "Now I better get my ass moving before my crew leaves without me."

A few days later, his routine of doing nothing produced a feeling of increasing frustration. He attended the service in the station's chapel for Eric Spencer, spending a few minutes talking to the former crew of the Gladiator. The captain was still under suspension, but the rest of the crew, other than himself, were employed. McLeod felt sympathy for the captain, who made an emotional speech concerning his fallen crew member. He also felt sorry for Tia Dermott. The engine mechanic was an extremely important member of the mining ship. Appointments for that position were hard to get, primarily because captains had a tendency of choosing their engine mechanics from working with them before. Dermott was still developing a name for herself and hadn't received an offer from another ship yet. Instead, she gained employment at the space station's ship repair facilities. After McLeod had coffee with the former Gladiator crew, he made an appointment with the personnel office, hoping they would allow him to begin active duty again.

The space station did have a recreation and exercise area, but it didn't appeal to him. He, like the rest of the workers, was out in the asteroids to work and make money. There wasn't any other reason to be there. The company he had a contract with, Gibbston Space Lines, was a medium sized operation. They owned a share of the space station Terra Nova with eight other corporations. The mining of asteroids was a high risk, high pay-out for companies as well as individuals. So far, McLeod was earning good bonuses as well as his salary. Without work, those bonuses disappeared, and the bonuses were a major component of his compensation. The next day he stopped at the personnel office.

The personnel officer, a woman who hadn't reached thirty yet, greeted him in the small, but well-organized office.

"Sorry I couldn't see you this morning." She shook his hand and gestured to a chair in front of her desk. "I had to take care of payroll first, otherwise there would be hell to pay from upset miners."

"That's okay. I have more time than I know what to do with. I'm wondering when I can return to work. I feel I can do my regular job again." He shifted on the plastic chair, trying to get comfortable to no avail.

She checked her monitor. "The medical report says one more week. I can push for an earlier release, but that would be still a few more days. The issue is safety. In an emergency, there's a concern you wouldn't be able to respond quickly enough."

He nodded. "Ironically, the issue of safety is why I am injured." He let that statement dangle for a moment. "My lawyer has indicated there may be cause for compensation because of the actions of the Gladiator's captain. I haven't decided yet if I want to go through that process."

She returned to the screen for a moment, her fingers touching a few points on the monitor. "How about if we continue to pay the same bonus amounts since the time of the incident? We could average out your last month of bonuses to arrive at a figure."

"That would be fair. No need for a lawyer to resolve compensation then."

"Good." She smiled. "We have recently purchased a new mining ship, actually a refurb, called the Nebula, and we're looking for a crew to operate her. Looking at your file, it seems you have held a few different positions on mining ships, including pilot, engine control and cable launch." She looked at him. "Do you feel you're ready to captain a ship?"

"I do."

"Okay, I'll send you a contract, plus a list of positions that need to be filled. There are a couple of personnel we highly recommend for particular positions, but you'll need to find others to fill the empty spots."

"Thank you. I look forward to going back to work."

She stood and offered her hand over the small desk. "Congratulations. I hope the Nebula does well under your command."

"Thanks." He tried to hide the excitement he felt in commanding his own ship. He left the office, making his way quickly to the elevators. This time when he stepped inside the elevator the smell of people inside didn't bother him. When he reached the cafeteria floor, he touched the earpiece hooked on his left ear.

"Contact Tia Dermott."

A few moments later, she answered.

"Hey, Jaret, what's up? Are you going to be allowed back mining again soon?"

"More sooner than later. Can you meet me for a coffee? There's something I want to ask you."

"What is it?"

"When I see you." He grabbed a serving tray and stood by a conveyor belt of snack food, giant automated dispensers of coffee and various drinks. McLeod loaded his tray with reconstituted scrambled eggs, imitation bacon, toast and orange juice.

"Alright. I can meet you in about an hour. I have to finish up adjusting a diverter coil regulator."

"Okay, the coffee shop in an hour and twenty minutes." He added a coffee to the tray.

"An hour and twenty minutes?"

"Yeah, I always add extra time for you. I swear you never learned to tell time."

She laughed. "Jerk."

McLeod moved past several workers and found an empty table with four, grey plastic chairs. They didn't provide much in the way of comfort but were durable.

Coffee, tea and energy drinks were the strongest drugs allowed on the space station with alcohol and non-prescription drugs strictly prohibited. Mobile units, half the size of a fire hydrant, constantly roved around. Besides cleaning the floors, they used sensors to detect the trace chemical signatures of prohibited substances.

One of the mobile units circled him as he carried his tray. McLeod considered the unit had detected the medication he was taking, and he wondered if security would pay him a visit. He found an empty table and sat down.

McLeod scooped the food into his mouth, not tasting the bland sustenance. Still, with its traces of vitamins, it filled him up. As he slurped his coffee, he looked around the large room that contained the dining area. Another section contained a conveyor belt of luncheon foods, a third with supper options and finally a section just for snacks. The high ceiling had giant air ducts to pull dust floating in the room. The purpose of the space station was to extract various minerals from the asteroids, with dust and ion laden particles constantly floating throughout the station. The space station was noisy with voices and the sound of heavy machinery located a few floors away that penetrated the eating areas. Occasionally the thud of an incoming rock made its arrival heard.

Most of the workers were men who spent most of their waking hours inside a mining ship. They didn't care to socialize and were focused on earning enough to later live a comfortable life on Earth or Mars after they quit. There were a few women as well. Mining ships, which ranged from a crew of two to a dozen, required people who were able to focus on doing a particular job in a less than ideal environment. Gender didn't matter, but fewer women than men wanted to put up with the isolation and danger near the asteroids.

McLeod obtained a second coffee and was glad the security hadn't been notified to see him. He sat at his table and saw Dermott approach.

"You finally shaved."

"Yeah, it only took me an hour." He chuckled. "My skin is still pretty sensitive." He touched his cheek. "Plus, I have to be bit more careful around this scar."

Dermott studied his face. "Hmm, I think it gives you more character."

He laughed. "Thanks."

"Did you hear they demoted the captain of the Gladiator? I guess they thought he must have screwed up in that accident."

"In a way, Franklin did. Tugging cables are designed for only so many hours of use. He exceeded the recommended parameters."

"Yeah, but cables have broken before. It was bad luck a rock was floating by right at that time."

"True. I'm just saying if I was captain, I wouldn't have left that to chance. That rock floating by…" He shook his head. "Franklin should have waited until we were clear of nearby rocks before initiating the slingshot manoeuvre. That's just my opinion."

She slowly nodded. "I think you'd make a good captain. You think ahead."

"Thanks." He took a drink of his coffee. "Actually, that's what I wanted to talk to you about. I'm going to be the captain of a mining ship, the Nebula. Do you want to get back into a ship in engine control?" The space station's engine repair facility pay was lower as she missed out on the bonuses, however, the work environment was safer.

She closed her eyes for a moment. "I thought you'd never ask."

"That's what I wanted to hear. Welcome to the Nebula crew."

2

Our galaxy is filled with star systems, lone stars and rogue planets that drift through space. Some solar systems have a single star and various planets circling around it. These simple systems give the planets the best opportunity to develop complex life. Other systems can have two or more stars and planets to follow more intricate orbits. Complex lifeforms are less likely to form, but it's far from impossible.

One of the star systems consisted of three stars and a host of planets. Over time one of its Jovian sized worlds was ejected entirely during a pass too close to one of the suns. The gas giant drifted into space, on a path of destruction.

In the same neighbourhood of stars, another star system, this one with a single sun and ten planets and a cluster of dwarf planets. The fourth planet in the system was named Hallia by its inhabitants, which roughly translated meant the giver of life. Of course, that was long ago. Now Hallia is a frozen, dead world, far away from the star that once gave it warmth.

CAPTAIN JARET MCLEOD PUNCHED A RED BUTTON ON THE front console with a dirty gloved hand. He watched as the intense gamma-ray laser beam cut into the rock almost five hundred metres below on the asteroid. His goggles protected his eyes from the glare of melting rock and the high ultraviolet rays. The asteroid reluctantly freed up a building-sized rock, and it tumbled down a slope in slow motion. From his vantage point in the Nebula, everything looked normal. So far, the mission was working well.

It was dangerous work, cutting out rock from the asteroids in the low gravity. Earlier, four members of his six-person team carefully tested the terrain of Asteroid Alpha 752, finding a promising indication of valuable minerals underneath.

A few months earlier when McLeod had been promoted to run the Nebula crew, he was given modest targets to achieve. His first few missions met his quota easily, matching the success of more experienced crews. He quickly took his crew from average production to being a top-rated ship and had done so without any crew member being lost or injured. A scar on his left cheek was a reminder of when he was a crew member on another ship that was lax on safety for a brief moment.

"Good job, people. The rock is free." McLeod swivelled the captain's chair back toward the console. He looked at the readout in front of him, the spectrum analysis confirming the properties of the rock before the laser cutting had started.

"How does it look?" The crew member who was responsible for the laser settings, Keith Gifford, called out.

"Still high grade." He turned to the back so his voice could be heard to the middle of the spacecraft. The ship was deprived of comfort and amenities. A narrow metal walkway from the control cabin to the rear engines was all that separated a person from the multiple conduits and wiring along the craft's walls. Sections of the floor were hinged so the entrance below wasn't a problem. It didn't look pretty, but it also meant everything on the ship was accessible. The mining ships were all much the same, regardless of their size or the number of the crew, small, with oversized motors, an exterior laser cannon, and battered on the outside from small rocks floating in the asteroid belt. The interior of the ship had a layer of ionized dust clinging to every surface.

The dust came from the cloud of particles constantly floating around the space station where chunks of asteroids were cut up. With the environmental laws preventing most of the mining on Earth, asteroids became the major source of metals and minerals. Mars had an abundance of minerals as well, but the government of Mars was also reluctant to mine the planet for anything but their own immediate use. The Terra Nova was one of four space stations responsible for mining the asteroids. Each station had dozens of mining ships that ranged in size according to the type of rock they were to bring in for smelting. The miners were well paid, but it was still hard to attract people willing to sacrifice part of their lives to make money.

McLeod made his way to where Trevor Roy sat, monitoring the screen in front of him. "How does it look?"

"Good." He pointed at the three-dimensional image on his screen. Like most of the three-dimensional screens, it gave a view like looking through a window with the images projected behind the screen. He flipped through various spectrum enhanced images, one showing where the rock was still hot when the laser had cut it free. "We have three strong targets for the cables."

"We're going to need them. That's one big mother we need to haul up."

"Ready when you give the command." Roy was the programmer for firing cables into the freed rock. On the outside of the spaceship a series of ridges housed rockets with cables attached.

McLeod looked around the ship, acknowledging the rest of the crew watching him. "Go." He turned his attention to the front of the ship, where the large screens gave an image of the asteroid below.

McLeod saw the bright light of the three rocket engines as they pulled the cables behind them. They struck into the rock surface, giving off a shower of dust and stones. Then three additional small explosions ignited at the rock surface where the small rockets buried themselves deeper into the hard surface. He frowned, not sure if one of the explosive charges was as strong as the other two.

McLeod spoke into his microphone, knowing that the ship's

engine engineer could have trouble hearing him over the rumble of the engines even if he yelled across the small spaceship. "How's it on your end, Dermott?"

"Ready at my end. We're in a stable position." Tia Dermott replied over the growl of the engines.

He nodded at Roy. "All good, let's grab it. Pull up the tension on the cables so there's no slack."

Roy pulled on a lever, watching his monitor. Like many of the other major controls on the ship, it had to be physically moved to operate. Electronic controls that reacted to touch could be accidently activated. "Done."

"How does everything look?"

Roy spoke in a calm voice. "Looks good. One rocket may have been a partial, but it still buried itself. Want to fire another?"

McLeod thought about it. The computer had already picked the three optimal points for pulling the rock. Adding a fourth cable might cause them to tangle during the transport. There was also a danger that another rocket could cause part of the rock to break apart or split it in pieces. "No, I think we're good to go."

"Alright, increasing the cable tension."

McLeod watched on the monitor as the cables continued to retract back to the ship on the three cranes supported on the hull of the ship. When they became taut, he observed the rock slightly wiggle as the ship changed position.

"Are we still stable, Dermott?"

"Yes sir." Like the rest of the crew she kept her spacesuit on minus the helmet. In case of the spaceship suddenly losing air, it was best to have to only worry about one thing to put on. The incident that left McLeod injured was still fresh in her mind.

McLeod and Dermott first worked as a team in a two-person ship, responsible for clearing out rocks that were too close for comfort for the space station and later on other ships. When McLeod was made captain, he knew he wanted Dermott to be part of his crew, impressed with her ability to keep the engines firing at high output.

McLeod felt and heard the rumble of the ship's engines as it pulled at the cables tethered below. He returned to the front console, checking the readouts on the various monitors.

"You have engine command." McLeod announced to Dermott. The engines could be operated either at the front console or at the rear. Since the ship would be using maximum safe power to pull the rock free of the asteroid's weak gravity, it was prudent Dermott should be in control in case quick adjustments needed to be made. There was also a chance of engine failure and Dermott would have the best chance to shut it down before a disaster struck.

"Aye, sir." She pressed a yellow button that would flash a warning on the front console, letting him know the rear controls had now taken priority over the forward ones.

McLeod felt the Nebula jerk as the engines quickly rose in power. The sound and the rumble caused everyone to concentrate on the monitors in front of them in case an emergency arose. The vibration along the deck and walls of the ship surged. As McLeod watched, the rock slowly lifted off the asteroid surface and began to increase in speed.

The big rock lifted off the surface with bits of material falling from it. Minutes passed. The vibration and noise in the ship went across in waves, droning on as the fight against the asteroid's gravity for the rock continued. Suddenly there was a slight decrease in the rumble from the engines.

"Captain, we have rock under our control!"

He heard the grin in her voice. They had searched the asteroid belt before finding the right mineral content on the odd kidney shaped asteroid and finally found a perfectly shaped rock waiting, ready to be cut away.

"Let's bring her home." Home was the processing ship, an ugly, dirty, monstrous sized floating space station. Besides providing sleeping accommodations, it also served as a repair and storage facility for the mining ships. It was similarly a place of boredom. Food and supplies could be had there, but with alcohol and drugs strictly prohibited, it was void of any parties.

The men and women who worked the mining ships were not interested in spending time at the processing ship. It was there to accept their chunks of rock, make sure their mining ship was functioning and to transfer payments. An idle mining ship lost money for the owners. The crew used the space station as a place to sleep, eat and get the mining ships ready for the next excursion.

The noise level dropped after the initial lift and lowered again as the rock floated behind them. Once the desired speed was obtained the engines were set on cruise. Dermott joined McLeod at the front. She punched him on the shoulder as she sat on the other chair.

"This could be the big one."

He nodded. "Great readings on the surface for content. If they're indicative of what's inside, this will be a very nice prize."

"Nice prize?" She laughed. "We're in for one healthy bonus."

He smiled. "This crew does a great job."

She looked at the artificial gravity meter. "Damn AG keeps fluctuating. That needs to be looked at when we get home."

"What about you? How long do you plan to do this?"

"Getting closer to calling it quits. I hope to get on one of these days with the passenger ships. That would be more relaxing. Either that or find a rich husband."

McLeod laughed. "You playing the pretty girl just to catch a rich guy? You're pretty, but the pretty girl batting her eyelids is not in your genes." He looked at her, a shapely, short woman with short blonde hair. "Most rich guys like having things their own way. Anyone trying to control you would find they have a wildcat on their hands."

Dermott shrugged. "Okay, so I'm my own woman. That means more work for me then." She looked at him. "Hey, you're good looking and almost rich. You should marry me."

McLeod started to laugh, and Dermott soon joined him. McLeod wiped away a tear from his eye. "Lord, can you imagine us married? We'd be either divorced or dead in two weeks."

"You're right. But I think you're one great captain. I'll always work for you if I have a chance."

"You do know you're one of the best engine mechanics around the Terra Nova? Make sure wherever you land that you get paid that way. You kept this piece of metal working when other mechanics would have it sitting idle at the spaceport waiting for parts. You saved the company a lot of money."

"Does that mean I get a raise?" She smiled.

"Sure, same time as I do."

———

The space station Terra Nova floated along the inner ring of the asteroid belt. At one time, the giant cylinder-shaped station was gleaming white, but now a thin layer of dust gave it a grey appearance. A small ionized cloud of particles constantly floated around the Terra Nova from the processed rocks.

McLeod watched as the massive doors of the Terra Nova opened to the processing centre. In the front of the doors were giant rings that guided the rocks to the middle. He took a slow deep breath, looking at the monitor's read out of the rock's velocity. A computer calculated the ideal time to release the rock. A green light glowed, and unless he hit the abort button, the cables would automatically release the prized stone. His hand hovered over the red abort button, and not seeing anything that would cause a problem, didn't prevent the cables from unlatching and sending the rock on its way.

"Done. It's all theirs now." He announced to no one as the rock glided to the bay doors of the processing centre. He resumed his attention to the ship controls.

Dermott grinned. "Let's dock and see what the damage is."

McLeod guided the Nebula to within one hundred metres of the Terra Nova, releasing the ship's guidance to the station. With a minor bump, the ship landed on the platform inside the hanger. The engines shut down and after a few minutes the exit doors to the ship sighed open.

McLeod waited until the last of the crew left the small spacecraft, noting the service technicians were already proceeding to inspect the ship and to check diagnostics. He caught up with Dermott as she approached the maintenance manager, Kevin Gill. She greeted him as he looked up from his workstation, cluttered with small parts and two computer monitors.

"Just wanted to tell you the AG is acting up again. It did the same thing a few months back. It was fixed, but its fluctuating again."

Gill, tall, slim with a touch of grey in the dark hair, nodded. "Did you feel any change in the gravity field itself, or was it just the AG detector?"

"Gravity felt fine. I think it was just the detector."

"The Nebula is a Northstar fourteen series. They're well made, but the AG detection circuit was placed at the base of the ship, which is too close to one of the exhaust ports. The AG module gets short circuited by the ions. We'll clean it out and seal it with a new compound that was developed to rectify this problem. They should have fixed this years ago."

McLeod liked Gill, impressed with his knowledge of the different type of spacecrafts that needed repair at the Terra Nova. "Thanks, Fish. Nice to know the Nebula is in good hands here."

Dermott added. "You're the best. Catch you for a coffee soon."

McLeod hated the first few breaths of the air in the station. He decided against going to his small room to wash up, electing to join Dermott for a coffee. The coffee, he once ventured, tasted like it was made from ground up rock with paint thinner thrown in. Still, it gave them a chance to wait until an assessment of their rock was done.

Dermott and McLeod shifted on the uncomfortable chairs as they talked about spending a few weeks vacationing somewhere, anywhere, on Earth.

As he chatted with Dermott, he received a message on his mobile from the processing side.

"Hey, they have an assessment."

"Great, that took long enough."

"Yeah, but this time they've asked us to come up to the assessment office."

McLeod wasn't bothered it took them longer than normal to make an assessment of the rock's worth. It likely meant it had more value and the assessment auditor wanted to make sure before offering a bonus payment.

Dermott stood, not wanting to finish her second cup of coffee. "Let's go and hear what they say."

They used the elevator to drop the fourteen floors to the processing levels. There they passed through an automated security door, authorizing only those with an appointment to venture inside. There were several assessment offices. Each office was enclosed by sound deadening fabric walls, except for the clear plastic wall that faced the hallway. Each of the large corporations that had a share of the Terra Nova had several assessment officers. McLeod and Dermott made their way to the officer that paged him. The assessment auditor waved them into his office on seeing their approach. Dark skinned, lightly built, he gave them a smile as he sat behind his desk.

"I don't meet every team when we push their rock through the recycler, but when we get a slice of heaven, I like to show them what we found."

McLeod looked at the monitor that was swung toward him. He understood what the phrase a slice of heaven meant. When part of the asteroid rock was cut with a laser, on rare occasions, unique minerals are exposed. What McLeod saw was a vein of brightly coloured metal inside the dark face. "Wow, that looks interesting. What is that?" He believed he already knew the answer from the readouts of the Nebula's spectrum analyser.

"Iridium. Very rare." He looked at McLeod and Dermott. "Somebody is going to be very impressed with you and your crew."

━━━

McLeod adjusted the course of the Nebula, checked the new coordinates, and announced to the rest of the crew "I've set the course for asteroid A4107. We'll arrive in less than two hours."

Tia Dermott turned to look at him. "This is a long trip. I hope it's worth it."

He shrugged. "If that rock doesn't produce anything, they'll be others close by that will. Besides, they're paying us well enough for this cruise." Earlier, McLeod and his crew, were asked to extend their search for mineral bearing asteroids further out from the Terra Nova. The space station was planning to move to a new area of the asteroid belt and wanted to have more information on the density of the asteroids and if they contained the more valuable minerals.

The journey slowly went by. The crew was bored but couldn't fully relax in the small spaceship. As they approached their destination, they were happy to begin routine checks of the instruments. McLeod established orbit around the asteroid with Trevor Roy studying the spectrograph readouts.

Tia Dermott peered at the surface below. The elongated asteroid had an uneven surface made up of grey and brown streaks of impact craters. "Pretty rocky surface. Only a few smooth areas. This asteroid looks like it's been smashed a few times."

"That will help to loosen a rock if we find one worth taking." McLeod answered as he adjusted the controls for maintaining the orbit. "Damn gravity fluctuates."

"That probably means this asteroid isn't just iron. Maybe we'll get lucky and find a rock with a nice deposit."

McLeod grunted an acknowledgement. If the asteroid was composed mostly of iron, the gravity would be steady as they orbited. If some rock contained lighter or heavier material, the gravity would vary.

During the second orbit the Nebula received a radio call from another spaceship.

"This is Captain Devon Morgan of the Consuela. Is that you, Jaret, doing the dance with that rock?"

McLeod grinned. "Hey, Devon, are you following me or just lost?" He looked at a monitor, showing where the Consuela, a four-crew mining ship, was located.

"I might as well be lost if I'm in the same area as you. I've heard you still don't know your left from your right."

Dermott laughed. "Hey, Devon, at least he found a rock while you're still sailing around."

"Tia, what strings did Jaret pull to get the prettiest woman in his tin-bucket?"

"He asked me nicely."

Morgan chuckled. "Now I have to learn to be nice. Were you sent by Gibbston to search out new asteroids? General Mining strongly suggested it would be in my best interest to lead our crew to check out this region of asteroids."

"Same here, except they gave us a nice bonus to go fishing," McLeod answered.

"Yeah, well, G M is giving us an incentive to do a search as well. I wouldn't be surprised if a few other mining ships make a trip out here as well. Good luck on striking gold."

"You too."

Tia Dermott glanced at the display, watching the spectrograph list various minerals next to coloured lines looking like the outline of a mountain range. The data had to be interpreted by Trevor Roy to know what was worthwhile to go after. "Devon always has a joke to make. You met him during a safety and security orientation class?"

"Yeah. We get along pretty good." McLeod adjusted for orbital correction again. "He likes you."

"No surprise there. With the ratio of men and women out here, every female appears like a goddess."

He laughed. "So you're the goddess of the asteroid belt."

"Don't be a wise guy."

"Captain! We have a strong reading of platinum," Trevor Roy called out.

"Coordinates?"

"I'll mark it on the topographical map."

McLeod peered at the three-dimensional map, spotting the boulder shaped like a giant thimble. "Nice find. Now let's get it free."

———

McLeod watched as Everett and Tobias prepared the blasting holes at the bottom of the boulder. "It's amazing how much we mine from the asteroids, send it to Earth, and still it can't keep up with the demand."

"Part of the problem is Earth doesn't want to dig out its own minerals for fear of damaging the environment. The other factor is Mars doesn't want to extend mining rights to any Earth corporation. So everything has to come from the asteroids." Roy added.

"At least it keeps us employed."

The Nebula hovered above the boulder.

McLeod swiveled his chair toward Roy. "When you're ready, fire the cables to that rock." He turned back to the front console to watch the firing of the three cables.

Moments later three rockets left the Nebula and buried into the boulder. Small explosions ensured the cables held fast.

"Cables are secure."

"Tia, you have engine control."

Dermott went to the rear of the spaceship, increasing the power of the engine. The vibration and rumbling of the motor filled the cabin as the boulder slowly lifted from the surface of the asteroid.

"We got it!" Roy called out.

McLeod watched the boulder wobble as it left the asteroid, causing it to sway on the cables.

Suddenly a warning bell rang out, followed by an urgent message.

"Mayday. Mayday. This is the Consuela. We have suffered containment damage from an errant rock and have a life threatening injury. We require immediate assistance. Our coordinates will be relayed at the end of this message."

McLeod looked at the coordinates of the Consuela as the emergency message repeated. He checked the time for the Nebula to reach the Consuela.

"Devon, this is Jaret. We can arrive in forty-five minutes. What's your situation? Have you lost all air?"

"Affirmative. A rock has punctured the ship. One of my crew is unconscious from the impact and his suit is leaking air. He doesn't look good. The emergency rescue ship is an hour and twenty minutes away."

McLeod understood the first choice was normally to use the emergency rescue ship, which was capable of providing immediate medical aid and do repair work on a spaceship. He used the intercom to address his crew. "As you heard, the Consuela is in distress. We can arrive over thirty minutes before the emergency rescue ship. That means we need to release our rock. Any objections or concerns?"

Dermott called out. "This is life or death. Let's do it."

The Nebula released the boulder and initiated full thrust toward the Consuela.

McLeod radioed Morgan. "Devon, we're on our way. Our arrival time is forty-three minutes."

"We have released our load and are now drifting toward your ship. That won't save much time but be aware our coordinates are slowly changing."

"Acknowledged." McLeod looked at Dermott as she monitored the engine, pushing its limits. He didn't have to check the console to know the engine readouts were all in the yellow warning zone. He released his breath and waited as the seconds ticked by.

Chug announced. "I have the Consuela on my monitor. She's tumbling, but not excessively."

McLeod used a headset to talk to Tia Dermott. "How do you want to approach them?"

"Hard. When we're close, I'll reverse the ship and use the full throttle to brake. I think it'll be easier to match their speed and position that way."

"Okay. I'll let the Consuela know what we're doing."

The Nebula pivoted during the braking maneuver, giving McLeod a visual of the Consuela less than one hundred metres away. The spaceships moved closer as the velocity was matched.

"You made good time, Jaret."

"Tia pushed the engine hard. Can you stop the tumbling?"

"Yeah, I think so. We still have positioning jets."

"Good. When you're stabilized, open your exit door and glide to the Nebula."

"Acknowledged."

McLeod announced to his crew. "Helmets on. We're going to depressurize the ship and open the airlock doors. It'll take too long to use the normal procedure of using airlock to bring in one person at a time."

Two crew members guided the unconscious man from the Consuela to the Nebula. Once the four-man crew were inside, McLeod quickly closed the exit doors and re-pressured the ship. A green light indicated normal pressure was achieved.

"You can remove your helmets." McLeod's attention went to the injured man lying on the floor. Two men were quickly pulling off his suit, exposing a red blotch on his left side. A first aid kit was passed to them.

McLeod quietly asked Morgan. "You okay, Devon?"

"Fuck, Jaret. I don't know if Nigel is going to make it. He lost a lot of blood and we couldn't do a damn thing other than patch his suit from the air leak. Damn rock punched a hole in the ship and the metal tore into him. Damn it to hell!"

"I'm going full throttle," Dermott announced. "It's going to be noisy."

McLeod looked at the bloody ripped skin of the injured man, wondering how he was still alive. An oxygen mask was covering his mouth as his vital signs were being monitored. They didn't look good. He placed a hand on Morgan's shoulder and pointed to the co-pilot's seat.

Over the noise of the engine, Morgan nodded.

McLeod sat in the pilot's chair and handed Morgan a headset after putting one on himself.

"You need to record what happened while your memory is still fresh of the details."

"You're right." He rubbed his hand across his face. "It was damn bad luck. One of the cables holding the rock slipped from its anchor we were pulling. The rock jerked and swung to the top of a cliff, jarring a rock loose. That rock sailed upward while the Consuela swung into its path as we fought with the cables. There was nothing we could do. That rock smashed into us. Poor Nigel. He had just put on his helmet. I couldn't hear him, but I saw his mouth open in a scream." Morgan took out a tablet from his suit's pocket and started to fill in the incident report.

McLeod contacted the Terra Nova. "We have a seriously injured crew member that requires immediate medical assistance."

"Understood, Nebula. You have priority over all ships. Port Seven is reserved for you."

"Port Seven is confirmed. The Nebula will be coming in at maximum speed and hard braking."

"Affirmative, Nebula."

McLeod looked at the engine parameters. All of them were in the yellow zone and he knew Dermott was pushing the engine to its limits. *There's going to be some maintenance work needed after this run.*

▭

As soon as the Nebula stopped inside the Terra Nova, medical crews rushed inside. McLeod and the others exited the ship and waited, talking quietly. Shortly later, the medical team carried Nigel out on a stretcher. An intravenous bag hung from the pole attached to the stretcher.

McLeod placed a hand on Morgan's shoulder. "We got him here alive. He's got a good chance with our medical staff."

"I sure hope so. Thanks again for coming to our rescue."

"You'd do the same."

"Captain McLeod? I'm Gerald Zetter, Gibbston's assistant general manager of mining ship operations. I would like to speak with you concerning this incident."

McLeod walked a short distance from the others. "What do want to discuss?"

"I'm curious about your decision to abort your mining operation in response to a distress call from another spaceship, a spaceship not belonging to Gibbston. There was an emergency rescue ship available at the time."

McLeod frowned at the tall, thin man who looked several

years younger than himself. "My decision was based on the fact I could arrive thirty minutes sooner than the emergency ship. And to clarify, the call was not a distress call but one of emergency."

"Regardless, I believe it would have been prudent to have the emergency rescue ship carry out its duties rather than have the Nebula step in. Your decision has cost Gibbston lost revenue."

McLeod stared at Zetter for several seconds. "Mr. Zetter, have you ever been in a mining ship during an operation?"

"No, I haven't."

"Then you wouldn't understand why I made the right decision to help the Consuela." He walked away leaving Zetter to stare at his back.

Dermott came up to him. "What was that all about?"

"He didn't believe we should have rescued the Consuela. Lost revenue, if you can believe it."

"He can go to hell."

"Mr. McLeod." An older, heavy-set man approached him.

"Yes."

"Lawrence Reznor, general manager of General Mining ship operations."

"Good to meet you, Mr. Reznor." He stuck out his hand. "This is Tia Dermott. She's in charge of the Nebula's engine."

"Excellent to meet both of you. I just want to thank you in person for what you and your crew did to help the Consuela. I will discuss with Gibbston on the transfer of compensation for your swift action."

"Thank you, but Mr. Zetter does not seem to share your opinion that we made the right decision to help the Consuela."

Reznor patted his hand downward. "Don't worry about that. Mr. Zetter is still learning. I'll have a chat with my counterpart at Gibbston." He lowered his voice slightly. "Mr. McLeod, the Nebula is drawing a lot of attention for its operation. All of it positive. If you ever want to progress past being the captain of the Nebula, there'll be a lot of interest from other corporations. Don't misunderstand, I'm not trying to poach you from Gibbston. But after you saved the crew of the Consuela, I'll have your back if you need any assistance."

After Renzor left, Dermott poked McLeod at his side. "It sounds like you've made a name for yourself."

"Thanks, but it's the crew of the Nebula as a group that deserves the credit."

"Don't be so damn modest. You're our captain. As the saying goes, no such thing as a good ship and a bad captain."

"Thanks." McLeod excused himself, going to an appointment he didn't share with anyone.

3

AFTER HE DEPARTED FROM THE GROUP OF MINERS, MCLEOD made his way to the bank of elevators. He stepped off on the level where the Gibbston Space Lines personnel office was located. McLeod had applied to work as an executive officer on a transport ship, wanting to get out of the mining ships. Most people lasted only a couple of years before the work of constantly mining the asteroids wore them down. The mental fatigue of dangerous work made a long career working the asteroids almost impossible. When the personnel office contacted him, he hoped they had found a position for him. McLeod had also watched out for similar positions with other companies, although most corporations preferred to promote within. This was especially true for executive positions on ships where the companies wanted to know exactly who was going to be an executive officer on the very expensive spaceships.

The personnel officer was the same one he had spoken to when he returned to work from his injuries.

"Gloria, if I remember right." He glanced at her name tag on the desk, 'G. Bishop'.

"That's right, you have a good memory." She looked at her monitor. "I have some good news for you. I know you were looking for an executive position on a transport ship, and it turns out we have an opening that is a step up in that area. The transport ship, the McKenzie King, needs a new captain. The present captain is retiring. If you're interested, we can start the paperwork."

"I'm very interested. When would this position be open?"

"Three weeks. There's a situation where you would need to look for some replacement officers, as well as securing the services of the present executive officers. The way most contracts are written, when the current captain is being replaced, contracts for executive officers can be cancelled by either the new captain, or by executive officers."

"So that means I need to contact the executive officers."

"Yes. I suspect most will want to stay on board, but there may be one or two positions you may need to fill with junior officers or have someone do dual positions. I will send you a file of interested candidates once we know which positions are open."

"Thank you. I'd best get started."

"Congratulations, Captain McLeod. I know your name was one of the first to come up when this captaincy became available. Let me know if you need help with any replacements."

McLeod was given the use of a small private office in the Gibbston section to contact the executive officers of the McKenzie King. The first few calls went well, with the officers agreeing to stay on, and he was hoping not to have to worry about hiring new executive officers. His first rejection came from the chief engineer officer, the one responsible for the operation of the motors and power.

"I regret to inform you that I have been offered another position and have decided to accept the proposal."

"I see. Well, congratulations on your new appointment."

"Thank you, Captain McLeod. The McKenzie King is a tough ship. She has a few peculiarities but won't let you down."

McLeod frowned on losing the chief engineer. He quickly scanned the crew that worked under him and saw most were mechanics low on experience. The engines on the McKenzie King were not highly sophisticated and served as a good place for new mechanics to learn the trade. It did require an experienced executive officer who knew about engines, and how to deal with those still learning.

He decided he needed to look for someone to be chief engineer who wasn't currently on the McKenzie King. *Maybe Tia could do this. It's a bit of jump from the mining ships to a transport ship, but she's smart, and has that attitude that she can beat any machine.*

He pushed that thought away and contacted the first officer, Lexanna Shultz. After a brief conversation, she indicated she wanted some time to think about the offer.

"I've worked on this ship with the same crew for a few voyages, and now I'm wondering if I should explore other opportunities. Can you give me twenty-four hours to decide?"

McLeod agreed, not sure if there was another officer able to take on the responsibilities of a first officer. *I can always promote a junior officer while I closely supervise their work. Not ideal, but I can work through that. When we get to Mars, there will be more opportunities to hire someone.*

McLeod left the administration office, deciding he needed to talk to someone about Tia Dermott as a suitable chief engineer. He used the elevator to enter the maintenance facility for the mining ships. As usual, noise and the smell of ozone hit him. Occasional blasts of air hit him from the air locks opening and closing. He looked around but didn't see Kevin Gill. He saw a familiar face of one of the older mechanics.

"Hey, Stu. Where's Fish?"

Stu frowned. "He's not here anymore. He got some promotion. Gibbston offered him some job that he couldn't turn down and left with only two days' notice. It must be something big for him to up and leave like that. Now we got some new guy. I guess he'll be alright, but Fish was the best I ever saw."

"Thanks, Stu. I appreciate the information."

Damn, losing Fish is going to hamper the repair facilities here. He knew every engine and all their weird perks. Now what do I do about Tia? Go with my gut, or look for someone who has more experience?

McLeod decided to stop worrying about it and focus on the

next mission of mining asteroids. He took a short nap and prepared for work.

Six hours later the Nebula circled an asteroid slowly, scanning the pockmarked surface for traces of valuable minerals. McLeod asked, "Anything yet?"

Roy frowned. "Minor stuff. Let's go to the next rock."

McLeod announced, "Okay, we're moving to Asteroid Alpha 558 to go fishing." He engaged the controls to accelerate the Nebula to the next large asteroid. It was difficult to establish orbit around asteroids with their weak gravity and required constant adjustment of the spaceship's positioning rockets. He followed protocol to see if another mining ship was already nearby or orbiting the asteroid. He didn't find the presence of any other mining ship and focused on the job of maintaining low orbit around the asteroid.

There wasn't a law against two mining ships working on the same asteroid, and in some cases that occurred on the larger asteroids, but miners had a tendency to be possessive of an asteroid they were working on. Those that chose to mine the rocks were risk takers with an aggressive personality, which made conflicts dangerous.

Due to the potential for conflicts, and to help with the prevention of pirating processed ore, Interplanetary Enforcement Police was formed. The I. E. P. worked under the jurisdiction of the International Space Agency but was considered autonomous in most of their operations. Their actual size, including the number of personnel and ships wasn't widely known. Their presence was noticed around all space stations, patrolling the asteroid belt and the Mars-Earth corridor.

"Scanning."

McLeod heard Roy's announcement. He looked at the pear-shaped rock below, not noticing anything remarkable about it.

Roy added, "We have a signature of tungsten, magnesium and whole lot of iron."

"How much tungsten and at what location?"

"Maybe three per cent. I've highlighted the location."

McLeod looked at the green circle on the three-dimensional map of asteroid on a monitor. "That doesn't look too easy to break out that rock."

Chris Everett tapped into the discussion. "Captain, I don't like the look of this rock. I think it's a composite."

"Then this isn't worth the effort." McLeod respected the opinion of Everett when it came to asteroids. The veteran miner knew better than most how to dislodge rocks from an asteroid. He was very good at understanding what may hide below the surface of the odd shaped rocks that floated in the belt. It this case, the term composite referred to what appeared to be a solid asteroid, but was actually a collection of gravel and large boulders that clung together by a very weak micro-gravity. A thin surface dust coating hid many of the cracks between the various stones. A ship, or a person, touching down on the surface would quickly find the ground giving way.

McLeod didn't want to spend time and energy taking a rock that was mostly iron. That didn't pay the cost of running the mining ship. "We're moving on to the next asteroid."

Almost an hour later they reached another target, and the Nebula established orbit again.

"Scanning," Roy announced. Moments later, "We have a hit. Tungstate, wolframite. Looks like a good vein."

"Coordinates?" McLeod checked his own monitor. A flashing green dot showed on the brown and grey surface of the asteroid. "It looks like our site is accessible. It's in a ridge." He knew from experience many of the valuable metals and minerals were often exposed on the asteroid's jagged surface from the countless collisions with other rocks. The surface didn't usually show much valuable minerals or metals, but violent collisions exposed the material below the surface. "I'm taking her down."

Landing on an asteroid was difficult, requiring an extremely slow descent. Just as the landing struts touched the surface, gabbling cables buried into the hard surface to prevent the spaceship from bouncing off.

"Helmets on everyone. Let's take a look and see what we've got."

The small airlock allowed for only one person to exit at a time. McLeod went first, and a few minutes later Roy joined him. The rest of the crew waited in the Nebula, removing their helmets after Roy successfully exited the ship.

McLeod and Roy moved in long leaps along the surface. They each had a rocket pack, in case one of them lifted off the surface, and in addition they were tethered by a cable to each other. Floating off the surface was a possibility, although it was considered more embarrassing than dangerous.

Roy grunted as he carried the analysis equipment in the metal case, banging it on his leg as he made each long leap. "I hope this is worth it." The bulky case swung wildly as his arms floated up to maintain balance on each jump and then dropped as he landed. After a series of jumps the case in his hand would occasionally move close to his body.

"I trust your earlier readings on it." McLeod matched Roy's leaps and paused in front of the ridge. He watched as Roy set up the equipment, a black box with an array of sensors on a tripod. A cable anchored it to the ground.

Roy announced, "Okay, switching on." He peered at the monitor with McLeod standing behind his shoulder.

The equipment sent a series of electromagnetic pulses to the ridge. A laser beam flashed at selected areas of the rock face.

"Looks good." Roy pointed at the monitor. "Fairly well-defined area. We can likely blast out a section without much wastage." He used his finger to circle a region. "Let's see what it has to say about blasting." The 'it' he referred to was the Integrated Spectrometer and Location Blasting Points Analyser. The machine displayed a three-dimensional image of the ridge and where optimal locations were to be set explosives to free the massive rock.

McLeod asked, "Do you see the marked areas, Chris, Tobias?" When he heard them reply in the affirmative, he added, "Okay, get your gear together. We'll be back in a few minutes, and then you can leave."

McLeod was glad he wasn't responsible for putting in the blasting charges. The laser drill equipment used to make the holes was tricky to set up, and together with the power supply to run the lasers, they were awkward to handle. The work wasn't technically challenging, but a long time was spent out on the surface of the asteroid. It was physically tiring trying to work in the low gravity.

As they waited in the Nebula, the remaining crew sat around, occasionally checking a monitor.

McLeod noted the presence of a spacecraft above them, the dark green and white markings distinctive of the Interplanetary Enforcement Police.

"I. E. P. are giving us a scan." He gave it a mental shrug. They usually left miners alone, and just monitored their presence. Occasionally, they would check that a mining ship had all the correct certificates that allowed them to mine the asteroid, including having all the required safety equipment. "They're moving away."

Roy diverted their thoughts. "Any of you see a USO?"

The letters referred to an Unidentified Space Object.

"Just as sensor blips," McLeod replied. He didn't reveal when he was on a three-person crew, along with Dermott, he had seen an unknown spacecraft. The long ship was too far away to make out details, but he was under the impression it was observing them as well.

"Not yet," Chug, the youngest of the crew members, replied. "I hope to see one."

Dermott shook her head. "I'm always too busy working on the engines. Have you?"

Roy wet his lips. "Yeah. I was on Mars, working on a water line project. We were pretty isolated, and we had to use a shuttle, and not a buggy, to reach the area. It was damn unlikely we'd come across anyone, let alone a spacecraft. There were four of us hooking up the line management flow controls, and we were wearing those thermal protective suits, plus helmets, because it was damn cold where we were. Those helmets are great for protection from the elements but obscure the vision a bit through the face shield. All the same, we all saw this ship just cruising. Real slow like. Then suddenly it was gone."

"Did you report it?" Dermott asked.

"No." Roy shook his head. "We all saw it, but what could we tell them? Our face shields gave a slightly distorted view and there was nothing around that could give us a reference of its size. We only saw it for about ten seconds. All I know is that I believe there's more to this USO stuff than what the official reports say, namely their claim that it may be a natural phenomenon we can't explain yet. Besides, no one wants to be interrogated by the I E P about an alleged sighting."

"I heard there were other strange things on Mars, creatures that are not from our selected Earth collection we placed there," Chug added.

"But no one has any physical proof of anything but transplanted Earth animals," McLeod replied in a calm voice in contrast to Chug's excited one. "Now there is Martian simple plant life that has survived. But that's a long way from complex life forms existing."

A loudspeaker broke up their discussion.

"We have the holes drilled, and the explosives set. We're coming back to the ship," Chris Everett barked.

Following protocol, the Nebula lifted off prior to the explosives being used. There was a very slim chance the explosions could trigger a fracture under where the Nebula rested. McLeod checked the monitor readouts one more time and turned to Roy. "Fire when you're ready."

"Three, two, one." Roy pressed the fire button.

McLeod watched the silent explosion. The dozens of holes shot up streams of yellow fireworks along the back of the ridge, followed by a series along the sides of block of stone. Suddenly the giant block dropped perceptually.

"It's loose," Roy announced. "I guess it's time for the cables."

Dermott plopped in the chair next to McLeod as he guided the ship back to a port in the Terra Nova. Cables towed the massive block of stone behind them.

"Okay, what's up?"

"What do you mean?" He gave her a small smile as he glanced at her.

"That." She pointed a finger at him. She knew their conversation was relatively private; the engine noise drowned out normal voices beyond the front of the ship. "Something is going on with you. I know you, I can tell. Plus, I heard some interesting stories. Did you know that Fish is gone? Is this part of the secret you're keeping?"

He sighed. "What is it with women that figure out personal stuff without being told?"

"We pay attention to faces. Talk."

"A few weeks ago, I applied for a position on a transport ship. It was approved and I was waiting for an opening. A day before we left on our rock hunt, I received word that I'm being made captain of the cargo ship McKenzie King."

"Congratulations!" She reached out her hand and squeezed his arm. "When does this happen?"

"In about two weeks when the McKenzie King makes port." He paused, then said, "Some of the crew of the McKenzie King will be staying on, but I'll also be adding my own personnel as well." He paused again and made a decision. "Are you interested in running the engine department?"

"You mean as in charge of the engines?" Her eyes brightened at the thought of the promotion. The occupation of engine maintenance was dominated by men. Being made in charge of an engine department, even in a transport ship, was a significant accolade for a woman who had been in space only a few years.

He nodded.

"Are you sure?"

"That's what the head of crew placement asked when I said I wanted you running the engines on the Nebula. I said I wanted the best I could find, and I'd trust her with my life. The same is true now."

"I could kiss you. Thanks." Dermott took a quick glance toward the back of the ship and leaned over to kiss him on the cheek.

━━

McLeod washed up in his room. Earlier he had received news from the assessment office of a positive result on the latest rock they sent in for processing. He was pleased with the additional bonus, but a second message was even better news to him. Lexanna Shultz had agreed to continue on as the McKenzie King's first officer. He sent a message to the Gibbston personnel office indicating to extend a contract to her immediately. *I don't want her to change her mind.* He had checked her résumé and thought her expertise in running the McKenzie King would be difficult to replace. A minute later, Gloria Bishop sent a request for him to come by her office to discuss the leadership of the Nebula.

I'm not doing anything now, so I might as well see her. He took the elevator to the Gibbston personnel offices, and soon was able to sit in her office.

"Thanks for coming by. I know you're winding up operations as the captain of the Nebula, which creates a minor problem on who to promote as the new captain." She clicked a few buttons on a keyboard and stared at a monitor. "Since you're taking Dermott as your chief engineering officer, the new captain will have to find someone to replace her. Before I look at various personnel files, do you have any recommendation of who could take over as captain of the Nebula?"

"Trevor Roy." McLeod scratched the back of his head. "He may be young, but he's smart and stays calm during the missions."

Bishop nodded. "The Nebula has been very successful, and I would prefer to keep as much of the crew together as possible. Promoting within the crew would help that." She tapped a few keys and looked at her monitor. "He has piloting experience when he was on a two-person ship, so there is that." Bishop peered at McLeod, waiting for him to respond.

"He was great on reading where deposits were hiding and can

use that skill in helping the Nebula stay successful. I recommend you give him this chance."

"Okay, thanks for your input."

He stood. "By the way, do you know what happened to Kevin Gill? He was running the maintenance department on the Terra Nova."

She smiled and laced her fingers. "Sorry, that's classified."

"Okay, I understand that. I was just concerned that he was okay."

"He's fine. Just a new position." She hesitated and revealed more information. "It's a secret where he's working now. Sorry, I can't tell you more."

4

THE MCKENZIE KING SLOWLY MOVED AWAY FROM THE TERRA Nova station. Filled with resources gained from the mined asteroids, the McKenzie King's enormous mass took time and power to reach its maximum operating speed. Besides carrying the smelted metal from the asteroids, the oblong ship also had a passenger section. Almost all the passengers were workers, having finished their contracted terms to mine the asteroids of their precious metals. On the return trip to the Terra Nova, the ship would bring their replacements.

The fourteen-hundred-metre-long McKenzie King was far from elegant. Those familiar with spaceships often referred to transport ships as a long pipe hit with an ugly stick. Identical rectangular sections were joined together to make a long train. A smaller module was attached to the front section, containing sensors that helped to generate the diversion field. The information from those sensors were relayed to the control section at the rear of the ship.

The rear of the ship held a spherical section that was dwarfed by the rest of the space craft, but it contained the control module, the passenger compartment and the all-important engines. The engines, nine Mark Two Industrials, pushed the giant craft. The industrial motors were designed to operate at near peak power for long periods of time required to accelerate the ship. This made the engine crew subject to constant work to maintain them, and McLeod was glad he didn't have to spend long hours in the noisy engine room. He was pleased Tia Dermott was running the engine crew, feeling there were going to be fewer problems with her in charge.

McLeod settled down in the captain's chair, preparing for the long and usually boring journey between the mining station and Mars, and occasionally the trip was extended to Earth. He checked the readouts on a monitor and determined all was normal. The round command section had four areas that extended past the square face of the mining section. This allowed a visual past the rectangular sections if the front section sensors failed to communicate to the control section.

The ship didn't take the shortest, straight line route to Mars. Rather, it travelled in an arc slightly above the plane of the solar system, avoiding millions of small rocks and larger ones that orbited the sun. The rocks were the fragments of the asteroids, and generally continued along the same plane as the original bodies. While moving above or below the plane, the McKenzie King avoided most of the loose rocks. The remaining ones could still impact the ship and potentially cause damage. However, the ship generated a diversion field that was able to deflect rocks containing metal, in particular iron. If a rock was too large, moving too fast, or didn't contain enough metal, then it had the potential to collide with the ship. Thus, although the trip was long and could be mind numbing, there was the small possibility of a sudden disaster from a rock strike at the wrong place.

"Captain, we are now ten kilometres away from the station. Shall I make the announcement the passengers are free to walk around?" First Officer Lexanna Shultz spoke from her seat near the pilot's console.

McLeod confirmed. "Yes, we're officially past the danger zone now." Safety protocol meant all passengers and crew, unless duties required otherwise, remain seated when within ten kilometres of the space station. He was pleased to have the experienced first officer on the ship, and in particular having done several runs between the asteroids and Mars or Earth. As a first officer, she also took turns at piloting the ship, although it usually ran on automatic guidance. He listened to her rehearsed speech to the passengers and glanced once more at the monitors surrounding his chair. Satisfied that there wasn't any imminent danger, he stood. "I think I'll take a walk and do a visual inspection. Ms. Shultz, you have command."

McLeod exited to the control module and entered the passenger department, passing through the kitchen and the maintenance crew cabins area first. His own cabin was located there as well, although his larger suite contained superior amenities.

The passengers were moving around the level where seating and their suites were located, with most heading to one of two places. One was the lounge where alcoholic drinks could be purchased. After spending months on the mining space station where alcohol and recreational drugs were prohibited, the opportunity to indulge in drinking was very tempting. Unfortunately, for those wanting to celebrate too much, the ship's lounges restricted the number of drinks each passenger could consume per day. The restriction was slightly relaxed on the latter part of the voyage, but incidents involving alcohol were largely reduced due to ship's lounge policy.

The other area the passengers headed was to the showers in their suites. After living in the stale air of the space station, working long hours in difficult conditions, the workers were eager to stand under the hot water until their skin wrinkled.

One other place some passengers used was the recreation level where games, videos, music and exercise rooms could be experienced. The recreation level was nearly empty, but as days passed on the long voyage it would be become busy.

McLeod acknowledged a few of their guests as he passed through the passenger area and to the engine room. He had to use a thumb scanner and punch in a pass code to open the door. The heavy sound of the engines filled the room, making the floor vibrate. He quickly put on one of the yellow headphones that were hanging on a wall. A glowing sign warned that ear protection must be worn at all times. *The room of a hundred warning signs.*

The engine room was cavernous. Looking up, he could see the white ceiling four stories above with a series of catwalks, partial floors and permanent ladders criss-crossing the open space. Holographic signs floated in the air, warning of uneven flooring, high voltages and a myriad of other dangers. He saw robotic carts carry various parts along the floor as he made his way to where a cluster of workers were studying the readouts on various monitors. McLeod passed several doors to the rooms where different generators were housed. The generators created the artificial gravity, the diversion field, and the critical space compression field. Each door had a sign warning of the danger inside.

"Chief Engineer Dermott," he called out.

Although the environment was noisy from the nine engines, the headphones effectively cancelled out their sound. They allowed normal voice to penetrate, thus avoiding the need for additional communication devices.

Dermott turned in his direction, her gaze acknowledging him. She redirected her attention to those around her, spoke a few words, and walked toward him. "Captain, anything wrong?"

"I hope not." He grinned. "I suspect you may know more than I do back here." He looked at the massive motors at the rear of the ship, three rows of three engines.

"Everything is running normally. In an hour, we'll start maintenance level one." She brushed back her hair with her fingers.

McLeod had studied the maintenance guidelines for the ship. He understood maintenance level one meant shutting down an engine for half a day to replace filters, ion plates and recalibrate the various inputs versus output. It meant that instead of nine engines, eight would be working instead. "Good to hear. I only came down here because I don't have any pressing duties. Are you off duty at eighteen hundred?"

"Likely, unless there's a problem."

McLeod knew how Dermott would often forget about time and stay working long hours on a repair. "I was thinking we could meet for a beer and a burger."

"Sure. Nineteen hundred? I'll need time to clean up."

—

McLeod wasn't surprised Dermott was late showing up at the lounge. He relaxed at a table, drinking a non-alcoholic beer. Although regulations permitted him to have alcohol while off duty, being a new captain of a cargo ship, he didn't feel comfortable in indulging in a drink yet.

"Sorry I'm late." Dermott sat across from him.

"No problem. Extra repair work?"

"I called a meeting at the end of the shift and included the next shift. I wanted to make sure the process was being followed for taking an engine offline and putting it back on afterward. It's a safety issue. The process is simple, and has built in safeguards, but some of the engineers are new and I want to make sure there aren't any errors."

"That's what I like about having you as chief engineer." He approved her explanation. "You don't make assumptions and don't leave anything to chance."

"Thanks. I'm starving. Let's order food before I faint."

The ordering of food and drink was done on a tablet attached to the table. Although the food was partially prepared by a robotic chef, the food and drinks were brought out by a human server. The server, along with the cleaning crew, was considered a safe position to determine if the candidate was suitable for long journey spaceflights. After working the entry position, they would be considered for a career in the spaceships. Many of the maintenance and hospitality crews were working through a college or university program that would lend itself to a career in space.

McLeod took a bite of his burger. "How do you like working on the Mark Industrial Engines?"

"They're monsters, but actually quite simple to work on. The problem is they require a lot of maintenance because they're running under full power for long periods of time."

"They're also noisy."

"No kidding." Dermott laughed. "That ear protection is mandatory for good reason."

His mobile chirped twice rapidly, indicating a message from

bridge command. He listened to the message and sent an acknowledgement signal back. "Looks like a rock managed to press past the diverter field and hit a sensor array on the front module. It's not serious, we can use the other sensors to compensate."

"Are you just going to leave it?"

"No, but I'll wait until we're above the solar plane by a few degrees first."

"Less rocks and other debris to worry about there."

"Right. No point in fixing a sensor and then have another get smashed an hour later. I don't like having to shut down the compression field for repair any longer than I have to." McLeod referred to the field used to compress space in front of the ship, allowing it to travel much faster than engine power alone would allow. The compressed field pulled the ship like a boat in the wake of a large ship.

The repair work was done by a robotic repair probe the size of a small car. It was capable of autonomous repair anywhere on the outside of the ship. The self-powered device robot did not have compression field capability, thus the field had to be shut off during repair. The diverter field was also turned off as it would also repel the probe, however once they moved above the plane of where the asteroids circled the sun, the chances of collisions dropped considerably.

"Good point."

"I'm glad we both had an opportunity to get out of the mining ships. They do wear a person down."

"They sure do, and not much rest to be had at the Terra Nova either. Also, with me being a woman, I had to put up with being hit on every time I went anywhere on the space station. I tell you, some of those guys could be real assholes when you tell them to screw off." She frowned at the memory.

"Sorry, I didn't know how bad it was for you. The men in the Nebula seem to treat you okay."

"Well, there were a couple of reasons for that. One is that everyone was pretty focused on their job when we were in the ship. You made sure of that. I was working on another ship where you weren't there, and I was hassled a couple of times."

"That shouldn't happen." McLeod shook his head. "The captain wasn't doing his job."

"I agree. But if you're a woman in male dominated space, it goes with the territory. I had my eyes wide open when I decided to pursue this career."

"Why did you want to be an engine mechanic for spaceships?"

"Money. I get paid three times the amount I would doing the same job on Earth, or even Mars."

"Makes sense."

"There's one other reason I didn't get hassled on the Nebula as much as I did on other ships."

"What? Your ability to turn into a tiger if some guy got too insistent?"

"Yeah, my morphing ability." Dermott laughed. "No, seriously, it was you. When I'm around you, men just leave me alone. I think they know you won't put up with any shit. You're my protector, even if you didn't know it."

"Damn, I guess I learn something new every day. And here I thought it was you protecting me." He laughed with her. "I better check on that sensor array damage, and make sure there aren't any other problems."

"Okay, thanks for the invite. See you later, it was great talking to you."

━━

The command centre was quiet, and Shultz gave him a questioning look. "I didn't expect to see you back here this evening."

"I wasn't planning to, but just wanted to check on the damaged sensor array."

"No worries there. The other sensors can cover the same range. Nothing else is happening." She smiled. "You better get used to this. Transport ships just plug along. Usually the most excitement is generated by the passengers who get a little antsy about returning home. Maybe an argument or two happens along the way." She put a hand on his shoulder and pushed him back. "Go and have a drink or watch a video. Leave us to our boredom here. We'll call you if something exciting happens."

McLeod grinned. "Aye, aye, madam." He understood his presence wasn't doing her any favours. Shultz had moved up the chain of command slowly, largely due to her lack of formal education. She had finally obtained most of the required degrees by studying in her off hours. Part of the decision whether to promote her to being captain of her own ship was the perception of her abilities by her subordinates. They were less likely to give her a glowing report if he was there for every minor incident.

McLeod spent the evening walking around the ship, inspecting various areas of the ship for any deviance from regulations. He stopped a few crew members, even those only involved in cleaning, to say hello and tried to memorize their name with their faces.

One young man appeared nervous when he greeted him, stuttering out a reply. "Hel-lo, Captain...McLeod, s-sir."

"Relax. I'm just saying hello. Ronald, is it?"

"Yes, Ronald Brown."

"Your first time working on a spaceship?"

"Yes sir. I'm a repair technician for climate control."

"I remember my first job on a spaceship. It was a pretty nerve-racking experience, but I asked questions from the older guys, and learned a lot as I worked different jobs. Enjoy the experience of working on McKenzie King, Ronald. You may end up like I did and make a career out of it."

"Thank you, sir. I hope to be working in space for a long time."

Brown looked less nervous after McLeod finished speaking with him and decided he would check to see how he was doing in a couple of days.

McLeod returned to the bar, and ordered a proper drink, a straight rum. He inhaled the alcohol fuelled aroma from the rim of the glass and set it down. He tried to calculate the number of months it had been since his last drink. *Damn, that's a long time. This rum is going to taste real good.*

He sipped the rum, letting the flavours trickle over his tongue. He marvelled at the change from being a captain of a mining ship to that of a transport. *On the mining ship, I had to be ready for any of a hundred possible disasters. On this, nothing but the calendar to mark off.*

He ordered a second rum. *I never considered how hard it must have been for Tia. I heard that some women feel slightly intimidated by the number of men on a spaceship, but on the mining ships and the processing space stations it must be a lot worse. A lot of the men there don't give a damn about any niceties. You have to be tough-minded to work mining asteroids, doubly so for a woman.*

He finished his second drink and made his way to his suite. Instead of going into his room, he continued to the command centre. The amber light above the entrance indicated it was operating on night mode. The few personnel working were quietly monitoring readouts, not expecting any problems. If a situation were to come up, Lexanna Shultz would be called, being in charge of the night operations.

He studied a monitor, showing a view of the front of the ship. The sun was easily identified as the brightest object, and it appeared as a small round globe. Everything else was just bright dots of light. He left the command centre, satisfied everything was boring and in control.

Everything is good, and I'm not about to wish for any excitement. Boredom can be good.

[5]

THE HALLIANS HAD DEVELOPED A CIVILIZED SOCIETY, AND EVEN reached the technology level to land on their two small moons via rockets. It was an enormous accomplishment for the bipedal species, but the same science that allowed them to reach space, also showed them their world was doomed. They spotted the giant rogue world enter their star system, and calculated a near collision would happen with Hallia.

There wasn't any way to escape the world moving toward them. They saw the frozen atmosphere thaw and boil along coloured bands as the visitor approached their sun. It was both a beautiful and a horrible vision.

Meanwhile scientists designed several globes that would be placed in orbit, hoping they would survive the close encounter with the gas giant. While Hallian life wouldn't survive, the satellites could leave a record of it when it was a living world.

The launching of the satellites was cause for celebration for the Hallians. It was also to be the last celebration on Hallia. Some Hallians did survive the horrific storms and earthquakes as the two worlds rendezvoused. Hallia didn't break apart as it was feared but was pushed out of its solar system.

50

After a small breakfast, McLeod entered the command centre. Shultz was already there, working on the logbooks for last night's work. There weren't any major incidents to report, so she finished up quickly.

McLeod stood next to her as she signed off on the log entry. "That was a nice quiet evening. I took your advice and decided the ship was in capable hands without my presence. In fact, I treated myself to a couple of drinks. First ones I had since I left for the mining station."

"That must have tasted good."

"It did, but I'm not used to alcohol anymore. Two drinks and I slept like a log."

"Captain, there's an unidentified space object at 32 dot 073 by 143 dot 255. Distance and speed unknown."

McLeod heard the excitement in the corporal's voice. *Likely his first USO.* He looked at his own monitor in the control room, noting the pulsing light that showed where the USO was located relative to the McKenzie King. The object was too far for the distance to be calculated. Electromagnetic waves were used to determine distance, and if the distance was too great, even the speed of light didn't cover the distance quick enough to be effective. He saw the readout of the location and the change in the numbers as the USO moved. "What would be the speed of the object if it was at the Kuiper Belt?"

"Sir, the speed would be 2 dot 43 times the speed of light."

"Very good, corporal. Save and send the information to International Space Agency." The USO sightings had been a mystery since humans first colonized Mars. At the same time UFO sightings had dropped dramatically, leading to speculation the two phenomena were tied together somehow. Still, the USO had a second mystery to them. If they were travelling near the outer regions of the solar system, then they were moving at enormous speeds, often breaking the speed of light. The speed of light was thought to be a barrier for all physical objects, and many scientists scoffed that the USOs represented real objects. Those scientists suggested they were an illusion they had not discovered the basis for yet. The USOs were also known as ghost shadows.

Several years previously, a space telescope was searching the Kuiper Belt, the region of comets far past Neptune, when an anomaly was discovered. Photographs showed a shadow crossing in front of the backdrop of the millions of stars, the silhouette approaching the size of a Kuiper object. At first, it was given a number to identify it as a member of the solar system, when additional calculations showed it was moving over the speed of light in the Kuiper region. Theories on what the object was ranged from alien spaceships to an optical illusion due to the affect of a gravitational lens.

McLeod went over to Lexanna Shultz, who was checking navigation monitors. The three-dimensional images of graphs and vectors required special training and experience to interpret the information. "Seeing anything special?"

"Just a hunch I had. This is my third USO, and I was curious to see if it matched the other two in direction." She pointed at two thin lines, one blue and the other red.

"Do they? This is my fourth USO, but I never thought to look at their apparent direction. Of course, that was when I was running a mining ship, and I didn't have the time to do anything but to note and report them."

"No, this one was moving in the opposite direction." Lexanna indicated the red line with a finger. "Although it was at the same angle as the other two."

"Like if they were spaceships going to a specific location and returning?" McLeod asked.

"That was what I was thinking. The I. S. A. is collecting all the data on USOs but won't release any information. I'm sure they've figured out what they are by now but governments like their secrets."

"They sure do. You're relieved of duty. I'll resume command."

"Thanks, I think I'll grab some dinner." Lexanna stood and left.

A few hours later, he placed a hand on the shoulder of his third in command, Henry Lee. "I'm going to grab a coffee and do a physical check in the engine room. You have command while I'm gone."

"Yes, sir." He looked up at the captain. "Take your time with the coffee. There's not much going on in here."

"Let's hope it stays that way."

McLeod made his way through the passenger area, stopping to chat with a couple of men he recognized from his time working on the mining ships. "Hi Pete, Jamie. Finally heading home to stay, or just a rest period?"

"This cowboy has had enough of this crap." Pete shook his head. "I've saved enough to buy up some nice property and take a safer job."

"I have a wife and kid," Jamie added. "If I spend any longer out here in the rocks, I'll be paying alimony and child support. It looks like you've done alright for yourself. Captain of this hauler has to be lot a easier on the body than smashing asteroids."

"Yeah, I don't have any complaints. Except this is a bit boring compared to the mining ships."

"Boring is good after risking your life every day out there." Peter laughed. "Now you just need to find a pretty woman to help you spend all that money you made."

"It has crossed my mind. Good to see you guys are leaving with your bodies still intact."

McLeod walked to the engine room, complimenting a woman that was cleaning the floors as he went by. "Great job, Nickie. The floor looks clean enough to eat off."

"Thank you, Captain." She laughed and added, "But tables are easier to sit at."

He put on the ear protection and approached Dermott as she directed two crew members working above her on one of the engines.

"When you pull the filters, inspect the inside for anything unusual. Don't just slide in the new filters."

He waited until she finished her lecture and turned away from the crew. "Everything good, Tia?"

"All good." She smiled and briefly touched his arm. "They're new at engine maintenance. Well trained, but no experience, so I have to babysit them."

"Did you hear about the USO we spotted yesterday?"

"I did. If they're spaceships, I wish I could see what engines they use."

"Whatever they use, I'm sure you could fix them."

"Thanks." She gave him a light punch on his shoulder. "And thanks again for getting me off the mining ships. I had my fill of those tin buckets."

"You're welcome, but you're the best there is when it comes to keeping engines running."

His mobile beeped twice quickly. "Captain McLeod. Go ahead."

"Space emergency, Captain. The Nevada Queen is broadcasting for help."

Dermott's eyes opened wide. "Oh, my God. That's a passenger ship!"

McLeod turned and hurried back to the command centre, speaking as he did so. "I need the position of the Nevada Queen and how long it'll take for us to get there at maximum speed. Call First Officer Shultz to report to the command centre."

[6]

*THE ENDLESS NIGHT ARRIVED AS LIFE ON HALLIA CONTINUED TO
vanish. Dark dust clouds covered the sky, making day and night
impossible to distinguish.*

*As death wrapped its cold arms around the planet, a group of
Hallians huddled on a high plateau. The hundreds of scientists,
engineers and technicians, along with their families, were the ones
responsible for the launching of the satellites, and now used what little
time they had to fire small positioning rockets on the satellites to
ensure they had achieved a stable orbit. Directly around the facility a
town had grown. The last Hallians collected together to try and
celebrate what their world had accomplished.*

*The final signals the scientists sent to the satellites caught the
attention of alien ships.*

*These aliens normally didn't care to try to make life better for
other species but decided they could save the last inhabitants on
Hallia. They landed and took on aboard the few thousand Hallians
left on their ships.*

———

McLeod sat in the control room, reading the updates to the
Nevada Queen's situation. "The passenger ship was stranded on its
run from Mars to Earth after it had completed about two-thirds of

its journey." He turned to Shultz. "Lexanna, it looks like both engines shut down. They're just sitting until help arrives. It appears that they're not in any immediate danger. Another ship will be able to arrive at their position in half a day. That's a lot better than our three-day voyage to get there."

"Thank God. How in the world did both engines fail? There's going to be hell to pay for that."

McLeod guessed how both engines likely failed. *The captain, and some of the crew, are getting paid bonuses for keeping expenses down. They cut down on basic maintenance and now that's biting them in the ass.* "They're going to be some lawsuits out of this. Passengers on inter-planet flights are usually well heeled, and don't appreciate interruptions or danger on their voyage."

Shultz looked upset. "This is just stupid." She slowly breathed out, visibly trying to relax. "I was once on a ship where the main engine blew a reducing coil. That's pretty rare and we had to put the auxiliary engine on-line. One tenth the power, but we made it back to the space station. I have to say it scared the shit out of me when that coil went, like an explosion in a bell. There wasn't anyone at fault, just a fluke occurrence."

"Those things can happen on any ship."

"True. But this old crew member took it all in stride. He told me you can't worry about the one in a thousand stuff. If it's going to happen, it's going to happen. But, if you want to be on a safe ship, look at the captain. Don't get on a ship where you wouldn't trust the captain in a two-man lifeboat to get you to home port."

"Good advice."

"Yeah, it is." She peered at him. "Just so you know, I checked your record before I agreed to stay on here. I talked to some of your colleagues. They would follow you to a black hole."

———

Dermott heard the news about the Nevada Queen and quickly summoned her crew. "What happened to the Nevada Queen is a perfect example of what happens when you assume basic maintenance is sufficient. Look for anything that shouldn't be there. Believe me when I say you do not want your name written as the last maintenance person on the checklist before engine failure. That can be career ending." She looked at each crew member in turn. "Let's make sure we stay diligent when servicing the engines. Lives depend on us."

She left the engine room, now officially off duty. In fact, her shift had ended two hours previously, but she wanted to go over all the engine records before she made the speech to the crew. Everything was exactly as it should be on the records, but she felt the need to push the point home even more. *I never had a mining ship stranded due to engine failure. Others did, but my record is clean. Why some of these techs feel they can just slap on a new filter and it's good to go I'll never understand. Thank the heavens Jaret appreciates my ability. Too many captains ignore women, thinking they're incapable of doing anything in a spaceship.*

She went to the lounge and ordered a beer and pizza. She refused to meet the stares of the mostly male patrons around in the bar, knowing that might be taken as an invitation to join her at the table. In the past she did allow the occasional man to take her to his cabin, but she wasn't in the mood tonight.

The ice-cold beer tasted wonderful and was prepared for a second gulp when a female voice interrupted her thoughts.

"Hi, may I join you?"

She looked up at a blonde with shoulder length hair. The pretty young woman had a cheerful expression on her face. "Sure."

"Thanks. I want to have a drink and a bite to eat, but a woman sitting alone here sometimes get harassed by these men. They're like wolves let out of cages after working the rocks."

"Yeah, that about sums it up. I'm Tia."

"Tracie, otherwise known as the pizza girl." She giggled. "My nickname given to me when I first started here a year ago on the nightshift. Now I run the daytime kitchen, but the nickname stuck. How about you?"

"I work in the engine room."

"Oh! I heard there was a woman who was in charge of the engine room. Wow, that must be something to work in there and be in charge of all those men. I'm impressed."

"I learned my trade while working on mining ships."

"You must be tough to survive that. I hear the men are pretty rough and demanding among the rocks."

"They can be, but you have to stand up for yourself and don't take any shit. Once you have their respect, it isn't bad. Plus, I worked with a guy who acted like my big brother."

Dermott finished her beer, ordered another, and announced it was time to turn in. "Let's get together again for drinks or a movie."

"That'd be great. It'll be fun to have a female friend on this ship."

McLeod ordered the robot maintenance vehicle to begin the repair of the front sensor module. That involved shutting down the diverter field and the compression field for the robot vehicle to do its work. He noted Dermott was happy to show her crew the proper shut down sequence for the diverter and the compression field. He visited the engine room to watch how it was done, feeling a captain should know as much as he could about each aspect of the ship operations.

Once again, he was impressed how Dermott used every opportunity to create a teaching moment. She made sure every crew member in engine maintenance was familiar with the procedure.

After they shut the two generators, McLeod walked over to her. "Are you interested in watching the repair robot at the comm?"

"That would be great."

"Good. It'll also give you a chance to say hello again to the comm officers. They should know who you are other than through the electronic communications from the engine room."

"This sounds special. Should I comb my hair first?"

He laughed. As long as he knew her, she had kept her hair a short, no nonsense length. "No, but maybe put on a dress."

This time she laughed. "Too bad. I don't own one."

They reached the command centre, and after Dermott said a hello to everyone, they watched a monitor with the image from the robot's own camera as it moved into position and began the repair work.

The machine replaced the sensor module and did an inspection of the other sensors, using an array of instruments. It replaced a second module that was functioning according to the readouts in the control cabin, but the robot may have seen visual damage that suggested failure was a future possibility. Two hours later, the robot docked back into its cavity, a cover slid across to protect it, and the mission was completed.

"That was great to watch." Dermott sounded excited. "Thanks for inviting me up here. It was also great to see the officers up here."

"It was good for us see you as well. Before you go back and turn on the diverter and space compression fields, I want you to promise me that you won't be a stranger up here. Come by occasionally." Shultz gave her a smile. "I could use another woman to talk to."

"Okay, I will. Now I better run so we can make time again."

After Dermott left, Shultz came up to him. "I know it's none of my business, but did you apply for a new position?"

He shook his head. "Why do you ask?"

"I received a questionnaire about the ship operation and you as a captain. It's a bit unusual. I always have one to fill out at the end of a voyage, but never near the beginning."

"I honestly don't know. Maybe they're planning to fire me."

His mobile chirped twice, and he briefly touched his earpiece to hear the new message. The electronic voice stated he had an urgent message pertaining to the operation of the McKenzie King.

THE SURVIVING HALLIANS WERE DEPOSITED ON A WORLD WITHOUT any sentient species on it, and they began to develop their adopted world. They survived and prospered on the world, adjusting to the warmer climate and heavier gravity over generations. They were aided by the aliens that initially saved them and developed an understanding with their saviours.

Hallia became a distant memory, but the inhabitants kept track of where their former home travelled. They calculated that it was possible it might actually leave the galaxy, but circumstances led it to enter the gravity field of another solar system. The aliens showed the Hallians, via video images, where their old world came into contact with the outer reaches of the new solar system, interfering with a pair of minor planets. The minor planets' orbit was jarred from a circular orbit to an elliptical one that no longer stayed on the same plane as the other planets. Hallia joined the new solar system, orbiting even further above the plane.

———

McLeod read the new manifest. They were now within two days of Mars, and instead of docking the ship in orbit and enjoying two weeks off until the voyage back to the asteroids, they had only a few days off. Just over half of their cargo was going to be left at Mars, the rest of the shipment was going to Earth. Some of the passengers would be continuing on with the journey to Earth. He didn't mind but suspected some of the crew had plans to stay on Mars. All crew members had signed a contract, agreeing to work on the ship for the duration of the voyage, even if it was diverted to a different destination. It would be difficult to replace some of the crew members on short notice when they arrived on Mars.

He relayed the new information to the crew and suspected there would be some groans that their work wasn't done yet. They would get additional pay, which would help make the extended trip a bit easier.

McLeod confirmed his hotel room booking but cancelled the additional days he had originally planned. The penalty for the short notice of a cancellation would be paid by Gibbston Space Lines.

He met with the officers in the command centre, including Tia Dermott, and suggested they take advantage of their shortened leave the best they could. "I know Red City isn't exactly made for tourists, but there are some interesting places to visit, besides bars." He paused as the officers chuckled. "I'll be available if anyone has a problem. Don't hesitate to contact me. Okay, everyone here knows when to report. Have a safe time on Mars."

The shuttle took him down to the Mars Port Two. The newer port featured a magnetic rail from the facilities to Red City, the capital and largest city on Mars. He always liked how the city was designed, looking completely different from Earth cities.

When the dome that protected and covered the original colony on Mars became too small, the Martian people decided that they didn't want a second, larger dome. Instead they built unique, independent buildings exposed to the Martian environment. The buildings were tall, thin and shaped to help counter the high winds that often crossed the planet. During wind storms the buildings profile would help turn the wind against itself rather than trying to block it. The result was little wind near the interior of Red City.

From a distance, the odd shaped buildings looked alien, especially in early mornings when a fog occasionally shrouded the lower parts of the city.

He checked into his hotel and left his travel case on the bed. The room consisted of a dresser/desk, a small closet and a washroom with a shower. He looked out the window, seeing the odd twisted shaped buildings and the desert beyond. One wall in his room functioned as a TV or could be set to show as a window looking at various parts of Mars. He first checked the local news and noted there wasn't a dust storm advisory. He set the TV to scan various parts of Mars as he changed clothes, getting out of his captain's uniform.

The views showed Mars was still mostly red sand and rock, but terraforming showed there were small patches of life. McLeod had heard that some areas had successfully established a few insects and tiny lizards as part of a few isolated ecology systems. Life wasn't alien on Mars, as ancient remains of plants and tiny fossils had shown. After McLeod changed, he caught an elevator just outside of his room.

The elevator had two other occupants, and both men were too tired to engage in a conversation. He entered the lobby, and then a set of double doors to the outside. A sign warned of the reduced air pressure and gravity when leaving the confines of the building. McLeod gazed at the brick pathway that went from the hotel to the main walkway with plants in large pots marking the hotel property.

McLeod walked down the walkway and headed to the downtown area of Red City. Red City was the oldest and largest urban area of Mars and held most of the corporate offices and their government. A few other towns and cities were on Mars, but they didn't cater as much to visitors. The shops he came across were small and many carried a variety of goods. McLeod wasn't interested in any of them, but rather one of the bars in the area.

He picked one by the sound of its name that was situated at a corner of two streets. He entered the Opus Bar and Grill and made his way past the tables to sit on one of stools around the curved metal bar.

The blonde bartender, who hadn't reached middle age yet, greeted him with a smile as she wiped the bar portion in front of him.

"Just a drink, or would you like to see the food menu too?"

"Your coldest beer, and I'll look at the menu."

She poured him a gold coloured beer, setting the plastic mug in front of him. She handed him a plastic sheet, detailing the food choices. "Avoid the fish burger. I don't know what they do to grow fish fillets, but it tastes like flavoured dough."

"Sounds bad."

"Been like that since I've been here. I grew up in Nova Scotia, and I know what fish is supposed to be like."

He took a long gulp of his beer. "Cheeseburger safe?"

She grinned. "Not for the cow."

He laughed. All meat and fish products were grown in vats from protein strings. Some vats, which used a combination of art and science to make synthetic food, could produce excellent products. Others were a hit and miss. "Bring me another beer when the burger is ready." He watched her walk away, wearing a thermal suit with a colourful design on it. People who lived on Mars the year round generally wore a thermal suit every day, often not knowing when they might have to leave the safe confines of a building and have to travel outside. While men often still wore pants and a shirt over the thermal suit, younger women usually just wore the form fitting suit. The bartender's suit had the front closure partly undone, and he suspected the reason for that was to help generate tips. On Earth, tipping had largely disappeared, but for Mars tipping had become a necessity to help keep those in the service industry to stay on Mars. The high cost of living on Mars, plus its isolation from Earth, meant wages alone weren't enough to warrant people like her to stay.

The bar had a steady flow of customers. By the time he

finished his second drink, a second bartender had arrived to help with the evening crowd.

"Looks like it's going to get busy in here."

"Not much else to do in this town at night. A lot of people here are just passing through and need to blow off a bit of steam. Some can't drink much on ships, so when they get here, they make the most of it."

"I'm guilty of that."

"Earth run passenger ship?"

"No, ore from the rocks. Stop off here and then on to Earth with the rest of the cargo." He paused, "I'm Jaret."

"Leana. That's a hell of a long journey. You piss someone off?" She gave him a wink and hurried off to pour a few drinks. She returned to lean on the counter in front of him.

"What do you do on the ship?"

"I'm a captain."

Leana pursed her lips and nodded. "You act like a captain. In control and smart."

"Thanks. Did you hear anything about the Nevada Queen?"

"Just rumours. A complete breakdown in space. They had an emergency generator for life support, but it took a couple of days to rescue them. I guess they gave up trying to fix the motors and had to tug the ship to an Earth port."

"That can't be good."

"No. I heard some of the crew, including the captain, are being let go. In fact, the ship itself may be sold as scrap."

"Too bad if they do scrap it. It may be an old ship, but it had some style to it."

She put another beer in front of him. "On the house."

McLeod felt light-headed as he made his way to his hotel. *Combination of thin air and not used to drinking has hit me a bit hard. Nice bar. Nicer bartender. I'll have to go back before I leave Mars.*

McLeod woke up with the morning sun coming through his hotel room's window. He marvelled at the sight. For the past few years living in space far from the sun, he had forgotten what the sight of a sunrise was. He stayed in his bed for several minutes, staring out the window. Finally, he rolled out of bed and prepared for the day. He dressed and peered at the sun as it rose. He saw the red sand beyond the buildings and knew what he wanted to do.

The older man was friendly enough at the counter of Red Sand Tours.

"Well, we don't normally rent out the small shuttles, except to corporations who need them to check out a pipeline or something like that. Their drivers are licenced and experienced on the Mars terrain. Most of the time we give people a guided tour in one of the large shuttles. There are safety reasons for why we don't just allow newcomers to take a shuttle. You understand what I'm saying?"

"I hear you. Let me tell you a bit about myself first before you make up your mind. I'm a captain of an ore ship stopping over at Mars on my way to Earth. Before that I spent two years at the asteroids running the mining ships. I know safety, I know how to pilot a mining ship, and after being on a ship in close proximity to others, I need some away from humanity time."

"I see your point." The man nodded. "Well, I reckon anyone who can operate a mining ship can handle a shuttle. It'll cost you though, but I suspect money isn't the issue here."

"No, I can't say that's a problem."

"Okay, ever wore a thermal suit before?"

"Never."

He pulled one from underneath the counter. "This won't fit you, but they're all the same. Tight fitting, and not comfortable to wear as far as I'm concerned. But women wear them all the time. They must like the feel of them I suppose, or the fact it shows off their bodies real good." He chuckled. "Now the suit is breathable but holds in the heat extremely well. It comes with a utility belt that holds a water bottle, oxygen enhancer mask, battery pack and a hand-held power generator." He opened a pouch in the utility belt to reveal a small disc with a handle on it. A wire with a jack dangled from the device. "Now if an emergency arises where you need to power up the battery, you simply plug this jack into it and crank the handle. It'll charge up the battery pretty good. I doubt you'll need to use it. The battery also receives a charge from the suit's layer which is also a solar collector.

"Sounds simple enough."

"Okay, now I'll go to the back and find one that'll fit you."

McLeod received more basic instructions on the shuttle. He found the controls simple and didn't really need any explanation. He set the control on automatic and picked out a random destination, an ecology centre thirty-seven kilometres away. He relaxed as the Martian landscape rolled past him. He thought it really did look like the bottom of a dried-up seabed, which helped explain the numerous fossils they found in the area.

A half hour later, he switched the shuttle to manual, wanting to control the craft instead of being just a passenger. It was slightly different than that of a mining ship, but easy to maneuver. The shuttle was limited to two metres above the ground, while every move the mining ship did included an up and down component. He skirted around a series of columns made of wind blasted sandstone and accelerated along an open plain. A light flashed on the control console indicating he was close to his destination. He slowed and drifted toward where the guidance system indicated the location of the ecology centre.

He shut down the shuttle and stepped out onto the rocky soil. The cool air felt good on his face. He took a drink of water from the bottle attached to his utility belt and made his way to a fenced off green oasis beyond. A sign warned all visitors to stay strictly on the pathway and listed several other 'Do Not....'. A verbal warning also came through his earpiece. He went past the entrance, suddenly aware of the smell of plants and water. He understood the ecology centre was built into a hill, protecting it from wind. With a southern exposure and the hill protecting it, that made it slightly warmer than if it was fully exposed to the elements.

The centre used small mammals as the higher form of life. The ones using lizards were less successful, but biologists were still making adjustments to their DNA, hoping to establish a thriving species for Mars.

The path went along the outside of a pond, with the broad leaf plants growing along the edges. Water plants slowly waved under the cold water. McLeod didn't see any of the small animals but spotted a few of the insects. Water was pumped up from an underground reservoir and heated slightly before being poured into the pond via an artificial waterfall. The pond slowly drained back into the reservoir. Power for the pump, and heat lamps, came from solar panels on top of the hill.

From what McLeod had read, the success of the ecology centres depended on a very careful selection of supportive species, and their ability to survive the very cold conditions of Mars. Some centres successfully went into hibernation for several months, coming back to life during the Martian summer. Other centres were less durable, and biologists worked to fine tune the species. Occasionally, a rodent or insect was found a considerable distance from an ecology centre, giving rise to hope some were evolving to Martian climate. The lost rodents were also suspected of being the source of sightings of Martian life, although the believers of Martian life refuted that possibility.

McLeod took another drink of water and finished the loop around the ecology centre. He returned to the shuttle, considering where to go to next. The where to go to next turned into a random journey among the rocks. He avoided the small craters and ridges that littered the Martian surface and gradually made his way back to Red City.

The same older man was waiting for him when he returned.

"I was going to call you to see if you were planning to stay out all night. Some people sleep in the shuttles."

McLeod laughed. "No, I'd wake up and think I was on a mining ship again." He headed back to his hotel room, feeling much better mentally from his excursion on Mars.

J. H. WEAR

McLeod returned to the Opus Bar and Grill the next day and was pleased to see Leana working behind the bar again.

"Rum and cola this time. Less chance of a hangover I think."

She laughed. "It's just a different tasting poison."

"So, do you recommend any other activity besides consumption of alcohol in Red City? I rented a shuttle and drove around Mars and went to one of those ecology centres."

"Depends what you like. There's the usual movie and gaming places, but I'm guessing you've seen all those before. There's a museum of Martian history that's actually pretty interesting. They have a replica of the original mole diggers. Just a monster of a machine. There are fossils and models of the supposedly extinct Martian life."

"Supposedly extinct?"

"Let me just say there are reports from reliable people of sightings of creatures that are not of Earthly origins. I've taken a few trips outside of Red City to see if I can find any strange creatures. So far, no ghosts."

McLeod remembered reading the reports about *something* seen around Mars. The problem with the reliability was the thin air of Mars could cause hallucinations. Coupled with even a light alcoholic drink and suddenly the mind could play tricks. "Nothing has been caught yet though. And so far, no physical evidence of anything but humans walking around on the surface."

"That's not entirely true. They have established small, protected areas with plants, insects and small animals. What if some Martian life managed to survive in volcanic vents, and is now able to return to surface for short periods of time?"

"Possible, I suppose. There's a lot about Mars we don't know." He decided against mentioning when he visited one of the ecology centres he saw how difficult it was for anything to survive on Mars that wasn't carefully cared for. He didn't believe any Martian life, other than the simple plants, could have survived on the harsh conditions of Mars.

"They've found life on Europa, Enceladus, and Ganymede. And on Venus."

"Venus just has those strange microbes, although I agree

Enceladus has those swimming eels that represents complex life. I guess we don't know yet."

"Tell you what. I have tomorrow off. How about I take you to the museum, and then for some dinner? Just so you know I'm doing this as a friend. I kind of just broke up with someone."

He grinned. "First time I've ever looked forward to a date at a museum."

[8]

The Hallians were excited that their old world, while it never would be able to harbour life again, had found a star to call home. It became a quest for every Hallian to visit their old world at least once in their lifetime.

The Hallians would have eventually discovered faster than light travel in the normal course of scientific discoveries. However, they had the advantage, thanks to the aliens who had rescued them from their old world. While the aliens did not directly tell them how to accomplish faster than light travel, the fact that Hallians knew it was possible meant they could discard theories that prohibited faster than light travel.

When they travelled to their old world, they were often tempted to investigate the new sentient species that was taking the first steps in exploring their own solar system. They tried to be discreet, agreeing with their alien rescuers that the species must be allowed to advance at their own pace. The Hallians understood how the new species had been in contact with various aliens in the past, but once civilization had progressed to the point of landing on other worlds in their own solar system, isolation had been agreed upon by the sixteen space faring species.

McLeod walked to Leana's apartment building, which contained stores on the lower two levels, and a few floors of offices. He wasn't surprised it was located only half a block away from the Opus Bar and Grill, making it easy to get to work. With the Martian climate still on the cool side, it made sense to avoid being outdoors too long. The summers on Mars were cool, but quite tolerable. It was the winters that made sure people didn't want to stay outside any longer than absolutely necessary.

The security entrance gave him permission to enter the residential side of the building, and he made his way to where the elevators waited. A minute later the empty car opened its doors, and McLeod voiced the destination floor.

He pressed the glowing visitor indicator and moments later, Leana opened the door.

"Hi Jaret. Step inside. I'll be ready in minute."

He stepped inside her apartment as she walked back to her bedroom. She was wearing a thermal suit made of a bright yellow top that faded to black on the lower half. It also featured random cut outs of curved objects on the suit. The cut outs were of a semi-transparent mesh. From what McLeod heard they did not, despite the manufacture's claim, provide the same protection against very low temperatures. Still, he did appreciate the design of the thermal suit on her.

The apartment was efficient in space, with the kitchen occupying a small area with a minimum amount of counter space. It was separated by a counter from the living area, with one wall of the living area currently showing a forest scene from Earth. He understood that many transplanted people from Earth loved having a wall sized image of an Earth scene. A thin membrane capable of video images could be made as large as needed and be wrapped around curved surfaces.

The furniture in the room was modular, with two chairs joined together to serve as a couch. It, in turn, could be converted into a bed for an overnight guest. He walked over to the window, saw several of the thin towers that dominated Red City, and understood why she wanted an image of green Earth.

Leana returned from the bedroom, and he noted the cut outs appeared at the front as well as the back.

"I'm ready. Let's go to the museum."

He followed her to the elevator. "Tell me, does that suit really protect you from the cold, or is it a just a fashion thing?"

She laughed. "Come on, it's always at least partially about fashion. It does work well as a thermal suit. The transparent parts are not quite as effective, but it's a balance of fashion and practicality."

"Does that mean bikinis are out?"

"Unfortunately, for the time being they are. But if you find a way to make it hot and sunny here, I'll be happy to wear one."

McLeod looked up at the large curved door entrance. Above the stone perimeter, the name E. Evans Martian Museum stood out in black metal letters in front of lights. "Ellie Evans was that biologist who discovered the first large marine fossils." He saw her thermal suit had the front closure slightly lowered.

"Right. I saw a documentary about her. She was quite the woman."

They moved past the front entrance and immediately came to the exhibit of the mole machines used to dig deep inside the interior of Mars. After reaching their maximum depth, the mole machines used nuclear fusion to heat the iron core of Mars.

McLeod was fascinated by the huge model of only the front of the mole. "Good lord, that is one giant corkscrew. No wonder it could get to the Martian core." He walked to the side, curious how much power was required to turn the mole as it buried through rock. Next to the exhibit was a complete miniature model of the machine. The reduced model was still taller than he was, and he tried to envision the machine burrowing into the crust. He saw that the giant machine had only small access doors that allowed technicians to do a final setup before the mole was put into operation. Once the mole was operating, it was on its own. Each mole was self-repairing; if it failed to work no human was going to repair it. At a screen by a wall, McLeod peered at the three-dimensional simulation of the moles, appreciating the complexity and ingenuity of them. He turned on his earpiece to listen to the voice describing the moles.

"The first generations of the great moles, enormous building sized machines, dug deep into Mars. Weighing over seven thousand tons each, the moles used giant rotating corkscrews to dig through the rock. In addition, the moles used microwave lasers to melt and vaporize the rock in front as each large corkscrew relentlessly churned the rock behind it. If it began to slow down or get stuck, the mole could send out low frequency sound waves to create a minor earthquake. Of the first twelve moles sent deep into the crust of Mars, nine reached their final destinations.

"In a synchronized pattern, each mole ignited nuclear fusion, spreading heat that penetrated inside the Martian core. The first stirring of a long dead core began. The next wave of moles, bigger and with improved technology, fired up the core even more. When the last wave of moles were finished, the core finally awoke from its slumber. The iron flowed like taffy with the eddy currents generating a magnetic field around Mars for the first time in eons. The magnetic field was shut down millions of years previously when an asteroid crashed into the southern hemisphere, leaving only a weak field primarily near the north pole. The magnetic field, like that on Earth, protects us from the solar wind that can strip Mars of its atmosphere and hit us with harmful ultraviolet rays. Before life could return to Mars, we needed a magnetic field to protect us from the sun's radiation.

"The warming of the core had additional benefits. Mars' dormant volcanos came back to life, spewing out molten rock and gasses. The gasses, much of which were carbon dioxide, methane and water vapour, contributed to the warming of Mars. Trickles of water flowed near the equator as Mars warmed, spurring the return of Martian lifeforms in the form of microbes. The microbes in turn released more greenhouse gasses.

"Climate control scientists worked on Mars as well, using a black dye on some parts of the surface and a white dye on other parts to stir the atmosphere into winds, bringing warm, moist air into selected regions. Warm is a subjective word; most of the moisture that fell was sleet. However, now some hardy plants could survive on the open Martian plains.

"Today we have the emergence of more complex Martian plants, although still simple compared to Earth varieties. Earth based life is able to survive in controlled environments on Mars as well. From a dead world, Mars is returning to life. To the great mole machines, and those who designed and built them, we owe a debt of gratitude for giving us a world we can live on."

McLeod finished listening and joined Leana again as she had moved on to read about climate control changes being done on Mars to help terraform the planet. A statue of Riley Evans, husband of Ellie Evans, showed a tall, slim man looking up at the sky. He was considered a genius for his methods to change the weather on Mars. A story was told how he caused the first snowfall on Red City at Christmas as a gift to Ellie Evans just before he proposed to her.

The rest of the museum was largely devoted to Ellie Evans and her countless discoveries of fossils, including the giant rhodosaurus. The twenty-metre monster resembled a seal's body with the head of a fish.

"Ugly thing." Leana studied the holographic image.

"True. Very alien looking."

"From what I understand the DNA from the remains indicate Mars and Earth had a common ancestor. One theory is life on Mars may have seeded Earth from meteorites."

"I guess it's possible." McLeod added. "The same is true for Europa and the other moons. There seems to be a lot of similarities in the DNA of all the worlds. Except for Venus. Those microbes are pretty unique."

"They use sulphuric acid as food. What do you expect?" She laughed.

The statue of Ellie Evans stood in the centre of a collection of core samples taken from former lakes and oceans that existed on Mars. The cores revealed the small fossils that Evans studied and catalogued during her time as a biologist. Later she was appointed as director of the Martian Life Institute that researched past life on Mars, Earth life that could survive on

Mars, and the search for Martian life that still existed. So far, only simple plant life had been officially recognized as being original Martian life.

McLeod acknowledged her accomplishments. "She certainly accomplished a lot during her working career."

"There's more to her than that. She apparently had to go to Mars to avoid detention time on Earth for debt problems. I guess when she first arrived, she was quite the party girl. At least until she met her husband to be and settled down. She also initiated the Flash Club."

"Flash Club?"

"If you live on Mars, you have a few drinks and travel out to where you're well away from Red City or any of the posts. Then you take off your clothes and run around naked. It's become a ritual for adults after they've lived on Mars for a year. It supposed to mean you're now officially a Martian and are one with the planet."

"It never really gets that warm on Mars. It would be a chilly run."

"Usually you do it in a group on the warmest day you can find." She laughed. "And it helps to have portable heaters nearby."

"You've done it?"

"Of course. I consider myself to be a Martian."

"I'd love to see an enactment of that celebration."

"You first." She giggled.

They stopped for a coffee, conversing about how she ended up on Mars.

"I had options, but I was fascinated with the possibility complex life still existed on Mars. I watched the documentaries and read enough to know that we actually know very little about this planet. We have the surface mapped out, but nothing really about what lies below the surface."

"Do you think there's something underground?"

"Why not? It's protected from solar radiation and warmer than the surface. Life was on Mars in the past, and life has a way of adapting when things change. You know there's life in the Antarctica. It has adapted to the cold. Mars life may have done the same. I'm a believer we'll find it has happened here, if we know where to look."

"You have a good point. Say, I'm getting hungry. I think it's time we ate."

"Okay, I know a great spot nearby."

McLeod commented, "I think Red City would appear to be a lot smaller if they didn't make every street curved. Straight lines are usually the fastest way to go between places."

"True, but curved streets look nicer." She pointed at a sand coloured building. "La Concha is on the ninth floor, so you can now stop your whining."

"I was merely pointing out routes could be more efficient." He laughed. "However, you're correct about the streets looking better than if they were in a straight line."

The elevator was located on the outside of the building, giving them a view of the evening light on Mars. Red City lived up to its name with the sun appearing red as it set through a distant dust storm.

They were shown to their table by a young woman who acted like she knew Leana. After they sat down, McLeod asked her, "Do you know her? She acted like you've been here before."

"A lot of us in the industry know each other. We're kind of on the bottom of the professions here on Mars. Most people here are engineers, geologists and other high paying professions. So we stick together. I come here to eat, and she has dropped by my bar."

"So, what's good here?"

"Everything." She smiled. "Dina is the cook in the back. She won't disappoint you."

The dinner was better than he expected, and he said so to Leana, "I guess I'm used to food they serve to miners and the transport ship. Filling, but not necessarily high quality."

"A lot of people working on Mars make a high salary. They want good food and don't care if it's expensive. Thus, we have some pretty good bio tanks."

"Fair enough. Except for the fish?"

"That's just our supplier. Some others do a better job."

"Shall I order another bottle of wine?"

"Sure." She paused and continued. "I really like going out with you and hope we can do it again. But just so you know, I don't take anyone home on the first date."

"I'm fine with that. Actually, tomorrow is my last day on Mars, so I have to get up early."

"On route to Earth." She sighed. "I do miss that blue globe."

McLeod walked her to her apartment. Her suite on the twenty-third floor meant she was on the lower levels. The highest floors were more expensive to rent, one of the few symbols of affluence on Mars. Nearly everyone used the same shuttles when required to travel a distance. Clothes were usually of the casual nature, and even the most expensive clothes didn't look any different from the plain version at a distance. Unlike Earth, everyone on Mars was employed, made good money and didn't lack necessities.

The majority of the population on Mars arrived from Earth, although a growing percentage were born on Mars. Some people were now the fourth generation and biologists were studying the differences in the Martian born physiology from those living on Earth.

He gave her a long kiss goodnight and made a commitment to look her up the next time he was on Mars.

"I'll hold you to that promise."

He walked to the elevator, wondering when he would return to Mars again. *It could be months if I have to take the ship to Earth and then straight back to asteroids. Ah, the exciting life of running a spaceship.*

MCLEOD ARRIVED ON THE MCKENZIE KING THE DAY BEFORE it was due to leave Mars orbit. He found all systems were ready, with Lexanna Shultz working through the personnel check list.

"You must have arrived here yesterday to have the systems green lighted."

"Yeah, I didn't find much to do on Mars this time, so I thought I might as well get here early and check for any problems. All is good and we lost a good part of our cargo to Mars. That means we should be able to make reasonable time on the trip to Earth without all that extra mass."

"Thanks for doing the extra work. Sorry you didn't have a better time on Mars."

"I was fine, just maybe a bit anxious to get back on the ship. How about you? What did you do?"

"I rented a shuttle and did a bit of a tour outside of Red City. I also went to a local bar and the Ellie Evans museum. That was pretty interesting and worthwhile visiting."

"I'll have to check it out next time." She looked at him. "You going to a museum. I never would have thought that of you."

"I went with a friend."

"Oh, perhaps a female friend, as in on a date?"

"No comment."

McLeod compared the running of a transport ship to being on a train. Once it was set in motion, there wasn't much for him to do other than making sure nothing went wrong. There were fewer rocks floating through space between Mars and Earth compared to the close proximity of the asteroid belt where they started. The chances of damage from rocks was greatly reduced and less of a concern for him.

He had received warning of a solar flare that would increase cosmic rays, and he decided he would personally relay the information to the engine room.

"Lexanna, you have command. I'm going to the engine room."

"Sure, leave me with this mess here." She gave him a grin.

McLeod strode down the corridors to where Dermott ran the engine room. After entering the secure door and putting on the required ear protection, he made his way past a couple of mechanics working on parts at a work bench. *Looks normal here.* "Hi Tia. How is your crew doing on the second leg of the journey?"

"Great. Less babysitting I have to do. They understand more of what is required, and I've made a couple of them supervisors. They know how I like things to be done, and I can rely on them."

"Good. We just received word from the Solar Helio and Weather Institute that a series of solar flares will be occurring soon. I wanted to warn you to make sure the magnetic field generator is ready to counter a surge in cosmic rays."

"Thanks. I'll do a quick diagnostic on the field generator's detectors and do an inspection of the backup generator."

"Good to hear. I think I'll have an officer's dinner tomorrow, so try to leave that time available."

"Sounds good." She appeared to be wanting to say something more to him, but instead turned away to direct two crew members to follow her to where the magnetic field generator was housed in a separate room.

He briefly made his way around the engine room, saying hello to a few of the men working before exiting. *This is a nice easy job, but part of me wants to go back piloting those mining ships where you had to be ready for anything. There isn't any adrenaline rush on a transport ship.*

He wandered back to the command centre of the ship, coming across cadet Ronald Brown taking off a ventilation cover. "Good afternoon, Mr. Brown."

Brown looked startled at first but quickly recovered. "Good afternoon, Captain McLeod."

McLeod was pleased he didn't show as much nervousness as the first time they met. "Are you enjoying your first tour of space so far?"

"Yes sir. I realize there's a lot to learn, and I think I'll be taking more courses. I want to do more than just work on the climate systems."

"That's a very good plan. You never want a job that becomes too routine and without challenges."

When he finally arrived back at the command centre, his earpiece indicated he had a personal message waiting for him.

He went to his suite, sitting in front of monitor. The text message was simple. After docking the ship in Earth orbit, he was to report directly to the Gibbston Space Lines Administration Office. He left his suite, wondering why they wanted to see him.

———

The dinner, involving all executive officers, was held in the captain's suite. The front area held an oval table large enough to accommodate fourteen people, although this time there were only eleven officers. McLeod sat between Shultz and Dermott, feeling like he was being scrutinized. One of the servers said hello to Dermott, and McLeod recalled her name. *Tracie Thobes. I guess it shouldn't be surprising two women on a ship with mostly men could become friends.* McLeod made a toast. "I want to thank everyone for joining me on my maiden voyage on the McKenzie King. You've made it a pleasant, and stress-free journey." He raised his glass of wine, with the others following suit.

Shultz commented, "By stress free, I assume you mean boring."

He heard a few chuckles from the others around the table. "No, boring is not being on a spaceship."

That resulted in more laughter, and the conversation became lighthearted. At least until the subject of USOs came up.

Ales Rittmayer, a cargo integrity officer, added his position. "I saw two USOs when I was with a small science team visiting the Callisto Beta Base. We stayed at the base for two days, making measurements of Jupiter's ionosphere and magnetic fields."

McLeod listened to the hesitation of Rittmayer's voice, as if he was betraying a secret, but at the same time needed to, or wanted to reveal it. He knew that Callisto, with one side of the large moon tidally locked, was ideal to study Jupiter. There were several human posts located there, and all but one dedicated to researching the gas giant. One post was used to study the salty water ocean, and microbes, over one hundred kilometres below the surface. He was aware that USO sightings were not uncommon, despite the isolation from human space located closer to Earth and Mars.

"You see, we, that is the four of us, all saw them. One ship was large, maybe the size of the McKenzie King. The other was much smaller, kind of like a mining ship. They were close together and it was pretty obvious they were studying our base. One of our team members, Nicholas, was outside the base and setting up test equipment. He took measurements of the USOs and recorded them. He was really excited at the results. After we finished our work, we sent the information to the International Space Agency. We thought that was that." Rittmayer stopped to have a drink of his wine, aware everyone was quiet and listening to him. "A few days later we stopped at Argus Port to refuel and have a change of scenery from the spaceship. That's when the IEP made a visit to us. They took us to an office and asked questions, one at a time and together. It felt like an interrogation. Then Nicolas was taken away for a few hours. When we saw him again, he could barely remember the USOs, and not any of the measurements he took of them. And he sure as hell didn't want to talk about it anymore."

McLeod understood Argus Port, a space station located between Mars and the asteroids, was also a place where the Interplanetary Enforcement Police had their headquarters. The IEP could do pretty much what they wanted to do at that location.

"Anyway, I just want to say, if anyone here does come across a USO, keep it to yourself."

———

The McKenzie King made orbit around Earth, just outside where the moon circled the Earth. Safety regulations required the undocking of the ore ship to be done at a set distance from Earth in case of a mishap. A cargo container free falling to Earth could cause considerable damage. By having the operation done at a distance, there would be plenty of opportunity to take action in case of an incident.

McLeod waited with the rest of the officers as the shuttles arrived. The first shuttles took the passengers. The next one departed with the maintenance and kitchen staff. The final shuttle took the officers and support staff. McLeod was the last to leave, turning over the command to the crew in charge of unloading the ore and preparing the McKenzie King for its next trip.

The shuttles all stopped at Higalik Space Station where larger shuttles took passengers to Earth. McLeod would have liked to continue his journey on one of the shuttles, but instead took an elevator to the administration levels where several dozen corporations held offices. He made his way to the Gibbston Space Lines corporate office, where an automated voice invited him to sit in a waiting area. He barely had enough time to actually sit when a middle-aged man walked in briskly.

"Jaret McLeod? Please follow me to my office."

———

McLeod sat in the office with the director of personnel for Gibbston Space Lines. The office had a no frills look about it and the Spartan interior was dominated by a desk with two large monitors. The Higalik Space Station was owned by a consortium, with Gibbston controlling a minor stake.

Gerald Owen looked up from behind his desk. "I knew it wouldn't be long before they gave you another promotion, as you've been on their radar for some time. Top pilots often are progressed into captains, but this seems to be a bit more hurried than usual. You've done a great job with the McKenzie King crew. They'll be sending you an official contract soon enough, but I thought you should hear the offer from a live voice. Gibbston wants you to captain the Nevada Queen."

McLeod remained silent as he recalled information about the Nevada Queen. The older spaceship was smaller than most of the ships running between Mars and Earth. Like all ships it was divided between carrying cargo and passengers. He recalled the news of the ship becoming stranded on its way to Earth due to an engine malfunction. The perception of a spaceship marooned in deep space had hurt the company's image as a safe choice to travel with.

"I see. The Nevada Queen has an interesting reputation."

"Yeah, unfortunately it has a history." Owen frowned. "That's one of the reasons you're being moved to captain her. The last captain was straight out of training and wasn't ready for any of the hundreds of things that could go wrong. Gibbston decided that they needed a captain who could think on his feet. If you can keep a mining ship running in the belt, and then take on running a transport ship, a passenger ship on the Mars run should be a piece of cake."

"Good theory, but I knew every inch of the Nebula and the McKenzie King had a great crew already on her. The Nevada Queen is a whole new game."

"You're not seriously considering turning down this offer, are you?" Owen looked at him slack jawed.

"I'll take the job, providing I can take the best damn engine mechanic with me."

He looked at the monitor. "Tia Dermott? The same one you took to handling the engines on the McKenzie King?"

"That would be her."

"Sure, with the previous chief engine mechanic fired, you would need someone anyway."

"And Lexanna Shultz."

"Do you play poker? You keep moving up the ante." He sighed. "Yeah, I can see your point. Alrighty, I'll send in the request. I doubt they give a rat's ass about Dermott and Shultz as long as you're the captain." He stood and offered his hand. "Congratulations. You deserve this and I'll bet the Nevada Queen never makes the news again for floundering in space."

"Thank you."

"I'll forward the contract to you. There's a section on safety and budgets that I suggest you review. I believe Gibbston Space Lines will give you a bit more leeway on your first budget but be aware cost overruns are watched closely."

"I shall keep that in mind."

——

Captain McLeod entered the Nevada Queen, receiving a half-hearted salute from the commissioner in charge. The ship was docked at the Higalik Space Station and didn't require a captain during that time.

"She's all yours, Captain. I'm afraid to say I haven't made much progress in getting her ready for space. The interior is getting cleaned up, not perfect, but good enough for this class of ship. But the real problem is the engines. They're in very rough shape. It appears there is extensive repair work required, as you might guess if the Nevada Queen had to be towed into port."

"Fortunately, I have a great engine mechanic to fix them."

"That's good to hear. I wish you luck, you're going to need it."

McLeod walked around the ship, frowning at the wear and tear on the old ship. He knew most of it could be covered cosmetically but wondered about the hidden defects. McLeod sniffed the air. *Reminds me vaguely of the air in the Terra Nova. The air purification units can't be operating very well. There's a lot of repair needed on this boat, and it's going to be done right.*

[PART 2]

[10]

NELLIE WRITSON IGNORED THE FINE SAND BLOWING AT HER face as she made her way down Ellie Evans Avenue. Her eyes were protected by eyewear that also filtered out ultraviolet rays from the sun. Red City was made of a series of twisting streets. Straight roads were rare, as the design of the city was to make it difficult for the Martian winds to blow straight through. Still, the occasional gust of wind carrying the sandy soil made its way even to the centre of town. The tall blonde acted impervious to the cold, thin air. Her Martian genes gave her height and the ability to breath in the harsh environment. Although she had fine bones, she didn't look skinny, with muscles stressing the fabric of her thermal suit.

Writson could have used the underground tunnels instead to arrive at her destination, the Martian Government Administration Offices, but she was proud to be a Martian. Her definition of a Martian was that of a person born on Mars and not someone from Earth who decided to make Mars their home. Part of being a Martian, in her mind, was to face the elements whenever it was practical to do so. Less than twenty percent of the population on Mars was born on the planet, and thus could have her unofficial designation of being called a Martian. Writson was one of a handful that could trace her heritage right back to the original settlers, when almost everyone was either a scientist or a government employee.

Her high academics, coupled with a forceful personality, drove her to near the top of the Biological and Geological Department, becoming the assistant director. Most of those in her department appreciated her style of management, and she was respected for achieving high results, something that could not be said of the previous administration.

News of a surprising discovery by one of the research teams sent her hurrying to work. It was her day off, but that didn't matter to her. She was more than willing to put in long hours and extra days. While she didn't demand that of her subordinates, it did put pressure on them to work full days.

Writson entered the twin set of doors, immediately noticing the heavier and the higher percentage of oxygenated air. The gravity was also higher, closer to Earth normal compared to Mars' much lighter pull. Most of the people on Mars found the compromise acceptable. The eighty percent of Earth's gravity made it easy to move about. The air thickness was similar to being on a mountain on Earth, and most people didn't need to use an oxygen enhancer when they worked indoors. Outside, it became a necessity, with the oxygen levels lower. Writson was an exception. Everyone, when outside on Mars, carried an electronic device that filtered in additional oxygen, sending the vital air through air tubes. However, Writson only used the oxygen device when she absolutely had to.

Generations of living on Mars had changed the physiology of some humans. Writson had read the conclusions of doctors and paleoanthropologists. Humans born on Mars were exhibiting unique characteristics, such as lighter bones and smaller muscles. The lighter gravity was suspected of causing these changes, along with a slight increase in height. The multi-generation Martians were not thin. Instead their lungs had increased in size, expanding their chest cavity. They had also developed higher levels of fat and increased blood circulation. These adaptations aided Writson, and others, to live outside on Mars easier. Regardless of any changes in the human ability to live on Mars, everyone wore a thermal suit to protect against the occasional extreme cold that could cover the planet. Writson still had to use the oxygen enhancer outside on occasion, although she could go without it if she wasn't exerting herself. One item she and others always had to have was the water bottle. The dry Martian air made the water bottle a vital item.

The one-piece thermal, as with anything with clothing, the original practical, life-saving garment, was altered by fashion. Initially, the thermal suits were meant to be worn as an undergarment, but changes allowed for them to worn without being covered.

Men wore pants and a shirt over the thermal suit and were usually only black or dark grey in colour. Women would wear a cover up as well, depending on their comfort level. Writson was one of those who normally only wore a thermal suit. Her suits usually had various colours and patterns, sometimes with a contrast between the top and bottom. She had a pouch attached to one of the leggings that carried personal items.

Writson's body protested at the increase of gravity, but she proceeded to the lifts, where the elevator took her to the twelfth floor. She strode into the Biological and Geological Department that used the entire floor. She quickly acknowledged the young man who sometimes served as a receptionist, but usually was concerned with data entry. Information about Mars was being discovered faster than could be properly inputted.

"Jeremy, what's the situation?" Writson entered the door-less office of the manager of the geology department, Jeremy Tolmat.

Tolmat was born on Mars, but his parents took him to Earth for upbringing. He returned after obtaining his geology degree. Short, with a stocky frame, he kept his dark hair long. "Team Tharsis was investigating an unusual formation near the volcano Biblis Patera, an unusually low, flat area. They believe they have found signs of the remains of an artificial structure."

"Mother of Mars. Does anyone else know of this report?"

"No. I only contacted you."

"Good. Let's get our gear together and check it out."

The four-person shuttle left from the roof of the government offices building with Tolmat and Wriston inside. The thirty-two-story building's flat roof held several shuttles for government use only, and Writson quickly signed out one that could be used to transport any possible artifacts if necessary.

The shuttle flew on auto-pilot to the Tharsis Volcanic Region, located near the equator of Mars, an area of several extinct volcanoes. The Tharsis team was sent to explore the possible interconnections of the dormant volcanoes, and to determine if any could come back to life. As Mars continued to warm up, including the interior, there was concern on which volcanoes may become active again.

Just over an hour later, the shuttle landed where the research camp was located. Several temporary structures were dotted around the camp, including another, larger, shuttle.

Writson and Tolmat slipped on their protective goggles and gloves. The gloves were electrically connected to the thermal suit and could be heated as well. They exited the shuttle, feeling the wind blowing from the north. While the wind was fast, it was not strong due to the thin air. Still, particles of dust and sand hit their faces, making their short walk to the main building unpleasant.

The air lock was large enough for two people, and they entered the combination of an office and laboratory interior together, which held higher air pressure than the outside Martian atmosphere.

Only one person was inside working at the lab equipment. Shelly Madison, a petite brunette, greeted them, adding, "The others will be back soon. I radioed them when I saw your shuttle land."

Writson acknowledged her. "You're running the analysis of the area in question?" She was the junior member of the geology team and thus often had to do the more tedious tasks of running the computers.

"Yes. The region we're looking at is approximately sixty-five metres long and forty-three metres wide. Along the perimeter, we have what appears to be the remains of blocks that are at regular intervals, about every five point four metres. The blocks seem to be at one time square, maybe half a metre on the side. They're about two metres deep. They were hidden under the soil. We found them using ground radar while we were looking for lava tubes."

"What are they made of?"

"We haven't tested a sample yet, but it appears to be of Martian soil that was fused into blocks. Some of the remains have a glassy appearance to them."

Tolmat asked, "Are the blocks buried at the same height?"

"Yes, the tops are within a centimetre of each other."

"So, what is the initial impression you have of them?" Tolmat asked as he peered at the monitor over her shoulder. The monitor showed images of one of the blocks. Some of the polished pieces looked like pinkish-orange glass. One of the edges of a partial piece of a block appeared worn and chipped. "What were they used for?"

Madison took in a long breath before replying. "It seems to me that they may have been used to support a building of some sort. We use inflatable discs under our shelters to prevent corners from sinking, so maybe these blocks were used for the same purpose. If so, then at one time they were likely at ground level."

Writson added. "Those blocks, if they were used to support a structure, appear to be meant for a much more permanent structure."

A flashing light above the door indicated the arrival of the rest of the research team. It took several cycles for the two men and one woman to enter, along with the equipment.

Philip Norris, a tall blond-haired man and leader of the team, stuck out his hand to Writson to shake. "Nellie, it's great to see you again." He continued to hold her hand a few seconds longer.

"Quite the discovery your team has made."

"It was startling to find the remains of the first post, and then find several more in a pattern. We decided we better contact you immediately. We haven't reported the finding to the Mars Environment Preservation Department."

He left the statement open. Writson knew that once the findings were reported to the Mars Environment Preservation department, they would take over the rest of the investigation. The department would effectively stop any research until they deemed it was safe to do so, and that there wouldn't be any damage to the site.

"I'll make a report to the director and see if I can buy us some more time." The director, Gary Dorn, was a fair-minded boss, but he was also aware of the politics of the Martian Government. One did not want to get into a disagreement with the preservation department. They could stop work at almost any site under their mandate to protect the Martian past. Norris went past her, touching her on the shoulder, as he went to one of the laboratory tables.

Carl Duggan waved at Writson as he unloaded a case, placing a small black rectangular box by a computer. The tall, slim man quickly busied himself with transferring data from the box to the computer.

A petite, pregnant woman stepped forward. "Hi, I'm Lindsey."

"Hi, I'm Nellie Writson. You're the biologist on the team." She recalled reading Smyth's file, knowing she was born on Mars.

"That's right. I've been shifting through a few soil samples. Nothing too surprising there, but we have picked up some interesting gas readings. Somewhere there's a source of methane and oxygen. We speculated they have been coming from lava tubes, indicating that perhaps one of the volcanoes may be active underground. We were looking for lava tubes and found these posts instead. It's very exciting."

"It's a great find." Writson liked the cheerful woman. According to the reports Smyth rarely complained about anything and didn't use her pregnancy to get out of difficult work. "Now I have to send a report to my boss, who likely will have to inform the preservation department. We won't have much time before they seal off this whole area."

Smyth laughed. "Maybe we can just cover them up with sand again and pretend we didn't find them until we finish our other work."

"If only it was that simple."

Writson spent a few minutes carefully wording a message to the director, Gary Dorn.

It appears Team Tharsis has uncovered an abnormality while doing research. Mapping for possible lava tubes has uncovered what appears to be the remnants of artificial posts underground. I have arrived at the site and will investigate what the nature is of these posts, and to determine if indeed they are of a non-natural construct. I will immediately inform you of any progress.

She hoped he had finished working for the day and wouldn't see the message until the next morning. That would give her and the team more time to investigate the posts and the surrounding area. *This find is a game changer. Finally, proof of aliens. There's going to be a firestorm once the media learns of this.*

Writson and the others sat around the lab equipment resting on a table. As computers analysed their findings and produced spreadsheets of data, they conversed about Mars and speculated on the posts found in the Martian soil.

Duggan looked at a monitor as he commented. "According to this, the posts are about eighty-six hundred years old. I doubt they are the remains of any Martian civilization. If they were, then we would have found more evidence of that by now. These posts have to have been left by an alien species that stopped here to do some exploring."

"That's still pretty significant. I wonder what they were looking for in this area?" Norris asked.

"Maybe the same reason we're here," Smyth replied. The others looked at her, waiting for to continue. "Look, we were sent here to look at lava tubes, partly to know if there is a chance they will cease being dormant. Thermal images indicate they are warmer than the ground above and they may hold the last remains of life on Mars. Now it turns out they may be the cause of methane and other gases. There also just might be organic reasons for that, such as that life is still in those lava tubes."

Norris agreed. "Yeah, that makes sense. Aliens checking if there is any life on Mars, just as we do."

A hum from her mobile indicated Writson had a new message. She checked her messages, reading a new one from Gary Dorn.

I suspect that you already know whether or not the posts are artificial, and your message is meant only to give your team more time to do your own investigation until the Mars Environment Preservation Department is officially notified.

I will give you until noon tomorrow, and then I will pass on the required information to the Preservation Department. It is likely they will react very quickly to news of the artificial posts and stop any further work.

Writson sighed. It seemed Dorn had interpreted exactly what had happened but was willing to extend her a few more hours to do their own work.

"I suggest we all get a good sleep. Our director has given us until noon tomorrow to wrap up our research. Then the preservation department will likely shut us down."

"CAPTAIN MCLEOD, YOU WANTED TO SEE ME?"

McLeod looked at the short, middle aged man wearing the dark blue uniform of the Nevada Queen crew. Norm Javier was in charge of the ship's housekeeping and laundry. He gave the officer a frown to show he wasn't pleased.

"Mr. Javier, what do you see around here?" He swept his arm around the lounge area of the ship where passengers could mingle, have drinks, food and view the space beyond. Currently it was empty of passengers, with just the cleaning crew moving about.

Javier looked puzzled. "Sir, just the cleaning crew working."

"Do you know what I see?"

"No, sir." Javier's voice was reserved, as if expecting he gave the incorrect answer.

"I see people taking their time casually cleaning. What I don't see is any enthusiasm or purpose in their work."

"Sir, this is how they have done things in the past."

"That, Mr. Javier, is simply not good enough. This ship will be made sparkling clean. If you are unable to inspire your crew do so, please inform me right now."

Javier's eyes widened. "Captain, I promise I will do this."

"Thank you, Mr. Javier. When the passengers arrive on our ship, they don't see the engines. They aren't aware of the air fans, or the hundreds of other things behind the walls. They don't see the bridge. What they do see is where they will be spending five weeks. It is critical that we make a great impression here. I know your crew can make us all proud of the Nevada Queen."

McLeod watched as Javier went back to where the cleaning crew worked. He clapped his hands, drawing their attention, and soon was speaking to a circle of employees. Satisfied, McLeod made his way down the ship to the engine room.

"Problems?" He addressed Tia Dermott.

She gave a hint of a shrug and pointed at a bulkhead where part of the two engines could be seen. "Mark Twos. They're tough old blocks, but their maintenance schedules have not been kept up. They're also a couple of retrofits behind what should have been done."

"Is that why you said we might not be ready to go by the departure date?"

"I'm afraid so. Those retrofits will take time to do. The interior fuel manifolds have to be taken off. There are lots of parts that have to be taken off first to get there, and usually we find a couple of other areas to work on at that point. So, do you want me to hold off on the retrofits? Otherwise we risk missing the departure date."

"Go ahead and do whatever you feel is necessary to ensure a safe journey. I'm going to contact the space station maintenance department and see if there are any technicians we can use to help with repairs. I'm sure there are a few that would like the overtime pay."

━━

Lisa Wagner stared at the report on the monitor. *What the hell is going on there?* She touched a spot on her glass topped desk. The desktop was capable of displaying images, as well as allowing interaction with electronic documents.

"Mandy, do you know what's going on with the Nevada Queen?"

Mandy Kramer, the accountant for Gibbston Space Lines,

replied, "No. I noticed a lot of invoices coming in for the Nevada Queen and thought I should give you an update before their departure. I suspect there will be more expenses still to come. They're over budget as it stands now."

"Damn."

"That's the ship with the new captain?"

"Yes, and he may have the shortest tenure in history as a spaceship captain."

Wagner debated on whether to do a video call with the Nevada Queen, but decided she needed to do a face to face with the captain. She took the company's private shuttle to the space station, wondering if it would be too late to replace McLeod. She had never met him but had reviewed his file prior to his promotion. From all indications, he should be a top-rated captain, ideal for the Nevada Queen.

Wagner wore a pant suit, knowing from experience that skirts and high heels were a dangerous combination on a space station where the artificial gravity occasionally fluctuated. The Higalik was an older space station that had been expanded several times in its fourteen-year life. The expansion had led to challenges, among them was the consistency of the gravity field.

She entered the Nevada Queen through the short walkway that went between the station and the ship and was immediately greeted by one of the ship's officers who led her to the captain's quarters. The front part of his quarters served as an office and a meeting room.

McLeod stood by the oval table that could accommodate eight people for meetings. Three tablets were on the table, showing various charts and documents. He appraised her briefly before acknowledging her. "Ms. Wagner, it's good to meet you."

Wagner was confident in her appearance and was used to second looks she received. Tall, she had a pale complexion, shoulder length blonde hair, brown eyes and a slim figure.

"Captain McLeod, it's good meet to you as well." *Well, at least he looks like a captain. He does have that leader's look.* "We need to discuss the recent expenditures made for the Nevada Queen."

"I was expecting a few inquiries, but a visit from you surprises me a bit."

She stood at the table, facing him. "I thought we should meet so that you can explain how you managed to surpass your budget by one hundred and sixty-four percent." She watched his face, mildly taken back that he didn't flinch or even blink his eyes. She waited as moments passed. "Well?"

"How did the Nevada Queen do on previous budgets at departure?"

"It was under for the past four years."

"Were bonuses paid out for being under budget?"

"Of course." She leaned forward, wondering what he was driving at.

"The reason they were under budget was because they saved on doing proper maintenance. I'm merely trying to catch up on repairs and putting this ship back to where it should be."

"Do all of these repairs have to be done now? I see where you've authorized overtime pay for additional technicians, and these weren't even Gibbston employees. You have also hired four more cleaning staff crew members. How was that critical to the ship's performance?"

"In regard to the first question, may I ask what the cost was to rescue the Nevada Queen when the engines failed in the middle of space? Was that in the budget as well?"

"Careful with your tone, Captain McLeod."

"Have you been on the Nevada Queen recently, Ms. Wagner?"

"Not for a year or so."

"I suspect you prefer to travel on the Royal Venice, or other luxury ships."

"Where are you going with this?" The annoyance in her voice increased.

"Please, come with me." He gestured toward the door.

Wagner sighed. *This is not going as planned. He's not acting like he's worried about losing his job and has taken over this meeting.*

She walked with him, making sure he wasn't leading the way. "What's this about?"

"Seeing is believing."

They entered the passenger lounge. She stopped and looked around. "What did you do here? It looks brand new."

"The cleaning crew should get the credit. Along with the four extra cleaning staff that were hired."

"Impressive. But I'm still not convinced about the budget overrun."

"May I show you the engine room?"

"I suppose so." She gazed around, impressed by how clean and fresh the ship was. *Damn, this should have been done years ago. We can increase the ticket prices if we promote this as an intimate spaceship...no, space liner.*

She walked quickly to keep up with his longer stride, taking mental notes on the renewed interior. When they passed a worker, whether in housekeeping or a technician, they looked up at him with respect. McLeod usually addressed them by their name as he acknowledged them and adding a comment on their work.

"Do you know the name of everyone working on the ship?"

"Most of them. I make a point of reviewing the employee files and matching a name to the faces."

"Do you find that a worthwhile investment in time?"

"Ms. Wagner, this ship isn't being cleaned and repaired by unknowns. Everyone on this ship is important to ensure a safe and pleasant journey. I shouldn't fail to recognize them and acknowledge them."

She glanced briefly at his face, wondering if there was a hint of a lecture in his rebuttal. *He doesn't hold back on his opinion. Actually, a bit refreshing from the usual reaction I get from employees.*

They reached the engine room, where a crew of half a dozen technicians worked on the two motors. Two of the men were working on top of a motor, reaching inside. A woman with a short haircut shouted up to them from the floor.

"Tia," McLeod called out. "Do you have a minute?"

She turned, her face passive as she looked at Wagner standing next to him. "Sure." She gave a final instruction to the two men and strode over to them. Her green coverall had a tear at the right sleeve with grease and dirt marks at random spots.

"Tia Dermott is the head of ship's engine room. She's

responsible for the maintenance and running of the engines." He paused and introduced Wagner. "Lisa Wagner is the owner and CEO of Gibbston."

Wagner shook her hand, noticing it was a hand used to hard work. "I was asking Captain McLeod on the cost of readying the Nevada Queen for operations. One of the large cost overruns is occurring in the engine room." She let the sentence hang, wondering how Dermott would react.

Dermott didn't baulk. "There's a reason for the retrofits. Besides better performance, the retrofits can ensure we can make it to Mars and back safely. I won't roll the dice and risk everyone's life by not doing a job properly."

Wagner walked back with McLeod. "Well, it seems you have the crew working hard and getting the ship back to optimum standards. Just try harder to keep me informed of cost overruns in the future."

"I will do that."

Wagner left the ship, feeling slightly impressed by McLeod. *Maybe he has those captain's qualities we are looking for to run the Hendrik A. Lorentz.*

———

Lisa Wagner pivoted in her chair, staring around in her well-appointed office as she considered McLeod as a possible captain for their experimental ship. She had reviewed his file again and still wondered if she was overreacting on first impressions when they met. She stood and exited her office, walking on the tiled floor to the office of Matt Crowley, President of Ship Procurement and Technology. She smiled a hello to his assistant, a middle-aged woman of perfect hair, nails and work ethic. Wagner tapped on the door frame and entered the spacious office. His office had a view of the sprawling city of Calgary to the east. Her own office captured the western view as well as the Rocky Mountains.

"Matt, do you have few minutes?" She approached the front of his desk and sat down.

"No, but you're welcome to take them anyway." He gave a

grin, creasing his senior face. He had kept most of his hair, although he used pills to stimulate the creation of melanin and keep grey hair from taking over. Of average height and weight, he was a workaholic and failed marriages were proof that he couldn't balance work and a personal life.

"Our new captain for the Nevada Queen, Jaret McLeod, may be the one we're looking for to captain the Hendrik A. Lorentz. I'm not sure at this stage, so I want to run it by you."

Crowley leaned back in his chair. "Shoot me what you know." He crossed his arms.

"He went way over budget on the Nevada Queen. Spent money on everything. You name it, ship interior appearance, engine modifications and extra personnel. So, I made a personal visit to see what the hell was going on, prepared to even relieve him as captain."

"So what happened?"

"He didn't act intimidated in the least that the owner of the company went to see him about cost overruns. I walked around with him in the ship, and good lord, you should have seen how the crew was responding to him. All working diligently."

"The ship looked okay?"

"Better than okay. Like brand new okay." She frowned. "I was annoyed and impressed."

"A strange mix of emotions." Crowley chuckled. "You think this McLeod may be a good fit as captain of the new ship?"

"He's smart and determined to do things right. And he has that quality that's hard to define. He's more than a captain, he's a leader."

"So how sure are you that he should be the captain of our very expensive and one of a kind spaceship?"

"I'm not sure enough yet. I do know we would prefer to promote an interior candidate to keep information from leaking out, and he's the best I've seen so far. But I need to go to Mars to inspect on the progress of the Hendrik A. Lorentz anyway, so I thought I would use the Nevada Queen to get there and watch McLeod a little closer."

"Good plan, although the Nevada Queen is not the fastest ship in the universe."

"That's all right. I can do work on the journey as well."

[12]

THE COLD MORNING ARRIVED AND WRITSON PEERED OUT
the observation window, holding a cup of black coffee. She saw in
the window the reflection of Norris approaching from behind her
before he spoke.

"Good morning. Minus eighteen. Not too bad."

She turned partly around. "Yeah, and the sun will warm things
up. We should reach above freezing by this afternoon." She took a
drink of her coffee and faced him, leaning on the padded counter
in front of the window, surprised at his close proximity. "I think
we should break up into two groups. You can lead one team to
continue to research the blocks and see if there is anything else
unusual. I'll help investigate the lava tubes." She looked up at him,
wondering if it was Martian genes giving him height, or if he
would have been that tall on Earth.

"Sounds like a good plan. I assume you would take Lindsey, as
she's investigating possible biological trace gases from lava tubes.
Who else would you take?"

"It doesn't really matter to me. I was thinking of Shelly
Madison, as she may not be as much use to you in moving
equipment and digging." Despite the low gravity of Mars, the
equipment used to investigate the surface and underneath was
bulky and hard to manoeuvre over the boulder littered surface.

"An all-women crew for you." He grinned. "That means I'll be stuck with the men."

"Well, I certainly wouldn't use the word stuck." She laughed. "Let's get rolling now that we have daylight."

Writson told Smyth to lead the way, since she was the one most familiar where the lava tubes were located relative to the source of the methane and other trace gases. Writson and Madison carried the equipment cases, not wanting to cause Smyth any extra strain. Smyth did insist she was fine to carry one of the cases but gave in to their argument she had to be careful since they were climbing up small hills.

The three women all wore thermal suits of various colours, although Madison alone had pulled up the hood to cover her head.

Smyth called out to the others behind her, puffing as she did so. "Just after this rise, there's a circular depression. That's where there's a concentration of some of the gasses. There's not much methane, but it's lighter and most of it would have floated away." She paused to take a sip of water. "It's also right next to a lava tube, BP7."

Writson interpreted BP7 as lava tube number seven that came from the volcano Biblis Patera. Unlike Smyth, she didn't have trouble breathing the Martian air. She examined the pathway that ended at the edge of the slope. The ground was littered with sand and small pieces of gravel, making a crunching sound with each step. Writson checked the display softly glowing on her left sleeve just above her wrist, giving information on her own vital signs and the ambient temperature. She noted the temperature had risen to minus eleven degrees Celsius, and her own body signs were normal. She let out a puff of air, the vapour quickly dissipating. "Are the gases there from being close to the lava tube, or are they concentrated from being in a depression, collecting the heavier gases from farther away?"

"It just seems too much of a coincidence that the gases are right next to the lava tube. It probably does concentrate some gasses in the depression, but I'm positive they originate from the lava tube."

They stopped at the end of the slope. After the depression, a flat path continued. Writson peered at the at the rugged terrain that rose along both sides of the pathway. "How close is the lava tube to the path?"

Smyth pointed with her hand. "The lava tube runs under the right side of that rocky ridge, and partly under where we stand. The tube is about three metres wide, so we're near the edge of it."

Madison opened her tablet to a three-dimensional map showing the lava tube relative to the ridge and the pathway, passing it to Writson to look at.

"How far does the lava tube go?" Writson used her gloved fingers to slide the map down from their present location. She saw the lava tube was largely circular in diameter and was surprised how much volume it contained.

"It goes another one hundred and fifty metres, and then opens up to a cavern before coming to an end."

"It just closes off?"

"At one time we believe it continued on and poured lava into a sea. The lava eventually stopped flowing, leaving the hollow tubes. Later, when the sea disappeared, the ground around the exit collapsed."

Writson smiled. "Let's hope the ground underneath us doesn't collapse."

"No worries. The ground at the edge of sea was soft sand and was weakened by the drop of the water level. This area is mostly rock." Smyth patted her stomach. "It won't give way, although I've gained some weight lately."

"That's not extra weight." Madison quickly countered. "That's extra joy."

"Thanks."

Writson continued to study the area around them on the tablet. "It looks like there's a way to get to the top of the ridge. There's a gap from the pathway that looks climbable."

Smyth looked at the image on the tablet. "It is, I suppose. I think I saw that gap, or one like it. It looked like it was climbable, but I was by myself and didn't want to risk slipping. I need to be a bit more careful what I climb when I'm alone."

"Understandable. First, we should take some readings and compare it to those you made previously."

They opened the cases, lifting out the various equipment. Most of the units snapped together, quickly being made ready to use. Madison remained where they were, while Writson and Smyth each walked with a pair of sensors. The sensors were fist size, black oval devices. The two sensors were attached on each end of a short T-shaped pole.

"How's the pregnancy going?"

"Pretty good now. The first couple of weeks were rough, but now I feel good. Maybe I'm a bit tired at times, but not bad at all."

"Are you married?"

"Yes, three years in a couple of months. Roger arrived on Mars when he was a toddler. His parents wanted to work on Mars and took him and his sister with them. He loves it on Mars and has never left."

"You were born on Mars?" Writson recalled reading the information on her personnel file.

"Yes, actually I'm second generation." She gave a quick glance at Writson. "I heard you are a descendant of the original settlers."

"Yes, it's a bit unusual to be able to trace your heritage back that far. I feel pretty lucky that way."

"But you're not married? I know it's hard to meet the right person. We don't have a few billion people to choose from like on Earth."

"True. I guess I also want a partner who's also a multi-generation Martian, so that reduces my choices even more."

They went down through the depression and out, travelling along the path between the ridges. After fifty metres, they turned around and walked back to where Madison waited with the monitoring equipment.

Smyth took a sip from her water. "That was a good walk for me. I know you have those Martian genes that lets you breathe this thin air, but that walk really taxes me."

"It does give me an advantage out here. But I have to admit I suffer a bit inside buildings with the higher gravity and thicker air."

Smyth laughed. "That's where I feel the best."

Madison looked up at their return. "We have good readings. There are readings of trace gases all along where you went."

"Same gasses as our last readings?" Smith asked.

"Yes, besides methane, we have nitrous oxide, nitric oxide, carbonyl sulphide and oxygen." Madison showed her the tablet with the information displayed on a graph.

"How likely is it that this is from chemical sources versus from microbes?" Writson looked at the tablet as well.

"It's hard to say. Some of the trace gases may have come from microbes that died out long ago and now are just being released as Mars warms up. Oxygen can come from the ultraviolet light that's breaking up the carbon dioxide," Smyth answered. "So, all of these gasses can be produced without life being actually present at this time. Still, I suspect that there's a good possibility that microbes would be present underground."

They packed up the equipment and continued on the path, reaching the point where Writson had seen a gap on a ridge.

"I want to climb up there. I think it may be where the trace gasses are coming from. You can wait here as the climb may be a little steep. I can do this climb easily. I'll take a detector, and I'll check out the readings up there."

"I'll go with you." Smyth looked at Writson. "I'm pregnant, not helpless."

Writson planted a foot at the start of the narrow path, following Smyth. It appeared to have been formed by a stream of water washing down the ridge when Mars still had flowing water. She watched Smyth take slow, careful steps up the incline, not wanting to slip on the loose stones.

It proved to be a relatively easy climb for Wriston, although Smyth was needing to use her oxygen enhancer and was puffing when they stood at the top of the ridge.

"Are you okay?"

"I'm fine. I just need to catch my breath for a minute."

"Take your time."

"I'm envious on how you can breathe in this air. Is it just larger lungs, or is it something else that lets you pull in more oxygen?"

"Larger lungs, but something in my DNA was kicked in. It's the same with some other multi-generation Martians. Our lungs aren't just larger, but also more efficient at absorbing oxygen."

"Is that why you're particular about a partner? You want to make sure those genes are passed on?"

"Yes, partly. I also want someone who has the same feelings I do about Martians having to follow orders from Earth bound leaders. We need more independence from Earth politics and corporations."

"Well, we still need Earth for a lot of our technology and other stuff we can't manufacture here. So, I guess as long we're dependent on Earth, we won't be free of their influence."

"That's true. I'm not the most patient person when it comes to change." Writson laughed.

"Just keep in mind when you're looking for a potential partner, gene diversity can be an asset. I'm just saying there may be options for you."

"Thanks, so far I haven't had much luck meeting the right guy." She pointed along the edge of the ridge. "Maybe we start along here and do a grid to map out where the gasses are."

The top of the ridge was uneven, with the topography looking like a miniature mountain range. They walked along the side of the ridge, looking for anything unusual, such as a vent where the trace gasses could have escaped from. Writson carried the detectors, and shifted them around near the ground, trying to keep a rectangular pattern in her walk.

Near the middle of the rectangle, Smyth pointed at what appeared to be a cave opening in one of the sharp peaked hills. The opening was just big enough for a person to slip inside, and Writson crawled partly inside, turning on her torchlight.

The light revealed a rapid drop from the cave entrance. At the end of the four-metre drop, a grey-red floor showed in the reflected beam. *That looks like an interesting place to explore.* She held the sensors an arm's length inside the opening. *Okay, let's see what the readings have to say.*

"What did you see?"

"It looks like a way into the lava tube. If we used some cables, we could easily get down there and explore the lava tube itself."

"But we don't have time for that now."

"Unfortunately, no. We better return to Shelly and see what the readings are."

They made their way to where Madison waited. She didn't have to ask about the sensor readings.

Madison quickly pointed at the tablet. "Take a look at these concentrations. Right at the end it just spiked through the roof. Do you know exactly where that location is?"

Writson nodded. "We do. Unfortunately, we have nearly run out of our noon hour deadline. It's time we headed back to the camp." She paused before continuing. "When the Martian Preservation Department gets here, they'll want to obtain all of our data. That includes information on the lava tubes, and where the gasses originate on the top of the ridge. I wouldn't want them claiming credit for finding where the trace gasses are coming from." She looked at Smyth. "After all, it appears you actually did discover where trace gasses are escaping from an event."

Smyth agreed. "I'd hate for them to take over from our work."

"I could delete the last bit of data we obtained." Madison ventured.

"Perhaps you can save the data in an encrypted format and move it to our department server. We'll still have all the data at our disposal, but they won't."

When they arrived back at the camp site, Duggan, Norris and Tolmat were already packing equipment in one of the shuttles.

Norris explained. "We have a feeling that we may be shut down soon from exploring, and certainly this equipment will be redundant after the protection agency arrives. Anyway, if they're taking over, they can get their own equipment to use."

"Fair enough." Writson watched as the last piece was secured in the bay area of the shuttle. "Did you find anything new?"

"We did. I'll send you the data later, but it appears there was more than one structure in the area. We found the remains of more support pillars, but these seem to be for the support of two smaller structures. It was good to do some more work, and at least in my opinion, evidence of previous alien buildings. How did it go on your end?"

"We may have found the source of the gasses. But as with you, we'll have to wait to do more exploring until the protection agency gives us the all clear."

They all trooped into the shelter, deciding to have lunch. They sat around one small table that was intended for eating, and at a couple of nearby work benches. The food was all individually packaged, merely requiring heating up.

"I know this food has all the nutrition a person needs, but somehow any flavour it's supposed to have disappears into the plastic serving bowl," Norris grumped.

"For me, it's fine. But you guys have been at this site for over a week," Writson agreed. "I wouldn't be surprised if you're tired of this stuff. Fortunately, you'll likely have normal food soon enough when the preservation department arrives."

"Yeah, joy to them. They shut down a water drilling operation when a small fossil was discovered. A year later they're still carefully extracting the area. I can't imagine how long they'll have possible alien structure remains closed off."

The noise of a shuttle announced the arrival of the Martian Preservation Department team. The five-person group entered the building, removing any extra space.

"I'm Dr. Thomas Rigger, the lead on Area twenty-one investigation unit. Who is Philip Norris?"

"I am." Norris stepped forward to address Rigger. "How can I help you?"

"I need you to give me all the data that has been collected regarding the purported columns, as well as the surveys done in the surrounding area. We would like to start work as soon as possible, so please arrange to transfer that information immediately."

"I'm sorry, we can't comply to your request." Writson spoke up and moved in front of Norris. She appraised Rigger. The middle aged, distinguished looking man appeared to have been born on Earth. Short curly hair was receding on a light brown scalp. He stood ramrod straight on a tall, average weight frame. She tightened her lips.

"Who are you and what gives you the right to withhold data? We have official jurisdiction over this site." Rigger's jaw muscles tightened.

"Nellie Writson. I'm the assistant director of the Biological and Geological Department. As such, I'm head of this unit. This is still a site of importance to us, and we're still processing the data."

"Then give us a copy of the data. You can continue to analyze the information back at your facilities."

"No, with this I think we need to follow protocol. You can send me an official request for the data, and I will then give it due consideration."

"I remind you this may be an extremely important find."

"All the more reason to follow procedure."

"This is ridiculous. Who is your direct superior?"

"Besides God? Director Gary Dorn."

"I'll be contacting him concerning your attitude and lack of cooperation."

"That's your prerogative, but it's still my decision." She turned to Norris. "Let's get your team and our equipment out of here."

As they walked to the shuttles Writson spoke to Madison. "You need to separate the data into two parts. One that we keep, and one we will share with the preservation department."

"Can do."

13

CAPTAIN JARET MCLEOD STOOD AT THE UPPER LEVEL OF THE control deck, his arms behind his back, and fingers interlocked. When he entered the upper level after his obligatory visit in the passenger area, he sensed the change in the crew below him. He understood the crew's tendency to slightly change the posture and focus when the commander of the Nevada Queen was present. That was fine with him. He wanted the crew to be slightly reactive in his presence.

From his vantage point he could see the eight officers operating at each console. Nearby him on the upper level was his First Commander, Lexanna Shultz and Navigator Richard Combs. Each were focused on their own work. He was extremely pleased Lexanna Shultz took him up on his offer to move to the Nevada Queen from a similar position on the McKenzie King. Tia Dermott came over as well, which didn't surprise him. He was delighted when several other crew members from the McKenzie King also applied for work on the Nevada Queen, showing their admiration for the way he ran a ship. One of the few holdovers from the previous executive crew was navigator Richard Combs. The conservative officer was known for his high-quality work, if overly cautious in his personal life.

The navigator was third in command. He was responsible for

ensuring the ship followed the required course and gave instructions to engineering to ensure the proper route was followed to maximum efficiency and was ranked one level above chief engineer Tia Dermott. McLeod read the official logbook and reports from the previous voyage of the Nevada Queen when it became stranded in space. He noticed there were several entries where Combs had objected to the performance and condition of the engines, wanting additional work to be done before the voyage to Mars was to be undertaken. His concerns were overridden by the former captain.

Lexanna Shultz became the ship's commander only when McLeod was off duty or otherwise not available. On some ships, the navigator would have thoughts on moving up the chain of command to become first commander. In the case of Combs, a genius in math and vectors, he was quite willing to let Shultz make the hard decisions of running a spaceship. Watching graphs on his three-dimensional display screen was his true love, and he didn't have any desire to be a commander.

McLeod, taller than most men, maintained a body that showed he had previously done hard work mining asteroids. Muscles stressed the blue jacket of his uniform. His face still featured a scar from his left temple to his jaw, courtesy of the earlier industrial accident when mining one of the asteroids. He was an imposing figure and his face and voice were exactly what one expected from a leader. A light buzz in his ear from his earpiece signalled there was a situation and he turned to his own console. The multiple screens showed various parts of the exterior of the ship and his experience quickly spotted the problem. At the same time his earpiece relayed the excited voice of the far space observer Ensign Terrance Carter.

"Captain, we have a spook at coordinates 30 dot 75 by 94 dot 22 by 48 dot 02. Velocity at 0 dot 778 C."

McLeod watched the blip on his own console. He turned to Shultz. "Unidentified space object moving past us. Almost eighty percent the speed of light."

Shultz watched the object on the screen for a moment. "It's

not changing course. I guess we're safe from being attacked." She gave him a smile. "Should I log it and let the ISA figure out what to do with another USO?"

"Thanks, but I'll take care of that." He liked how the tall, shoulder length brunette could quickly analyze a situation, but also had a subtle sense of humour. The International Space Agency had been collecting information on the unidentified space objects for years. They weren't common, and this was only the sixth he had encountered with the first few occurring when he was on a mining ship. Most of the objects were moving fast, anywhere from ten percent to well over the speed of light. The images were blurs, not revealing what exact shape they were. He, and others, were quite certain the agency did have better visuals of the objects but decided the public didn't need-to-know everything they had learned. Speculation ranged from alien craft to pieces of rocks ejected from a passing black hole.

He spoke to Carter. "Object presents no danger. Good work, continue to monitor."

"How was the passenger walk through? Get hounded by the single women?" Shultz asked.

He heard the smirk in her voice. "All is well there. I escaped without incident." The trip to Mars carried more cargo than passengers, and most of the passengers were there to work. A few were traveling to Mars for the adventure of visiting another world. Regardless of the reason the passengers were on board, the owner of the spaceship wanted the captain to be seen by them. Occasionally, McLeod had to stroll through the passenger lounge area, comprising of restaurants, shopping kiosks, bars and entertainment rooms. He was often approached by passengers, particularly women, who had questions about the ship and the voyage.

"That's good. I'd hate to have to rescue you from the clutches of a rich woman."

He looked at Combs, who was ignoring their conversation. The average height, heavy-set man was one of the few who sported a beard, considered a slight hazard in space. If the ship air systems failed, and if a space suit was not available in time, an air mask would be a last resort. Facial hair could cause an improper seal, making the air mask less effective. When he was asked about why he didn't shave off his beard, the soft-spoken Combs replied it was because he liked to live on the edge. That usually brought about a few chuckles.

"Everything in specs?" he asked Combs.

"All good, although engine number two is showing higher than normal temperature levels for the out-take coolant."

"How much higher than normal?"

"Two point five degrees, well within tolerance. Just that last time I checked it was right on the mark. Now it's gone up a bit."

"Talk to engineering?"

"There was no reason to. That temperature fluctuation is to be expected from older engines."

"Okay, keep an eye on it."

"Seriously? You're telling me to keep an eye out for engine variations?"

McLeod grinned. "I guess that's rather superfluous. I'll be in the captain's lounge."

The captain's lounge, a few steps away from the control deck, also served as a meeting room. It led to the captain's suite, a spacious area including a kitchen and sleeping quarters. As usual, he checked the progress of the ship on the monitors attached to the walls. It was currently seven hours ahead of schedule, the retrofitted engines proving they could sustain higher output. He was pleased with his maiden voyage as captain of the Nevada Queen, especially so since Lisa Wagner, the CEO of Gibbston Space Lines, was onboard. She had made it plain she was not happy with the cost overruns to make the rebuilt ship ready for departure. However, on the occasion when he had seen her on the ship, she had been cordial to him.

A beep on his monitor alerted to a change in the ship's status at the same time his communicator buzzed. He touched the device located on an arm band. "Combs, are you calling about the temperature increase?"

"Yeah, another half degree."

"What does Dermott have to say?"

"She believes it's a sticky valve at one of the output manifolds."

"Thanks, I'm going to the engine room."

McLeod put on his cap and walked briskly toward the rear of the ship. As he entered the main lounge, he nodded at passengers and crew, trying hard not to show any stress in his face. He used a lift to drop two levels down, believing he could make better time going through the area of retail shops, coffee bars and lounges. His long strides took him near the edge of the shops, where more expensive items of interest were sold.

"Captain McLeod."

He closed his eyes momentarily at the sound of Lisa Wagner's voice behind him. He turned around. "Ms. Wagner, how good it is to see you. Are you doing a bit of shopping?" His hands fidgeted as he stopped to address her, noting she was wearing an expensive looking blouse and skirt. The shorter than average skirt was complemented by high heels, giving her height. Overall, her manner of dress made her look like a woman in charge.

"I'm just looking right now. Are you in a hurry, Captain?" She gave him a questioning look.

"Ah, yes, as a matter of fact. I have a situation I wish to discuss with one of my officers. If you'll excuse me?"

"Better still, I'll accompany you. I'd like to see how you handle situations."

"I didn't realize I was still on probation. Very well, but I need to walk quickly."

Wagner didn't have an opportunity to reply, half running to keep up to McLeod.

They passed the doorway that indicated ship personnel only and reached the engine room. A second sign read *Authorized Personnel Only* and finally another sign read *Danger. This Is A High-Risk Environment.*

"Dermott, what's the situation?" he called out to the woman on a stepladder next to the second engine.

"Higher than acceptable output temperature, captain. I just

did a visual, nothing obvious. I believe the problem is valve number five."

"I see. Ms. Wagner, you need to leave this area. There is some danger present."

"Captain, need I remind you I'm the owner of the Nevada Queen, and therefore I can be where I please?"

"With all due respect, as captain of a spaceship currently in deep space, I am the absolute authority here. I will request that you leave the engine room immediately."

"And if I don't?" Her face turned pink.

"Then I will have security escort you to your cabin, and have you confined there until further notice."

Her jaw dropped and she took a deep breath. She stared at him. "Well, captain, this act of authority will not be soon forgotten." She pursed her lips and walked out of the engine room.

Tia Dermott whispered, "God, I hope you don't get fired. She looked like she was willing to have you launched into space."

"So be it. I can always go back to mining asteroids. What's the next step?"

"Option one. We shut down engine number two and take apart the output manifold and replace the valve. Down time would be two days. We could still run with engine number one during that time, but our arrival time would be delayed by thirty-six hours."

"Option two?"

"I can attempt to free up the valve by vibration induced by a mass bearing tool."

"Really?"

"Yup, I'll hit the damn thing with a hammer."

McLeod watched as Dermott used a four-kilogram sledgehammer on the top of the manifold. After two strikes, a technician called out. "Valve is open! Temperature is dropping to normal."

McLeod breathed a sigh of relief. "Great work team." He exited the engine room and came across Wagner leaning on a wall with her arms crossed.

"Still feel like you're in charge, captain?"

"My apologies, but I couldn't have you at risk in the engine department. There was a danger of an explosion. If something were to happen in there, I would be held completely at fault, as I should be."

She gave him a short smile. "Well, I guess I should be thankful you didn't put me in chains and throw me in the brig. On reflection, I suppose I shouldn't have tried to exert my authority."

"Thank you for your understanding."

"Shall we have a drink and put this behind us?"

They choose a table in one of the small lounges.

"I want to ask you a few things about yourself, if you don't mind." Wagner took a sip of her gin and tonic.

"I thought you had everything you needed to know on my personnel file." He slowly turned his pilsner glass in his hand, not tasting the gold liquid inside yet.

She gave a long smile. "Oh, we do know a lot about you. But I was curious on your thoughts on spooks and USOs."

"Spooks and USOs?" He repeated the question to stall for time, unsure why she would ask it. He still expected a grilling for ordering her out of the engine room, and he wasn't sure if he was being led into a trap.

She peered at him. "Come on, just your thoughts."

"I believe the spooks are USOs, and that our esteemed space agency knows a lot more about them then they are willing to reveal to the public."

"And USOs are?"

"Advanced alien spacecraft. Something is going through our solar system at a high percentage of the speed of light, and even exceeding it. To me, that speaks of advanced technology and not a natural phenomenon."

"Interesting. I don't disagree with you. Just for the sake of argument, let's say an alien spacecraft was found intact. Would you be willing to try and fly it?"

He grinned. "I'm not normally a risk taker, but yes, in a heartbeat." He looked at her reaction and saw a pleased expression. *She's not bad looking, for a stuck-up CEO, that is.*

"Captain, you're a most interesting man. We may have to continue this conversation at a later date." She stood. "Now I have some reports to finish, and I should get back to them."

"It was good to talk to you as well." He stood and waited as she left the lounge. *That sure was an odd conversation.*

14

First Commander Lexanna Shultz approached McLeod as he stood at the back of the bridge. "Everything normal, Captain. No issues to report."

"Excellent to hear. We have just two more days to Mars orbit, and we're ahead of schedule."

She gave a smile. "I guess it's nice that you didn't have any more situations with Lisa Wagner. She does make the crew a bit nervous. They said she acts a bit aloof, as if they were invisible."

"Well, that may not be an entirely fair assessment of her. I came across her a couple of times while she was in a lounge and in the viewing area, working on reports. Both times she didn't acknowledge me until I approached her to inquire if she required anything."

"That was brave of you."

"What kind of a captain would I be if I was scared to ask someone how they were doing?" He chuckled. "One can't allow fear to stop from making the right choice. She deserves recognition, as any passenger does. She was quite grateful I asked, not annoyed I interrupted her work. She is the CEO of a large company and works seven days a week. She isn't aloof, just focused on work that needs to be done."

"Oh, do I catch a touch of admiration for a pretty woman?"

He laughed. "Why do women love to try to put together a romance where none exists?"

"Oh, come on, surely you can see this from my viewpoint. A single, and may I say handsome, captain meets a powerful, beautiful woman. How do sparks not happen?" She giggled as he blushed slightly.

"Ms. Shultz, I may cancel your shore leave."

McLeod smiled as the passengers slowly boarded the shuttles, shaking hands and offering them a pleasant stay on Mars. When most of the passengers had vacated the Nevada Queen, the crew were next to leave. The crew was replaced by other personnel, who were to do mechanical checks and repairs. After the crew left, the officers were next to leave, along with one final passenger.

"Well, Captain McLeod, I have to say that was a more interesting voyage than I had anticipated." Lisa Wagner stopped in front of him. "You certainly have made an impact on the authority of running a spaceship."

"Thank you." *I think.* "We're glad to know that you didn't find your trip boring."

"It certainly wasn't boring." She placed a hand on his shoulder momentarily. "I may contact you while we're on Mars. Maybe just to continue our conversation. Or maybe to offer you a promotion." She paused. "Or maybe to fire you."

McLeod smiled. "It's nice to have options."

She laughed. "You're very good at understating a situation."

McLeod watched her disappear into the shuttle. *For some reason, I hope I don't hear from her while I'm on Mars.*

McLeod boarded the nearly empty shuttle. In his company were First Commander Lexanna Shultz, Navigator Richard Combs and Engine Engineer Tia Dermott. The four relaxed with a drink each, dropping titles and chatting about what they were going to do on Mars.

Combs indicated it would give him time to read and to catch up on some videos he hadn't seen.

"Don't you do enough of that on the ship?" Shultz shook her head. "I think I'll rent a shuttle and go and explore Mars a bit. They say it keeps changing as the temperature and air pressure increase."

"Jaret, what about you? Are you going to explore the wilderness or the bars?" Dermott gave him a grin.

"No plans yet. I think I'll get my fill of alcohol the first night or two, and then maybe look for some more sober activities to use up my time. How about you?"

"I'm going to stay away from anything mechanical. I'm not planning to get drunk but will partake on some social activities in the local drinking establishments."

"I hope that doesn't mean karaoke. I've heard you sing, and it isn't pretty to hear."

She stuck her tongue out at him. "I've heard you talk, and I can say the same thing about you."

"So that's why you prefer the engine room." McLeod laughed. "You can't hear me."

"All the same, I plan to be in the Shifting Sands Bar for a few nights. Look me up and I'll buy you a drink." She looked at Combs and Shultz. "That goes for you two adventurers as well. It will be good to have a couple of drinks with people I know but normally don't have time to socialize much with."

15

McLEOD SURVEYED RED CITY FROM THE CLEAR SIDES OF the elevator as it travelled down to the main level. The forty-seven story Phobos Building housed business offices, a few coffee shops, a couple of lounges and a hotel. Gibbston Space Lines held an administration office in the building, and McLeod went there as a courtesy to say hello and made sure they received all the reports sent from the Nevada Queen. McLeod believed as a new passenger ship captain, it would be good for them to meet the person doing reports.

He remembered the first time he visited the capital of Mars, it seemed surreal and he marvelled at the engineering it took to make Mars habitable. The line of sight from his room was hampered by the various buildings in Red City that helped protect the city from the dusty winds that travelled around much of Mars.

McLeod walked down the familiar red rock path to the Marriott Green Isle Hotel. His room, a studio style apartment, was slightly larger than the normal rooms and afforded a view of the land beyond Red City. It was still mostly pink sand and rock, but terraforming had allowed a few green plants to survive in small caves where moisture could be collected.

McLeod checked the newscast in his hotel room. There wasn't much change in local news, other than a sex scandal with a board member of the Mars Traders Corporation. Many of the people on

Mars held shares with the company and were interested in how the company was run. The board member might be required to resign her position if it was found the company's interests were influenced.

McLeod exited the hotel, heading to the market section of the city. The shops were all small and many carried a variety of goods. McLeod wasn't interested in any of them, but rather the bar situated at a corner of two streets, the Opus Bar. He made his way past the tables and sat on one of stools around the curved metal bar.

The blonde bartender greeted him with a smile as she wiped the bar portion in front of him. She glanced at him a second time and a genuine smile appeared as she recognized him.

"Hello again. You're back for another tour of duty?"

"I'm afraid so. And you're still hanging around Red City to catch a ghost."

Leana laughed. "Someday, I will catch it."

"If it's there, you'll be the one to find it. Dark rum, cola."

The ghost commonly referred to was a spindly housecat sized creature that many people had claimed to have seen in the outlands of Mars. No photographs of the creature existed, except for a blurred shadow that could have been caused by a dust devil. What it lived on was also speculated, some saying it might be able to digest the various minerals in the ground. There were also rumours of a rat sized lizard and even a Martian flying insect. Seen, but not caught on camera.

Most scientists were of the opinion the creatures existed only in the imagination.

Leana placed the tumbler with the dark liquid in front of him. Of all the alcoholic drinks on Mars, McLeod found rum to be reconstituted the best from a dry powder. Some whiskies were okay, and wine was a hit or miss. Beer often could regain its flavour, but the carbonation added afterward didn't last, resulting in a flat taste. "Did you hear about the spook last week? A round one apparently."

McLeod nodded. "Yeah, near the West Post Observatory." He didn't like the name spook given to unidentified space objects. At one time, UFOs were commonly seen on Earth. As humans moved to space, exploring and inhabiting the moon, Mars and even asteroids, the UFO sightings dropped substantially. Now USOs were the mysterious crafts occasionally seen.

The name spook came from an astrophysicist who was doing timed photos from Hawking Space Observatory Delta. He noticed the star field he was photographing had stars and nebula blinking off for a microsecond or less, all in a straight line. He concluded something was passing in front of the stars. He made a bold, and controversial assumption; that whatever was passing in front of the stars and nebula was an object at the outskirts of our solar system. He then calculated that the object, judging from how many stars were covered at the same time, that it was almost two kilometres long and perhaps one half a kilometre wide. The cigar shaped object would be travelling at one point six times the speed of light. The name spook came about from the object not being seen but inferred from its silhouette.

His proposition was a hit with the news media. He faced ridicule from his peers, but he refused to back down. He challenged anyone to find an alternate hypothesis.

McLeod didn't voice his opinion on the matter. While working a mining ship, he was certain he had seen a shadow more than once on a deep scan monitor. Like the rest of those who mined the asteroids, he kept most sightings to himself. Reporting such USOs could mean being placed on psychiatric observation rather than working.

"Ghosts and spooks. Who really knows what's real?"

Leana grinned. "Well, at one time, people didn't believe a sasquatch existed either. Just saying."

"Hey, let me buy you a drink. Tell me about the Traders scandal."

She held up a finger, served two more customers and made herself a gin and tonic. When she came back, she was eager to spill the news.

"Our 'Miss my private life is not of anyone's concern' apparently with, or without, her husband's knowledge decided to have a threesome."

She paused as she took a drink. "With two other women. Can you believe it? This one is not going to blow away easily."

McLeod nodded. Bartenders usually knew the story behind the news when it came to people. His mobile buzzed and he looked at the message, frowning.

"Girlfriend wondering where you are?"

"Worse. The boss wants to meet me in a couple of days."

"That usually isn't good news. Did you piss her off somehow?"

"I threatened to throw her in the brig if she didn't leave a restricted zone on my ship."

"Maybe I better be the one buying you a drink then."

16

THE NEXT MORNING MCLEOD DECIDED HE NEEDED TO TAKE a few hours away from drinking. He rented a style of shuttle called a rover and left Red City on one of the roads heading out of the city. The rover style of shuttle had room only for a driver and two passengers. It was capable of only three metres of lift and depended most of its motion on four, flexible coiled metal wheels. Unlike the paved streets inside, the roads past the boundaries of Red City were simply hard packed sand and rock.

The rover drove on autopilot, although McLeod could drive on manual mode if he desired. The road he took weaved around various rocks and skirted a small canyon. The rover had a sealed passenger compartment, but he wasn't overly concerned about the outside environment.

The rover came to a stop at the entrance to Wizard Lake. The area around Wizard Lake had a small rest area, plus footpaths around it. An electronic voice inside the rover warned about coming in contact with the water, as there was a danger of contamination with microbes. McLeod stepped out onto to the red, sandy soil, making slow, deliberate strides toward the water. He wasn't sure how the lake received its name, other than it was a nickname given to the climate control engineer who first determined the area would support a large body of water. Of all the bodies of water on Mars, Wizard Lake was one of the largest.

It was shallow, covering a large irregular shaped area, and was considered more of a sea than a lake.

The mineral rich water was slowly rising, as the frozen water underneath and around the bed thawed. It meant the lake water was cold but was still able to support life. Plankton floated on the surface, and there were some types of hardy fish from Earth surviving in the cold water. It took a lot of trial and error to find species of fish that could live in the Martian lake, plus the supporting plant life and microbes.

McLeod followed a path to the rest area where a few stone benches and seats were located. He passed the rest area and continued to the edge of the lake, admiring the play of water from the wind. Occasionally a cloud of dust crossed over the lake.

I wonder if a sailboat would work here? The wind is certainly strong enough. Might have to employ a different technique as the water is choppy and likely require larger sails. He smiled at the thought of sailing on the lake and followed a path around the lake.

The hard, rocky path was mostly natural, with just a few of the larger rocks moved off the pathway. The walkway was kept clear of sand by the nearly constant breeze.

He took in the unique Martian landscape. Rocks were strewn about randomly between rock columns left behind when oceans of water disappeared. The columns had eroded from the constant wind but still stood, reaching like fingers to the sky. The only sound was his own breathing, and the different pitches of the wind as it was buffeted by the rocks. The trail rose slightly and went down again, skimming the edge of the lake.

The sun glinted from the water, momentarily causing him to squint and look away. A sudden movement captured his attention, a flash of red and grey by a boulder. *What the hell?* He hurried to where he saw the motion, stepping around the boulder.

There wasn't anything he could see. He examined the ground, but the bare rock didn't show any footprints. *Did I imagine it? Was it a dust devil?* He considered it looked too real to ignore the possibility of it being more solid than a collection of dust. He followed the trail again, keeping his vision far ahead where a creature might be scurrying about. He was trained on focusing for unusual objects from his time spent on the asteroid belt. His mind shut out the mundane rocks, ready for anything that moved. Fifty metres ahead, he thought he saw *something* darting between a rock and a column. He hurried, as much as he dared with low oxygen and gravity, to the spot.

He wasn't surprised he didn't find anything. The ground showed slight impressions which a clawed foot might have made, if he used his imagination. He looked at the rock column. *Better not risk climbing it, but it would provide a great vantage point.* He pondered what he thought he saw, reconstructing the brief image. *Short legs, skinny body with hair, short tail, small head with a long snout.* He advanced again in the general direction of where the creature, if there was one, might be going. He looped away from the lake, hoping to catch it unaware. He looked behind, wondering if perhaps the creature might decide to follow him. *It's smaller than a cat, and one isn't anything to be concerned about, but what if it was part of a pack? Maybe a dozen would be a real problem.* He saw his footprints had already disappeared, the shifting sand quickly obliterating any structure.

A chipping sound froze his movements. He turned in the direction and made his way to a rock column that had fallen over long ago, leaving a scattering of rocks and pebbles. *Might have been the wind making the sound.*

He studied the ground. His eyes caught the wind covering up what might have been scratch marks. A few feet away he saw a hole in the ground by a large rock. *Maybe something made that hole, and tunnels underneath this area. That would explain why it would be so hard to see.*

McLeod decided he had spent enough time outside and went back to the rover. He didn't see any sign of the creature again, although he was surprised how far he had travelled in pursuit of the whisper of something. *Maybe it's all my imagination. Maybe there's something when you're by yourself on a desolate world that makes you want to see something.*

The rover rambled back to Red City. McLeod relaxed, musing about life returning to Mars. *Could a creature as advanced as what I might have seen live on Mars? Maybe they were hibernating all this time until the planet became warm enough, or eggs hatched when conditions became right. Or maybe they were alive all this time and we only came across them as we invaded their territory. Or maybe there isn't any creature, just my imagination at work.*

He returned the rover as sunset arrived, and went to his room, sketching out the creature on his pad with the assistance of a software program that reformed his crude lines to an actual drawing. He left for the Opus Bar, finding Leana tending the bar.

"Hey." She gave him a smile and brought out a bottle. "New rum. Want a shot?"

"Make it a double." He placed his pad on the bar. "I think I saw this earlier today." He turned on the device, revealing the sketch of a furry animal.

"Seriously? Where did you see that?"

"Around Wizard Lake. Just a glimpse of it, and it might have been the wind and dust. But this is what my mind and imagination came up with."

"Wow. That's pretty close to what others have seen. Wizard Lake makes sense. Most sightings occur around water." She refilled his glass. "I'll have to go there again and take a look for myself."

"Go with someone. When you start wandering around there it's easy to get confused on how far you've walked. Also, the creature, if there is one, may feel threatened and attack. You don't know what it may be. I saw a small hole in the ground as well. It could be natural, but also it might be a tunnel a creature dug. Maybe they live mostly underground."

"That would help explain why we can't catch them."

"Perhaps. I wanted to let you know I don't think you're completely crazy for believing in them."

"Thanks." She laughed.

McLeod left Opus and headed to the Shifting Sands bar. Because the streets were all slightly curved, walking was more interesting. It also gave Red City a small town feeling as each neighbourhood had its own collection of hotels, shops and entertainment. The underground transportation system could move residents quickly to various parts of the city, but the streets above were used largely by transportation vehicles such as delivery vans, bicycles electric scooters.

Fifteen minutes later, McLeod entered the bar where Tia Dermott had promised to be. He quickly spotted her standing at a high-top table with two others. A woman was standing next to her, and he recognized her from the Nevada Queen, a member of the kitchen staff. He recalled she also worked on the McKenzie King as a cook, transferring to the Nevada Queen when he took command. Dermott gave him a wave as he approached the table. A young man at the table turned around, and quickly stood straighter as he recognized the captain.

McLeod smiled. "Good to see some of the crew is making use of time away from the ship. Daniel Roberts, isn't it?"

"Yes sir, Captain."

"Relax. We're not on board. How are you doing, Tia?"

"So far I'm catching up nicely to the lack of alcohol I had on the ship. Tracie is helping me with that." She gave the woman a slight nudge with her elbow.

"Tracie Thobes, you're part of the hospitality staff."

"Yes, I am. It's nice being on a passenger ship rather than a cargo ship. Definitely more interesting work and the customers are a little easier to deal with." The long-haired blonde gave her hair a toss back. "Some of those miners on the transport ship had lost some of their social skills."

McLeod shared a pair of drinks with the others. He quickly determined that Roberts was interested in both Dermott and Thobes and wasn't aware he was the odd man out. Dermott and McLeod didn't discuss details of their social life during their time working together, but he had hints that while she preferred men, occasionally she was quite willing to switch sides. This appeared to be one of those times when the soft skinned Thobes was the winner of her affections. McLeod put down his empty glass. "Time for me to get going."

Dermott looked disappointed. "Are you sure you have to leave? I was about to order some food."

"Thanks, but I have a meeting tomorrow. It'll be an early day."

"A meeting? I thought you were off duty until departure."

"I was. Lisa Wagner has requested a meeting with me." He smiled. "I decided I shouldn't say no."

"Oh no." Tia's eyes widened. "She's not still mad at what happened on the Nevada Queen is she?"

"No, I don't think so. It might be something else. Regardless, I'll find out tomorrow."

"Hey, if you're offered a position on another ship, you know where to find me."

"Thanks. I'll let you know what happens."

In the morning, McLeod first used a ground shuttle to the spaceport, and then a Gibbston Space Lines executive shuttle for transport to Space Station Delta. The station was used for non-scheduled passenger ships, restricted traffic for government and corporate flights. He was curious why Wagner set up the meeting at the space station rather than on Mars but speculated the answer would be known when he found out what the meeting was about.

He stepped out into the corridor of the space station, turning toward the elevators that would take him to the level where Gibbston Space Lines held their offices. The elevator opened to the reception, where a brunette with short hair gave him a pleasant, but short, greeting.

"I have a meeting with Lisa Wagner."

"Yes, Mr. McLeod." The receptionist gestured to a chair. "Please have a seat while I inform her of your arrival."

McLeod choose one of the four chairs in the small waiting area. He sighed and studied a print on the wall showing the surface of Europa.

He heard a woman's footsteps, turned his gaze and saw Lisa Wagner approach. He stood.

"I'm sorry to keep you waiting." She gave him a warm smile. "Please come with me."

They entered an office where a middle-aged man worked behind a computer desk. Two large monitors sat on his desk as he peered at one of them.

Wagner introduced them.

McLeod looked at Dwayne Bentley. There was something odd about him, and at first, he couldn't understand what it was. Then it occurred to him his face wasn't quite symmetrical. The left eye was lower than the right by a fraction.

"Good to meet you."

The heavy-weight man shrugged. "Likewise." His voice was flat.

Wagner looked at Bentley. "Inform Mr. McLeod about your theory."

Bentley shifted his position in his chair and a slight smile creased his lips. "Where to start?" The smile grew. "Tell me, what do you know about the speed of light?"

"It's about three times ten to the eighth power metres per second and is fast as you can go in space."

"Okay, is it a particle or a wave?"

"Both, from what I understand."

Bentley nodded. "Good, so far. Now if light is a wave, then how does it transverse across space? All waves, sound for example, require a medium to travel through. What do light waves use?"

"I don't know. Just another property of light I suppose."

"What about the photon? If it's a particle, then why doesn't it have a mass or a volume?"

McLeod shook his head. "I don't know. Not my field of knowledge."

"Not surprising. It doesn't appear that even the so-called experts know that answer either. Another question. Light will bend as it passes by a strong gravitational field. Since photons and light apparently do not have any mass, physics claim light bends because the fabric of space-time itself is curved. So, what is this fabric made of? And how does it make light follow its curvature?"

McLeod shrugged. "Like I said, not something I would know."

Bentley nodded. "Fair enough. Now to recap, why isn't light faster? Why is it at that particular speed? What is the medium a light wave uses? If it has no mass, why is it affected by gravity? What is the space-time fabric? Any other questions?"

"Yeah, why ask me these questions if they don't have an answer?"

"Everything has an answer. Some things we just don't know yet, so we make up some silly excuse like it's a law of physics. That's a cop out."

"I suppose you know the answers."

"To some things I do. Let's look at the speed of light. Why is it that speed?"

"Property of light I suppose."

Bentley raised a finger. "That's a misconception. It isn't light that established that speed, after all it's just an elementary particle or wave. Rather the speed of light, or rather maximum speed of any particle, is set by the universe." He held up a hand to prevent McLeod from possibly interrupting. "Light should be able to travel much faster, maybe almost unmeasurable. There's a hint of that when there are entangled particles, such as when two photons are created at the same time and move in opposite directions. Change the characteristics of one and the other changes immediately. Well, as much as we can determine anyway."

"You believe light should be able to travel an almost infinite speed, but the universe is holding it back?"

"Think of when you drop a weight, such as a steel ball, from a great height on Earth. The ball doesn't just keep accelerating, but rather reaches a limiting velocity due to air resistance. The same is true to light, although its velocity isn't limited by air but by a force in the universe that I call the Dowling effect."

"Dowling effect? What the hell is that?"

"The accumulation of all matter, including dark matter, in the universe produces the Dowling field that limits light, and all forces and particles to a finite speed. Einstein was wrong. It isn't the speed of light that limits our velocity, but rather light itself is limited in speed."

"Interesting theory. Why does it make any difference to us? Since we're limited to how fast we can travel."

"There may be a way to neutralize the Dowling field. If so, we can travel faster than light in our universe." Bentley grinned.

Wagner looked at McLeod. "Now are you interested?"

17

McLeod looked between Bentley and Wagner. "Hell, yeah, I'm interested. Are you going to tell me you already have a faster than light spaceship?"

Wagner answered. "That's a big maybe. We have the ship. Now it needs to go on a test run. To do that, we need a captain and a pilot. Do you want to be that person?"

McLeod's answer surprised her. "I'd want to see the ship first."

"I keep underestimating you." She gave a smile. "Okay, you get to see the ship first."

—

The spaceship was medium sized, just over three hundred metres in length. He looked at it from the spaceport window with anticipation. The body was a mix of bright white paint and black, sharp edged shadows. Long tubes held the ship to the spaceport, along with larger cylinders that clung to the entrances. Two entrances were large enough for people to enter while a centre entrance to the cylinder was oversized for cargo. The spaceship body was oval in shape with a pair of short broad wings at the back. On the top of the fuselage was a mounted cylinder. The mostly white spacecraft had a wide blue band and a smaller red one around its length. In the middle of the ship the logo of

Gibbston Space Lines was displayed. He saw several large black cables attached to various points along the ship. Space suited workers moved around the perimeter of the ship, occasionally inspecting an access panel.

"Nice looking bird. What's the cylinder for? It looks like a laser gun for blowing apart asteroids."

"It's meant to look like that is what it would be for. In fact, it contains the electronics to neutralize the Dowling field." Lisa Wagner paused. "In theory, I suppose. We have yet to have a successful test outside of the laboratory."

"What did the lab tests show?"

"There were effects that I will discuss later."

"You know more than what you're telling me. There's no way you converted a whole ship on a whim to test his theory."

"Let me show you the ship."

The elevator took them to the ground floor, and they walked through a tunnel that connected to the front of the craft where a sealed door stood. Wagner used a keypad to unlock the door. Slowly the door swung outward and to the side.

"We need to keep the door closed for safety reasons and to maintain security. We can't just have anyone wandering around our ship."

They stepped inside the ship and as McLeod looked around, she continued to speak.

"We made a prototype a few months ago. A robot ship that we transported near the asteroid belt."

"What happened?"

"As far as we can tell the Dowling field was neutralized and the ship exceeded the speed of light."

"What do you mean by as far as you can tell?"

"The ship sent back data that indicated it went faster than the speed of light, and then suddenly nothing."

"Nothing? No explosion?"

"Nothing. Silence. It was programmed to make a return to where it was launched, but that didn't occur."

"Space doesn't allow for room for error. One screw up and it's your last." McLeod looked around at the entrance and turned toward the control cabin.

The front was lit by soft light with the forward viewscreens currently blacked out. McLeod knew during normal ship operations the viewscreens gave a view of what was outside the ship in real time but also protected the occupants from sudden bursts of radiation and light with optical filtering. In case of electrical failure on the ship causing the viewscreens to stop working, the viewscreens could be swung down to reveal actual windows made of thick carbon-glass.

He saw the configuration of two rows of three control consoles with swivel chairs. Behind the twin rows a raised platform contained the captain's elaborate console and a smaller, secondary console for bridge's second in command.

"Looks normal enough." He turned toward the rear of the ship, noting the close proximity of the captain's and other executive officers' suites. Next were the officers' exercise room, meeting room and lounge. He went past various emergency controls embedded in the walls and through the kitchen and dining room. He suspected on the deck below, as usual, were the sleeping quarters for the rest of the crew plus their exercise room and lounge area.

Wagner followed McLeod as he left the dining room. An open doorway showed the two-level engineering room with a catwalk going through the centre and around the perimeter. Along the walls monitors and consoles dotted the available space. In between, conduits ran in what appeared to be a haphazard fashion. Some of the conduits were small, barely the diameter of a fist. Others were much larger and four were big enough for a person to crawl through.

"Must be some big engines in this boat." He walked across the centre catwalk to the engine room. The heavy doors were open, revealing four engines in a row.

"What do you think?" She smiled as McLeod took a deep breath.

"That is major power. Jefferson's Mark Sevens." He climbed

down spiral steps. "I haven't actually seen these before, only read about them."

"Now you can have a chance to see them operate."

He peered at the massive motors, seeing only the front portion of the square block of each. Behind a firewall were the rear ends of the motors. Each square block had a variety of panels, conduits and control panels attached to the face. Unlike the usual touch screen controls, the panels all used physical switches and buttons, preventing accidental engagement. Yellow lights were glowing from a number of the panels, indicating power was present at the motors.

"Are you still in the testing phase?" He pointed at glowing lights.

"Static calibration. We plan on initiating low level synchronization tomorrow."

"That should be interesting to watch."

"I'm sure it will be, for the captain." She let the sentence hang. "Let me show you engineering."

They stepped through to the engineering section and McLeod immediately smelled the mixture of ozone, oil and metal. He felt the air movement from fans, knowing it was critical that the control equipment for the motors were kept as stable as possible. Fluctuations in temperature could cause problems during the calibration and synchronization phase.

He saw a man in a blue uniform monitoring a large array of several monitors. Bar graphs with changing numbers covered each screen.

He approached the officer. "Fish?"

The officer turned to his voice. Tall with a bit of weight in his middle, the east-Indian heritage man sported a closely trimmed beard.

"Captain McLeod! So you're the new captain of this boat."

"Just Jaret. The captain hasn't been decided yet." He turned to Wagner. "Kevin Gill and I have known each other for some time. He is one fine engineer. You're lucky to have him doing the setup."

"We're going only for the best. That's why we want you to captain this ship."

McLeod walked with Wagner back to the Gibbston offices. "That is one nice ship. Can you tell me more about this Dowling field?"

"I can do more than that. I can show you."

They returned to the space station, going directly to where Bentley had his office and laboratory. The lab was spotless with white walls and a ceiling glowing with soft lights. Test equipment on trolleys surrounded a long black table. McLeod nodded his approval. "Nice setup. First rate stuff here."

"If you're going to ship up equipment to the space station, you might as well make it the best available." Wagner strolled to the opposite side of the table.

McLeod looked at a silver coloured ball resting in the centre of the table. "So what's this?"

Bentley, standing by the far wall, spoke. "This lab is set up to test the application of the Dowling field." He walked over to the table, powering on the equipment. "Pick up the metal ball."

McLeod hefted it as he carried it away from the table. "There's a few kilograms there."

"Three to be precise. Notice that it resists being lifted up, and if you try to move it side to side."

McLeod moved the weight side to side. "Yeah, inertia."

"That resistance to being moved is from everything in the universe pulling at it, trying to make it stay at rest. Whether you're in a gravity field, like in here, or in deep space, any mass resists a change in position."

"Newton's first law of motion."

"Correct, but there's more to that. You see, every particle in the universe interacts with every other particle in the universe. That's what gives objects inertia." Bentley turned a control on another piece of equipment, causing a whine to increase in frequency until it ceased to be heard. "Try moving it over the table."

McLeod held the ball over the table. "There isn't any weight, like you shut off the gravity field."

Bentley shook his head. "No, it's not like I shut off the gravity field. Try moving the ball around. You'll find Newton's first law doesn't apply to it."

"You're right. It's like moving a feather. What happened to its mass?"

"Technically it's still there, just that the Dowling field has isolated the ball from the rest of the universe and the collective mass of the universe. Because it's no longer part of the universe, inertia doesn't exist."

McLeod pushed the ball and released it. It floated a short distance and stopped. "Why does it stop?"

"That's a bit harder to explain. The ball is in its own universe. There is nothing to tell it of its location or speed. Therefore, inertia doesn't really exist for it and it stops moving. If the Dowling field we're generating here is stronger, it would completely insulate the ball from our universe and the ball wouldn't even float the short distance it did."

"What happened to its mass? It's still a solid object."

"Solid object." Bentley smirked. "Take any supposedly solid object. If you could peer at it with some super microscope, you could see that it is made up of atoms, electrons and a nucleus. Now the nucleus is made of protons and neutrons, which are in turn made up of quarks and gluons."

"Yeah, fundamental particles."

"True, but an up quark can change into a down quark under the right conditions, which implies that there is something that makes up quarks. My point is the more you look at matter, the less substance it appears to have. Mass is the simple attraction of particles with all the other particles in the universe. If we isolate an object from the rest of the universe, the mass disappears."

"If the ball is isolated from our universe, how come we can see it?"

"Photons don't have mass. They can travel from one universe to another, even through other dimensions. In our Dowling field, the photons are also free to travel whatever speed they want to and aren't limited to the so-called speed of light limit we have."

"So you have developed a Dowling field to envelope an entire spaceship?"

"Yes. Actually, we need a larger volume than the size of the ship. The field doesn't have a sharp cut off. It's like a magnetic field; it gets weaker in proportion to the volume it is occupying. The Dowling field of the size needed for a spaceship is fairly large and requires a lot of power to generate."

"That helps to explain the Jefferson's Mark Sevens."

Bentley grinned. "Well, actually it was a bit of an overkill there, but it's always nice to have a cushion. That ship will fly."

"So all it takes to going faster than the speed of light is turning on your magic field?"

"Dowling field." He sighed. "I simplified the explanation a bit. There isn't actually a Dowling field."

"You've been lying to me?"

[18]

"No, not exactly." Bentley grinned. "More like a little white diversion of the truth. Let's look at gravity for a moment as an explanation. Everyone has seen the simplistic model of a weight being put in the centre of a rubber sheet. A small ball is sent rolling along on the sheet and it spirals toward where the weight has made an impression on the sheet. According to scientists this is how gravity works. Except for a minor detail that it's a two-dimensional representation of gravity and we live in a three-dimensional world. Now it stands to reason, if we extend this model to our three-dimensional universe, gravity must then be part of a four-dimensional universe. In this case, what we call a gravity field is actually just a bending of space in a higher dimension."

"Alright, how does that restrict light's speed?" McLeod wondered how long the explanation would take.

"Remember my earlier example of how a weight falling from a height has a limiting speed due to air pressure?" He gestured with his hands in a downward motion. "Well, the extra dimension isn't just nothing. It's what light waves travel through and it's what sets the upper speed in our three-dimensional universe. We can't see any extra dimensions, but they exist. How many is a different story." He grinned. "My Dowling field actually distorts the dimension that slows light down. Let's just say it creates a hole in the universe where matter and at least one of the extra dimensions no longer have any influence."

"A hole in the universe," McLeod repeated. "Where nothing but our spaceship exists so we can go as fast as we want. Are there any relativistic effects from exceeding the speed of light? What about time and our apparent mass?"

"Mass remains the same. In our universe mass increases as we approach the speed of light. In our hole in the universe, the speed of light is much higher. Maybe not infinite, but damn high. The same thing with time. The one thing to remember is that the Dowling field doesn't perfectly isolate a spaceship. There's some leakage of the extra dimension and that will allow a small amount of inertia and set an upper limit to the speed of light. But don't be worried, we can still go as fast as hell."

"Well, are you convinced now to become the new captain of the Hendrik A. Lorentz?" Wagner asked.

"Do I get to choose my crew?"

"As long as they meet our qualifications."

"Then I think we have a deal."

"Great." Wagner grinned. "Just remember, not a word of what you saw to anyone about this. That includes your present position as being captain of the Nevada Queen. We still have you listed as her captain. We don't want anyone speculating about a new captain for the Nevada Queen. We're quietly assessing possible candidates. It would raise questions if we listed you as the captain of the Hendrik A. Lorentz before we left port."

"That means I'm a captain of two ships. I can work with that."

"Good. We won't be giving much advanced noticed when we do leave port. The less information we send out about the Hendrik A. Lorentz, the better."

19

MCLEOD CONTACTED DERMOTT VIA EMAIL, ASKING HER TO meet him. A few hours later, McLeod stepped into the Shifting Sands Bar, chose a table and waited as he nursed a rum and ice. Shortly later he saw Dermott enter the bar with Tracie Thobes. He stood and waved.

The women approached his table, with Dermott quietly speaking to Tracie, who gave a small hand wave at McLeod and went to sit at the bar.

"Sorry. She insisted on coming here with me. I think she's new to casual relationships and some women can be a bit clingy."

McLeod chuckled. "That's something I've discovered about women too. She seems really nice."

Dermott gave a small shrug. "I like to keep my options open. I usually pick men, but Tracie has been on my radar for a while and I thought, what the hell?"

"Pretty girl."

"She is. But you didn't want to meet me to talk about my dating habits."

"What I have to say needs to be kept strictly confidential."

"Okay. I'll keep this between us."

"I may be leaving the Nevada Queen. I've been offered the position of captain on a new ship."

"Oh, wow! Congratulations." She stepped around the table and gave him a hug. "What ship is it?"

"I can't tell you much, except that it's new and has some kickass engines."

Dermott grinned. "It sounds like you have your slice of heaven."

"It's more like a chunk. I'm going to need a first-rate engine mechanic. One of the best." He paused as he watched her hold her breath. "I want you. Interested?"

"Damn fucking right I am."

"Great, you'll likely be contacted tomorrow morning." He stood. "Please keep this to yourself. Don't let Tracie know anything."

"I won't. I'll celebrate quietly. Thanks for thinking of me."

"I was thinking of myself when I offered you the job."

———

After McLeod left, Thorbes walked to where Dermott sat.

"What was that all about? What did he want?"

"Nothing too serious. We may be losing one of our engine mechanics, and I may have to start looking for a replacement."

"He had to tell you that in person?"

"Look, there were a couple of other details as well that I won't discuss right now. New topic. I want to go to a bar tonight to drink and do some dancing. Do you want to join me or not?"

Thorbes smiled. "Dancing sounds great."

———

After McLeod said goodbye to Dermott and Thobes, he headed to meet Richard Combs. Combs wasn't the type to meet in a bar but did accept an invitation at a coffee house.

The coffee house was quiet. During the day, a server handled beverage and food requests. But at night the options were limited to what the vending machines would provide. McLeod repeated his information, including the need to keep what he said private, to Combs. "I want you to join our team."

"It sounds interesting, but I want more information. What kind of ship is it?"

"I can't tell you that. It's new, with the latest engines and equipment."

"Is it a passenger ship, a transport ship or a government ship?"

"No comment. All I'll tell you is that this is an opportunity to work on something new."

"This sounds a bit risky. Like I know the Nevada Queen is old, but she's in good shape, and I understand her. I'm not sure I want to be on another ship that I don't know anything about."

"Okay, I know you don't like to take chances. But the offer will remain open if you change your mind."

"Thanks, but you know me and change."

McLeod left the coffee bar, deciding it was time for a drink. He headed to the Opus bar.

━━

Leana placed the rum filled glass in front of McLeod. "Here you go, one dark rum double. What's the occasion? Were you fired?"

"No, something of the opposite. Actually, a bit of a promotion."

"Congratulations. You sure do have survival instincts. Insult your boss and get a raise. I'm impressed."

"Thanks. How about I buy you a drink to have with me?"

"Well, technically I'm not allowed to drink while working, but that's never stopped me before. I think a martini would be nice."

McLeod sipped his rum, looking at the half-filled martini glass on the table. Leana stopped by occasionally for a sip, then departed to serve other customers. It was her second drink, and McLeod was well ahead of her. He decided he better slow down his own drinking if he was going to be able to walk home.

"Want another rum? Last call."

"Okay, one more. Maybe you better bring me a coffee as well."

"Coming right up."

McLeod relaxed, draining the last of the drink in his glass. He looked up at Leana placing another drink and a coffee in front of him. "Hey, drinking proves Einstein's theory of relativity."

"How so?"

"Time, it's relative to the observer. If you drink, everything moves a lot faster. One moment you're walking away, the next you have my coffee."

Leana laughed. "That's not exactly relativity. That's being drunk."

"Kind of the same thing in my state." He took a drink from his glass in a jerking motion. *Damn, maybe I shouldn't have ordered that last rum.*

"Okay, I can see that." She walked around the bar, convincing the remaining customers to finish up their drinks and call it a night. She turned off the lights to the bar, finished her bar duties and returned to McLeod's table.

"I guess I stayed here a bit too long." He took a slurp of his coffee, deciding to leave the remainder of the rum in the glass.

"No, maybe too many rums, but not too long." She took his arm as he stood. "On Mars, we watch out for one another. It's too easy for a simple mistake to cost someone their life. You're in no condition to walk back to your hotel. I live just across the street, so that's where you'll spend the night. To sleep."

———

McLeod woke up, the lights in the room causing him to blink rapidly. Slowly he rolled into a sitting position on the couch. He pulled on his pants that were lying on the floor but didn't see his shirt.

"Good morning" he heard.

"I challenge that." He carefully stood and looked toward the kitchen.

Leana laughed. She handed him a cup of coffee, walking casually from the small kitchen separated from the living room by a counter with a pair of bar stools in front. "How are you feeling?"

"Okay. Minor headache. I deserve a worse fate for what I

drank." He saw she was wearing his shirt, looking far too big on her. He decided it still looked better on her than himself.

"I borrowed your shirt rather than get dressed. I normally don't wear anything until I have to leave the apartment."

"That's okay. Thanks for the coffee."

"Are you hungry? I can make you some breakfast."

"No, just coffee. Thanks for taking care of me last night."

"On Mars, we look out for one another. I wouldn't feel right just sending you out on your own last night."

McLeod nodded, deciding he needed a least one more coffee before he did any serious thinking. He sat at a stool in front of the counter with Leana standing on the opposite side. He listened to her make small talk, occasionally adding a comment of his own.

"What are your plans for today? Besides recovering from your hangover that is."

"I have some work to do related to being a captain of a spaceship. Nothing too serious, but I need to contact some of the ship's personnel."

"No rest for the wicked." She laughed. "A hangover and you're going to work. You would make a good bartender."

"No, I'd drink away the profits." His mobile chirped and a digital voice announced the caller's name. He answered. "Hi, Lexanna. Thanks for returning my call." He listened to her reply, responded and arranged to meet her in an hour. McLeod stood. "Sorry, I guess I have to take off soon."

"Then I guess I have to give back your shirt. I was hoping if I held your shirt hostage, you'd stay longer." She went to the bedroom, and emerged a few minutes later wearing a thermal suit. "Time for me to start thinking about going out as well." Leana passed over his shirt.

"Thanks for your hospitality."

"That's okay. But if the ship has a need for a bartender, give me a call."

"I'll give you a call in any event." McLeod smiled.

"I'll hold you to that promise. Drop by the bar soon, and don't take off in a spaceship without letting me know." Leana pointed a finger at him.

"Okay, I will." McLeod put on his shirt, gave her a kiss and hurried to meet Lexanna.

The Red Oasis was a popular breakfast and lunch spot, turning into a drinking lounge during the evening. McLeod accepted a bowl of soup and coffee, not wanting to try anything with more substance.

"You look a bit rough." Lexanna peered at him.

"A bit too much to drink last night."

"I guessed that. You didn't shave today. I'm going to assume you didn't make it back to the hotel last night." She raised her eyebrows.

"You don't miss much. Which makes you a great officer, but not someone to hide any secrets from."

She laughed. "Now what did you want to talk to me about? Must be important if you're meeting me with a hangover."

"This is information that can't be told to anyone else. I received an offer to captain another ship, which I accepted. I could use a second in command who knows what to do in any situation. Are you interested in joining me?"

"Perhaps. What kind of ship is it?"

"I can't tell you. It's new, latest technology and has big engines."

She took a drink of her tea. "Tia Dermott joining you on this venture?"

"She is."

"Combs?"

"No, he declined. You know how he is with the unknown."

"I do. If this was another passenger ship, you would have said so. That's a pretty safe ship and Combs would've hopped on board for that. That leaves military, government or scientific. You're not a military guy. Exploration? That would coincide with the news last night."

"What news?"

"Oh, you really did do one last night." Lexanna grinned. "Over the past couple of years, the data from the suspected new planet, Eris, has indicated that it was large enough to cause some of the permutations seen in the orbits of the Ort cloud as well as some of the other minor planets. But it still didn't explain how Pluto and Ciron ended with such a strange orbit. Some astronomers began looking for another planet and they believe they may have found it."

"Really? Another gas giant?"

"No, it appears to be a rocky world, not much bigger than Earth. It's faint and hard to detect, so there isn't much detail. But its orbit is really strange, almost forty degrees off the plane and crosses the path of Pluto. They think it was a rogue world floating through space and was captured by the sun, bringing it on a near collision course with Pluto and its moons."

"Wow. That's something. I wish I had been alert enough to catch the news."

"I believe they're calling it Meili, after a Norse god of travel. That makes me wonder if someone had known about the new planet for a week or so before they released the news, perhaps this has something to do with your new position."

"No, I don't believe so. This is a ship designed without a particular mission in mind."

"I have to admit I'm intrigued. Why did you take the offer? Money? Challenge? I know why Tia did. She'll follow you *anywhere*."

McLeod heard a slight change in the pitch in Lexanna's voice when she spoke about Tia following him anywhere. "I didn't ask about the pay. This ship is something any captain would appreciate."

"Man, you're coy with your information. Okay, I'm in."

"Great. I'll have them contact you. Be prepared to be surprised by some new technology. By the way, what do you mean Tia would follow me anywhere?"

A slow smile creased her face. "Oh, men are so slow to pick up clues. As a captain, you know everyone's name, what they do and how they help run the ship. You probably can do every position on the ship from cook to engine mechanic. Yet you miss the obvious. Jaret, she likes you a lot, and not just as a captain."

"What?" His jaw dropped. "But she goes out with others. I never receive much more than a let's get a beer together from her."

"Big deal, she goes out with others. She's lonely, and she dates those she has little long-term commitment to. But as a woman, I see how she acts when you're near her. Honestly, how do you not notice how she looks at you?"

McLeod went back to his hotel, feeling dazed at Lexanna's revelation about Tia. He took a short nap, showered, shaved and stepped out of the hotel, deciding he really needed to walk to clear his head.

As he crossed another street, his mobile announced a caller.

"Hey, Richard, what's up?"

Combs voice was soft, hesitant. "I was checking some listings at the space agency. The Nevada Queen has positions open for an engine mechanic officer. I checked the current roster at the Nevada Queen, and it looks like besides yourself, Lexanna and Tia have left. I'm guessing they decided to join you."

"That's right."

"I don't like the thought of working with new people. I mean it took a while for you to get used to my habits. I was wondering if you still need me as navigator."

"I do. There's some risk, as you pointed out before, of being on a new ship."

"Yeah, but it's less of a concern than working with new people."

"Then I'm glad to have you."

McLeod felt more relaxed as he returned back to the hotel. *I have Tia, Lexanna and Richard with me. All okay there. But that is a complication with Tia. What do I do about that?*

[PART 3]

20

WRITSON DIDN'T ENJOY HER TRIP TO THE MARTIAN WORLD Government offices. The sprawling, four story building held the ten elected officials in charge of Mars, plus the directors of each department. She entered the double set of doors and stopped at the reception desk where one of the two clerks checked her identification before allowing her to proceed to the elevators where the offices were located. The rest of the main floor was devoted to showing off the progress being made to make Mars a green planet by using large interactive displays.

She entered the second level, seeking out Director Gary Dorn's office. She took a deep breath and opened the door to where his secretary, a middle-aged woman, greeted her.

"You must be Nellie Writson." She smiled. "Please go in, he's expecting you."

Shit, I bet he is. "Thank you."

She entered his office and tried to force a smile as he looked up.

"Please close the door and have a seat."

She nodded, closed the door and sat in a well cushioned chair that failed to make her feel comfortable.

"Relax, you're not going to be sent to the north pole to collect ice samples." The big man gave a hint of a smile. "I did consider it though."

"I'm sorry, sir, for causing a problem."

He waved his hand downward. "It's not the end of the world. Dr. Thomas Rigger, despite his outward tone, is actually a decent investigator. He, like you, can be a little intense when trying to do a job. After I spoke to the director of the Martian Preservation Department, I called Dr. Rigger. In the end, he admitted he had been a little too direct in his request and apologized for that."

"Oh."

"I told him that we would be extending our fullest cooperation, and our files of the area in question will be forwarded as soon as possible." He raised his eyebrows. "Now perhaps you can tell me what happened, and why you made a pretence of following protocol in asking for an official request first."

"I was with Lindsey Smyth on the last day, following the source of trace gasses. It turns out they're coming from the lava tubes near the site of the artifacts. We found an opening to a lava tube, and we believed it would be interesting to investigate. Actually, the trace gasses were so high that Lindsey believes there's a good possibility they came from microbes living in the lava tube. I didn't want the Preservation Department to learn about that and shut us out of the lava tubes as well. So, I stalled for time before we gave them our data, hoping they would just concentrate on the artifacts."

Dorn closed his eyes momentarily. "So, you believe Lindsey and yourself may have found life in a lava tube and want to explore that possibility, without the interference from the Preservation Department. You do realize that if there is microbe life in the lava tubes, the Preservation department would take over that investigation as well."

"Yes, but I want Lindsey and our department to get credit for it. Then the Preservation Department can take over."

Dorn sighed. "I appreciate that you want our department to get credit if life is discovered in the lava tubes. However, withholding information from another department is not how we should be operating."

"I understand."

"I'll tell you what we can do. I want you to first send the

Preservation Department the files they requested. Then I want you to contact Dr. Rigger and apologize. You may then ask him if he'll give your team permission to continue with your investigation of the lava tubes. That's the best I can offer as a way to explore the trace gasses."

"Do you think he'll let us?"

"It can't hurt to ask. Remember, he is dedicated about doing research on Mars, and doesn't want to prevent others from doing so as well."

Writson left the director's office feeling relieved he hadn't torn a strip off her. She knew she had overreacted to Rigger when she demanded a formal request for the artifact data. She was pleased Dorn had smoothed out the situation and now she only was required to officially apologize to Rigger, that and ask if she could continue her research at the lava tubes.

She decided she would make sure the data was sent to Rigger's office first, and she would call him afterward. She hoped he would be in a good mood by that time. She made her way to her department's office.

All eyes were on her as she entered her department's office. She gave a forced smile, announcing the verdict.

"I'm still employed, although the whip marks will take time to heal." That brought a few grins from those in the office. She looked at Madison. "Can you send Dr. Rigger a copy of our files for the artifact region, plus those from the lava tubes."

"All of them?"

"Yes. I made an error in judgement in ordering the withholding of information earlier, so now we have to send everything." She went to her office, sat at the desk and stared at her phone. *I'm going to hate making this call.*

She contacted his office using her mobile. A woman's voice answered.

"Dr. Rigger's office."

"This is Nellie Writson calling from the Biological and Geological Department. Is Dr. Rigger available?"

"Dr. Rigger is currently out of the office and can't be interrupted at this time. May I take a message?"

Writson felt a wave of relief that she didn't have to talk to him. "Please inform him that I called regarding the transfer of files concerning the Tharsis Volcanic Region, and I'm sorry there was delay in sending them to him. I apologize for any inconvenience I caused. He can call me if he has any questions."

After the call ended, Writson left her office. She informed Jeremy Tolmat she was taking the rest of the afternoon off and he would be charge. "In fact, I may be late tomorrow morning as well. I plan to have a few drinks after having to call Dr. Rigger's office and apologize."

"No problem." He looked up at her from his desk. "We all appreciate that you stood up to Dr. Rigger and the Preservation Department. I'd like to buy you a drink sometime for that."

"Thanks. This time I think I better be alone. I won't be great company. See you tomorrow."

Writson wasn't sure where to go to have a drink. She decided drinking alone at her apartment was too much alone and headed to one of the bars she occasionally visited. She had developed a friendship with a bartender there, a woman she was able to talk to about Mars and the possibility of finding life on the planet above the microbe level.

She entered the Opus bar and sat at one of the high bar stools along the counter. Most of the Opus Bar consisted of tables with chairs, however, there were eight bar stools next to the curved bar. She gave a small wave at the bartender, Leana.

The bartender finished putting away cups under the counter and walked over to where Writson sat. "Hi, you're here early."

"Yeah, work issues. I decided I needed a drink or two to settle down." She noticed Leana was wearing one of her thermal suits designed more for appearances. The garment featured semi-transparent strips that ran along the outside of each leg up to her hips, and Leana had also undone part of the front closure at her neck.

"Do you want to talk about it?"

"No, suffice to say once again I opened my big mouth, and this time had to do a retreat."

"That sounds so unlike you." Leana laughed. "Rum and cola?"

"Please." She looked around the bar as Leana went to make her drink. There were a total of five people occupying two separate tables. All of them looked like they were visitors to Mars, their clothes looking like what off-worlders would wear. There was one other customer, and he was sitting at the other end of the bar. He was making a comment to Leana, causing her to grin. *Not bad looking. Tall and has that look of someone who has seen a lot. Scar on his face gives him that bad boy look.*

Leana placed her drink in front of her. "So, what else is going on? New boyfriend? Find any strange Martian lifeforms?"

"No, no boyfriend on the horizon. As for lifeforms, nothing yet showing up."

"Did you hear the rumours of some small creature seen out by Wizard Lake?"

"No." Writson gave a shrug. "Unfortunately, those that reported seeing something usually aren't the best observers. We normally don't bother to investigate those reports. Besides, we may have found...are looking into another situation." She took a quick swallow of her drink. "Could I have another drink?"

Leana raised one eyebrow. "Sure."

She left and Writson observed her making another comment to the man at the end of the bar. She returned with another dark drink in a tumbler.

"This one is a double."

"Thanks. Who's your friend?" She tilted her head toward the end of the bar.

"A rather charming man. He's a captain of a passenger ship, killing some time between voyages."

"Oh? And you two have hit it off?"

"He has a rather fascinating life. Nothing serious, just friends right now. Now, enough about my friend. What were you going to say about a new find? I know you, and you're hiding something."

Writson took another drink. "I can't tell you any details. This is very confidential. At one of the sites we discovered some unusual features that don't fit in with the surrounding area. Also, there we found some evidence that there may be some unusual chemistry in one of the lava tubes."

"That's pretty vague."

"I know, and that's how it's going to stay. When you work for the government, you have to adhere to a confidentiality agreement. I can't tell you anything more."

"So, I have to wait until there's some official announcement. That's okay, we can talk about other stuff. Excuse me, time for me to check on the other customers." Leana left the bar, stopping at the two tables with customers.

Writson relaxed, glad Leana hadn't pressed her for more details about the discoveries. *The problem is Rigger and his Preservation Department is likely going to get all the credit. Especially after the way I treated him.* She watched Leana return to the bar and carry a tray with drinks back to the tables. She stared at her drink, deciding she should consider having doubles more often. She felt a pressure at the back of her head that felt like she was being looked at. Writson casually turned her head toward the end of the bar, seeing Leana's friend, the captain.

He was looking at her and gave her a smile before lifting his glass in a salute to her. Writson returned a smile and returned to looking at her drink. *Interesting looking guy, especially with the scar. But you don't look like a Martian, so you're not going anywhere with me.*

She observed Leana return to the bar with a tray and empty glasses and proceed where the captain sat. They exchanged a few words, and she saw Leana laugh. She set another dark drink in front of him, and Writson suspected he was drinking rum as well.

Leana set another glass of rum in front of Writson. "It's from the captain. He apologizes for looking at you. He said you were one of the few interesting things to look at in the bar. Excluding me, of course."

Writson grinned and turned toward the captain. With a wave, she thanked him for the drink. "What's his name?"

"Jaret McLeod. He's not like most of the officers that come down from the passenger and supply ships. No arrogance, just confident and easy to talk to. Want me to invite him over?"

Writson shook her head. "No, he's not my type."

"Not your type? Just because he wasn't born on Mars? You don't have to produce his offspring. Just talk to him. Someday you may need to know someone who travels through space."

"Why? So, I can hook up with some cowboy who blasts off to space after one night?"

"No, because someday you may need to travel to Earth for a vacation. I have gotten a few free trips from knowing the right people."

"The way you look and dress, I don't doubt it."

"Part of the job." Leana laughed. "But it wouldn't hurt for you to talk to a few men just for the sake of talking. Establish a few more connections besides me and your co-workers."

"I suppose you're right."

Leana glanced at where the two tables were. "Be right back."

Writson touched her earpiece and spoke quietly. "Information on Captain Jaret McLeod."

"Jaret McLeod is the captain of the spaceship Nevada Queen. He has been employed by Gibbston Space Lines for the past thirty-eight months. His current relationship status is listed as unattached. His age is thirty-six Earth years. No other personal information is available without permission from his privacy account."

It was as she expected, the bit of information that was available about almost any person. Some individuals allowed more personal information to be known, but most withheld additional details.

Leana returned, "Shall I wave him over?"

"Sure. It might be interesting to talk to a spaceship captain."

Leana walked back to the end of the bar, spoke a few words with McLeod. A moment later McLeod and Leana joined Writson.

After they exchanged introductions, McLeod asked what she did on Mars. "I assume you live here. Your thermal suit is one Martians wear, not the plain style of temporary visitors."

She grinned. "Yeah, I have a closet full of them. Women aren't allowed to wear the same thermal suit two days in a row. I work for the Biological and Geological Department."

"In the field of research, I assume."

"Yup. I get to dig inside Mars. Lots of fun." She looked down at the table and then looked up at him again. "May I ask how you got that scar?"

"At one time I worked in the belt as a miner. We had an accident on our ship. I was pretty lucky, and only ended up with this scar."

"And now you're a captain of a passenger ship." *I don't want him to know I already looked up his public information.*

"Yes, the Nevada Queen."

"Nevada Queen? Isn't that the ship that got stranded when both her engines failed?" She looked around and realized Leana had disappeared. *She's determined to get us together.*

"That was before I took over, and that won't happen under my watch. I think the owner was a little pissed at how much money I spent on renovating the Nevada Queen, but she's safe to be in now." He took a drink. "Tell me more about your exploration of Mars. That sounds more fascinating than flying through empty space."

She laughed. "Yeah, digging a hole in the sand is more exciting than being a captain of a spaceship." She tossed her hair back. "Sometimes it gets to be fun. We send drilling equipment down and bring up core samples. We're trying to map out the oceans and seas of ancient Mars, because as this planet continues to warm up, the ice will turn to water and fill up the lakes and seas again. We want to know where the new coastlines will be. Also, it's easier pulling out cores now than when it's under water again."

"So, what do the cores tell you? Anything in particular you're searching for?"

"There's a lot of data. Not just in my department, but also other research teams want samples. Some are private laboratories that provide data to corporations. We occasionally find a bunch of fossils. Most of them are of very simple creatures. We also look for traces of certain minerals. There's a lot of untapped wealth on

Mars, although the government is hesitant about allowing actual mining. But money talks."

"Your department also has biology in its name. Does that mean you're also searching for life?"

Damn, he doesn't miss much. "We're supposed to be on a lookout for any signs of life, or recent life. There is some speculation the last of life on Mars only died out a hundred thousand years ago. Maybe a million years. But that's a tick on a clock in geological terms."

"But nothing yet?"

"No, but it's fun to look."

"What do you think of reports of seeing those mouse size creatures on Mars. Is it possible there's still Martian life around?"

"As they say, anything is possible. We know very little about Mars despite having colonized the planet a couple of hundred years ago. We have the surface more or less mapped out, but we know just a fraction on what is underneath. So maybe there is still life underground that occasionally pokes out onto the surface. We have also established small ecology centres at a few places on the surface. We make these niches warm enough to sustain Earth life and add plants, insects and a few hardy creatures. Then we observe how well they can adapt to the Martian environment. It is possible one of those Earth creatures left the compound area and was seen later in a different area, triggering those reports."

"You don't sound convinced of that."

"Where those creatures were supposedly seen is too far from the ecology centres we set up. I don't see how any Earth creature could survive a Martian night. People have a vivid imagination."

"So, no Martian life exists past the one cell variety?"

Writson hesitated before answering. "I wouldn't say that."

McLeod squinted at her. "Do you know something you can't tell me."

What is he? A frigging mind reader?

She forced a smile. "You know government policy. Don't reveal anything you discover in the field, even if it doesn't mean anything."

"I understand. I'm sorry, I didn't mean to pry about sensitive information."

"That's okay. You're just curious and that's a good trait to have. Tell me more about being in space. Like, have you encountered any USOs?"

"Encountered, no. But we have picked them up on our sensors. Most ships have reported USOs. They're not uncommon."

"What do you think they are?"

"Alien technology. It's hard to believe we're the only species to have space flight and I think we can assume some have technology years ahead of ours. How about you? I've heard that USOs have been reported near Mars."

"I haven't seen any. But yes, there have been reports of strange vehicles close to Mars. Of course, the official government response is that it is likely an unknown phenomenon of weather."

"Same here. The government asks for all reports of USOs, but never tells us what their conclusions are."

Writson was thankful that McLeod had taken her mind off her work, and the lecture she was given by Gary Dorn. Along with the drinks, she had forgotten about her earlier troubles.

"May I ask how long you've lived on Mars? Were you born here?"

She straightened her shoulders. "Yes. I'm actually a multi-generation descendent. I'm a true Martian."

"Did you attend the University of Aeolis Mons? Or did you take your education on Earth?" McLeod knew that while the University of Aeolis Mons was a well-respected university, it was more specialized on Martian sciences, rather than a curriculum that included arts and subjects more pertinent on Earth.

"I went to the U of A M and took additional virtual courses from University of Alberta on Earth. I decided I didn't need to go to Earth and get immersed in the culture there like most students from Mars. I'm happy living here."

"Fair enough. You should go to Earth as a tourist some day. I think you'll find it fascinating." He understood the virtual courses made it much easier for students to take courses from a university.

The holographic professor presentations made it seem the same as actually being in the lecture hall.

"I would like to. I'm a bit worried how the heavier air and gravity would make me feel. My body is designed for Mars, not Earth."

"I've heard that from other Martians as well. But bodies will adapt to an environment. You need to give yourself a few days first to acclimatize."

"Maybe I'll consider that on my next vacation schedule. There are only so many places on Mars to visit on a vacation."

"Tell you what, next time you have some vacation and want to go to Earth, check with me. As a captain of a passenger ship I'm allowed a couple of extra berths. I might be able to squeeze you on for free." He saw her look at him carefully. "And I do mean for free. Absolutely no obligation on your part."

"Okay, thanks. Maybe I need to get off Mars. I get a little too intense at work and sometimes forget there's a life beyond rocks and biology." She finished her drink. "I think I better head out while I can still walk. It was nice talking to you."

"Likewise. I hope to see again sometime."

Writson walked over to Leana where she was wiping a table. "Okay, nice setup there."

Leana grinned. "I thought you two hit it off okay."

"We did. At first, I was a little annoyed, but I have to admit he took my thoughts off my work troubles. So, thank you." She gave Leana a quick touch on her waist and left the bar.

The cool air helped Writson clear her thoughts. *I survived the day. I didn't have to speak to Rigger, and I met Captain McLeod. For an Earth man, he sure is interesting.*

[21]

McLeod joined the other members of the executive officers in the Gibbston offices on board of the space station. The meeting room featured the usual oval table with comfortable chairs around it. Lisa Wagner chaired the meeting but announced at the start it was not going to be formal.

"I'm not going to follow the usual rules of meeting protocol. We're all familiar enough with each other, and what the stakes are for the first human faster than light travel, that I don't want anyone to not voice an opinion or concern because of meeting structure. I will have a video done of this meeting, as I will review comments and make sure nothing has been left out.

"All of us have had one on one meetings with Dwayne Bentley." She glanced at the man sitting near the back. "I assume we all have an understanding of the theory behind our faster than light ship. We also have heard how our prototype spaceship disappeared into space, and obviously, that is of some concern. However, Richard Combs has a theory on what happened, and I would like him to express that now. Richard?"

Combs looked nervous, tugging at the collar of his shirt. "It's just that it seems obvious to me what happened. The test ship had a course calculated and it was inputted into the navigation control. It was to go on a route that avoided stars and other stellar objects. Because the test ship was placed in a field that isolated it from the effect of our universe, the navigation route ignored the gravity of stars and other high gravity it passed by. The gravity field wouldn't cause a direct effect on the ship. But the Dowling field the ship was enclosed in is inside our universe. When the field entered a high gravity field, it followed along the distortion wave of space. Space is bent near gravity wells, and our hole in our universe will follow that bend. My theory is that our test ship was pulled off course and was likely destroyed. Perhaps it even exited the galaxy."

"Wasn't it supposed to stop at a given point and return back the way it came?" Shultz asked. "Even if it was lost, couldn't it just examine the star field charts and calculate where it was?"

"What I would have done is build in a secondary navigation in case the first one was giving incorrect readings." Combs shrugged. "Apparently, that wasn't done. If the test ship ended up in orbit around a star or black hole, it wouldn't understand the star field around it. I'm just saying we don't know what the star field looks like beyond a few light years from here. If the test ship went off course, and I'm positive that is what happened, it wouldn't know which way was home again. Space is curved and warped. You think you travelled in a straight line, but the reality is when you look behind you, everything is different."

McLeod looked at Bentley, frowning as he rubbed his chin.

"Does that mean we need to have a redundant navigation system? Or is there another way to ensure we don't get lost?" McLeod asked.

"Absolutely. One has to be careful." Combs emphasized. "I suggest we take just small journeys close to our own system so we know where we are. I will also design software that can help locate us wherever we are in this area of the galaxy."

Bentley said in an irritated voice, "To be clear, it wasn't me who designed the navigation system. Richard's theory on why the ship disappeared is possible, but it could have been several other factors. Engine failure and electronic or equipment failure are all possibilities. I don't appreciate any inference I didn't do my job, and it's easy to look back and say this is what I would've done."

Wagner quickly moved to end any escalation of the argument.

"No one is to blame for the lost ship. It happened for reasons unknown. Speculation is fine, but that won't solve our immediate priority of ensuring the safe voyage of the Hendrik A. Lorentz. Let us focus on our mission."

McLeod took the opportunity to direct the conversation away from the test ship's failure. "I heard there is possibility of a tenth planet, Meili, that at one time crossed the path of Pluto, changing its orbit. Perhaps we can investigate this new world as our first mission."

The consensus around the table quickly agreed with his suggestion. Dermott added it wouldn't fully test the new engines but was fine with the short journey.

"New engines always should have a short run, and then be recalibrated and synced anyway. This will be perfect."

Shultz added another point before the meeting drew to a close. "When we finish our maiden flight above the speed of light, we need to celebrate the occasion properly. A Champagne toast and a speech by Lisa, all properly recorded."

That motion was endorsed by all, and the meeting came to an end. Bentley glared at Combs, but the bearded man didn't seem to notice as he walked out of the room.

McLeod returned to his hotel to change, trying to decide on what to do next. *I think I need a drink, but I don't want to go to the bar alone.* He sent a message to Gill, Combs, Dermott and Shultz indicating he was going to have celebratory drink at the Opus Bar and invited them to join him.

He received a confirmation from Dermott and Gill as he made his way to the bar, choosing to sit at one of the tables. Leana gave him a smile.

"You're too good to sit at the bar now? One promotion and it goes to your head."

He laughed. "Believe it or not, I will be having company this time."

"Alright, just wondering. Rum?"

"Please. Make it a double, hold the ice."

She returned with the rum. "Are these ship mates of yours that you'll be drinking with?"

"Yeah, we will be working together. I thought it'd be good to get together somewhere other than a spaceship."

She looked at the entrance. "Is that one of them wearing a beard? That's rather unusual, isn't it? I mean for those working spaceships."

"He's an unusual guy."

Combs looked at Leana quickly as he sat at the table and averted his gaze to Jaret.

"What would you like? I'm buying."

"Just a ginger ale."

As Leana went back to the bar, Shultz appeared, followed by Gill a few minutes later.

Gill asked, "Are we just meeting for drinks, or is there a problem?"

"Everything's okay. I just thought we should get together outside of a spaceship."

Gill ordered a whisky, while Shultz decided on a red wine. Only Gill wore the Gibbston Space Lines uniform, explaining he hadn't gone back to his hotel room yet. "I went back to the Hendrik A. Lorentz to check the engine synchronization reports one more time."

"Was Tia there?" McLeod asked.

"No, she said she wanted to explore Mars a bit."

"Good. I thought she was a little tense lately."

"A little tense?" Shultz laughed. "Brand new ship. Mark Sevens. No pressure at all for the only woman I know as chief engineer in a high-end ship."

"Good point." He looked at the entrance of the bar. "Speak of the devil."

"That's some thermal suit she's wearing." Shultz lowered her voice, sitting at the corner of the table from him.

McLeod had to agree with Shultz's assessment. The red pant portion of the suit broke into pixels that slowly transformed into grey at the top. "She looks pretty good in that Martian outfit."

"I think she's dressing to impress." Shultz pointedly looked at him.

Dermott sat next to McLeod, saying hello to everyone as Leana returned with drinks on a tray.

"Hi. I'm glad to see at least one of Jaret's friends decided to wear proper Martian clothing. It looks great on you."

"Thanks. I'll take a rum and cola."

McLeod thought the two-toned thermal suit showed off her curves. It surprised him slightly how slim waisted she was, realizing the space suits, coveralls and ship uniforms he had seen her wear previously didn't do much for her femininity. He felt a small kick on his shin from the direction of Shultz. "You look really nice. The Mars' fashions look great on you."

"Thanks." Dermott blushed slightly. "I wasn't sure if I should buy something like this for the short time we're here."

"I'm glad you did," McLeod added.

Leana returned with Dermott's drink, and McLeod raised a toast for all of them being together, concluding, "Planets today, the stars tomorrow."

After two more rounds, Gill, Combs and Shultz left the bar. Dermott passed on having another drink, opting for a coffee instead.

"I'm not used to drinking anymore."

"Yes, I learned that lesson not long ago. Where did you go on your visit on Mars?"

"Not far. I know I need to be ready to leave on short notice. I better get going as well. See you soon."

McLeod watched her leave, not noticing Leana had come up behind him.

"Pretty girl."

"Yeah. She's the ship's chief engineer and can fix any engine."

"Impressive. You have a special relationship with her?"

"No, why?" He looked up at her.

"I'm just wondering why she would be wearing a rather expensive thermal suit if she didn't live on Mars. Most visitors buy the plain thermal suits. What she wore was meant to show off what she's got. Just my opinion."

"I think I understand what it is. You see, she spends all her time in the engine room of a ship, and wears only loose fitting, unflattering clothes. She decided to dress up a bit. She makes a good salary and can afford a better thermal suit."

"Okay, just that it seems she dressed up for a reason."

———

Captain Jaret McLeod made a point of personally welcoming every crew member on the ship. The crew was still a skeleton for operations, with less than twenty personnel rather than the full operation of forty-seven.

He walked down the aisle, inspecting the stations and checked with each crew member on how they were doing. One extra person he had to deal with was Lisa Wagner. She didn't interfere with his duties, but he felt her presence whenever he was near the front of the ship. He reached the engine room and saw Gill and Dermott. He gave Gill a wave.

"Tia, are we ready to go?"

She turned from staring at the front of the giant engines. She grinned and practically bounced her way over to him. "Oh, we sure are. I'm so excited to fire these girls up."

He laughed at her excitement. "That'll happen soon enough." He was aware how close she stood to him, thinking of what Lexanna said about her. "Departure time is set for eleven hundred."

"Great. That'll give me time for a tea and something to eat."

When she didn't move from her close proximity, he briefly gripped her shoulder and walked back to the front of the ship.

———

McLeod checked the monitors one final time around the captain's chair. All systems were green. He touched a control on the arm of his chair. "Tia, are you ready to fire up the engines?" He didn't need to ask, merely wanting to give her notice that they were about to leave port. He imagined she was pacing in front of the giant engines, waiting for the go ahead.

"Yes. Fish and I are excited to see them actually run with power."

McLeod looked at Lisa Wagner and gave her a nod. "We're all set." He stood and walked behind Richard Combs and placed a hand on his shoulder. "Mr. Combs, please obtain permission for us to leave port and take us out of here."

"Yes sir." He focused his attention to the console in front of him. "This is the space craft Hendrik A. Lorentz requesting permission to leave port."

McLeod listened to the exchange between the port authority and Combs, reflecting that between the ship's autopilot and computer run navigation system, there wasn't any need for human intervention in leaving the space station. Despite all the advances in technology and automatic navigation, human voice remained the final protocol for ships arriving and departing spaceports. The worry of a computer error in ship navigation near spaceports was replaced with possible human ones. There weren't any fatal accidents using the human voice system, and there wasn't any pressure to change it.

McLeod smiled as he navigated the ship away from the space station. *Definitely not like piloting a mining ship. This is like silk compared to those buckets.*

The ship used normal propulsion to leave Mars orbit and proceed to the asteroid belt. It would take several days to reach the perimeter of the belt under normal propulsion, and McLeod didn't want to draw attention to the ship by running the massive engines near to their full capability. They wanted the space authorities and others to believe this was just another large mining ship.

McLeod approached Lisa Wagner, leaving the ship on auto-guidance. "Well, Lisa, it looks like the ship can at least run like a normal ship. I guess the question now is when we decide to punch a hole in the universe and see how fast this ship can go."

She smiled. "I don't believe the word fast really describes what this ship is capable of."

"You're right there."

"What do you think of Richard's theory on what happened to the test ship?" Wagner lowered her voice.

"He's very careful on how he operates equipment. He looks for details, and nothing escapes his attention. He doesn't normally say much, and when he does it is usually worthwhile to pay close attention. When he suggested that a gravity field pulled the test ship off course, I'll guarantee he went over the logbook to determine exactly where the ship was headed and what were the possible gravity fields interfering. He does everything by high mathematics and vectors. You asked me about his theory. I'd say his theory has likely been calculated the tenth decimal place before he'd say anything."

"Thanks. Richard seemed pretty certain when he spoke at the meeting, but I wanted to hear your take on it. I wish Dwayne would be a bit more relaxed about it. He's very smart, but he gets defensive very fast."

"So I've noticed."

"I studied your credentials before you were promoted as captain of the McKenzie King. I looked at every report with your name on it, as well as your crew's surveys. I don't believe there is a better captain for the Hendrik A. Lorentz."

"Thank you."

"I just wanted you to know that being the captain on this extremely important history changing mission is not by chance. You've earned it."

"Thanks, but I've had the privilege of a great crew. They deserve a lot of the credit."

She laughed. "Are you practicing your humble speech to the media?"

He grinned. "I guess that did sound a little corny. But it is true."

She placed a hand on his upper arm. "I don't want to sound forward, but what is your relationship between you and Tia?"

"She's my chief engine mechanic. What do you mean?"

"It's just the exchange of looks between you and her. You stand close to each other when talking. It has all the signs of interest beyond running a spaceship. That's okay, I just don't want to get in the way of any relationship."

McLeod initially was going to deny any special relationship with Dermott, but then he recalled Shultz's words on how she viewed him. "Our relationship is a bit complicated." *As in I don't know what it is.*

"I see. Well, most relationships worth having are."

McLeod wandered around the ship. There wasn't much for him to do. A brand-new ship with a small crew eliminated much of his work. He went past the lunchroom, spotting Richard Combs studying a tablet as he ate a sandwich at one of the tables.

"Richard, working through your lunch?" McLeod gave him a smile as he stood at the doorway.

"I'm checking for any relativistic effects on our navigation equipment that we may have missed."

"Find anything?" McLeod entered the lunchroom and sat across from him.

Richard frowned. "No, but that just may mean I haven't looked at everything. One cannot be too careful."

"In life sometimes we have to take risks."

"True, but right now isn't the time for unnecessary risks. Everyone should be focused on the task at hand."

"Fair enough. I better leave you to your lunch and your work."

He walked to the engine room and saw Dermott with another crew member.

"How are the new engines doing?"

"They're great. Mind you, at this speed, they're just idling."

McLeod thought she looked like she had just opened a present. "Eventually we'll be able to push them up a bit more."

"I can hardly wait." She stood close to him, smiling at him.

"Tia, let's go for a walk to my suite. There is something I want to discuss with you."

"Sure." She called out to the other crew member. "Jeremy, I'm off the floor for a bit. Keep me informed if there's any change in the operating parameters."

Dermott chatted about the engines and their special adjustments needed to perform at top efficiency. McLeod understood only half of what she was describing, occasionally adding words of agreement. They reached his meeting room that was part of his suite, where he offered her coffee.

"Tea, if you don't mind. I've already had too much coffee."

"Sure." He went to a small counter where he commanded a panel to produce a tea and coffee.

McLeod placed the tea in front of her and sat opposite her across the meeting table.

"So, what did you want to talk to me about? This seems rather formal."

"I want to talk to you about two things. One is your work regarding the engines."

"Is there a problem?"

"None whatsoever. You are a first-rate engineer and the best choice for operating the engines on this ship."

"So?"

"The other thing I want to talk about is our relationship, that is our personal relationship."

Dermott smiled. "Go on."

"I like you a lot, but I'm concerned about any distractions at this time. This ship is going to make history and I want to stay focused on being the captain of this ship. For the time being, I want to keep our relationship professional despite my affection for you. Please understand this is for the best interests in launching our new ship."

"I see." Her lower lip quivered.

"I'm sorry, but I have to consider the operation and safety of the ship before any personal issues."

She stood. "Does that policy include your dealings with Lisa Wagner as well?" She stood, ready to leave the meeting room.

McLeod stared at her. *What the hell is going on here?* "Tia, I don't have any personal relationships with any woman right now, other than as friends."

"Well, Captain, sooner or later I need someone who wants to be more than just a friend of mine." She walked out of the room.

McLeod stared at the open door. *I think I just made things worse.*

Writson was pleased she didn't feel any ill effects from her drinking yesterday, surmising that it was best she stopped when she did. She clipped on her earphone and stared at her closet, wondering which thermal suit to wear. She pulled out a thermal suit with red and black rectangles covering the garment.

She made a vocal request from her phone to check for any messages, finding only the usual office memos. She did a final check of her appearance and headed out of her apartment.

The elevator took her to the ground floor, and she was almost at the building exit when a call came in through her ear clip.

"Nellie Writson, this is Dr. Rigger's office calling. Are you available to talk?" a woman's voice inquired.

"Yes." *Damn.*

Riggers voice spoke a few seconds later as Writson stood by the exit doors. "I do hope I'm not calling you too early, but my day is going to be full and I wanted to contact you as soon as possible."

"Of course, Dr. Rigger. It's not too early at all." *Does he want another apology?*

"I'm calling for two reasons. First, I accept your earlier apology and now consider that matter behind us. The second item is that the artifacts that your team discovered have been analysed and it has been determined to be artificial in nature. One of the columns was transported to our main laboratory where more work will be done to investigate its exact nature."

"I'm pleased to hear that, Dr. Rigger."

"Thank you, but the reason for my call is to invite you to join me in announcing the discovery. Can you be at our laboratory by ten this morning?"

Writson readily agreed, surprised at his offer. "Thank you, Dr. Rigger. Do I need to bring anything? Should I wear more formal clothes?"

He chuckled. "No, no. Just bring yourself. Whatever you're wearing will be fine."

Writson ended the call and hurried first to her office, where she quickly told her staff of Rigger's invitation. "I'm sorry the rest of you, who really did all of the work, can't be there. But I'll do my best to ensure you do get credit for your efforts."

She cleaned up a few reports at her desk, had a coffee, and went to where the Department of Mars Preservation held their offices. She reached the building where the receptionist, a young blonde woman, indicated she was expected.

"Dr. Rigger is working by the laboratory, straight ahead through these doors." She pressed a button to open the dark glass doors.

Writson stepped inside the high-ceilinged room. The laboratory was large, although a sizable portion of it was dedicated to offices. The lighted ceiling and clean environment gave the impression of a business facility. An open area was in front of a glass wall, where behind it could be seen the artificial column on a bench with various pieces of equipment in close proximity to it. Rigger was standing in the open area directing a staff member when Writson entered.

Riggers noticed her standing by the entrance and waved her over. "Ms. Writson, it is good to see you again, and thank you for making it here on such short notice."

"No trouble at all, Dr. Rigger."

"As you know, the columns are artificial in nature. Our current hypothesis is that they are the remains of an alien structure. We have identified it to be eighty-seven to eighty-eight hundred Earth years old. That is the extent of the information we will be releasing to the press." He pointed at the space he was standing at earlier. "We will do the announcement there. I will be giving your team credit for the find. You may be asked a few questions, but I don't expect there is much to tell."

"Good, I'm not much for public speaking."

"Few are. I have learned the art of speaking in front of an audience, so don't worry about making a speech. I'll handle that."

Writson noticed a few other people entering the same doors as she did, and from what she could determine, they were reporters. They converged toward the open area. A few minutes later she stood slightly behind and to Rigger's side as he stepped up to a podium.

Rigger scanned the crowd in front of him and began his speech. "Thank you for coming to our press release. I have the pleasure of announcing a significant discovery that may well change our perception of alien life in our universe. Indeed, this may be the most earth-shaking discovery of modern times." He paused for dramatic effect and held out a palm to Writson.

"The credit of this finding goes to the tireless work done by the Department of Biology and Geology, in mapping out and researching the areas of Mars. A crew led by the esteemed geologist Nellie Writson is responsible for this most amazing discovery of an Alien artifact." He made a small gesture with his hand, and a holographic image of the column located in the laboratory appeared in front of them.

Writson heard the reporters gasp.

Rigger continued to speak. "We are looking at one of several columns unearthed. These columns are almost eighty-eight hundred years old. We can only speculate on their purpose and if other remains will be found. There is no doubt these have been left by an alien civilization, although we doubt at this time it is the remains of Martian beings."

Several questions were called out and Rigger gave answers that did not add to any more information. He concluded the news conference by again pointing out Writson's team made the discovery. "Thank you for coming. You have what information we have and anything else at this time is mere speculation."

Writson was glad she wasn't asked any questions. She was impressed by Rigger's demeanour during the press conference and realized why he had so much power in the academic world. He had the ability to make the world see him as the great scientist, and command research funds for what he found of importance.

And here I almost made him my enemy. That would have been a career disaster.

"Dr. Rigger, thank you for your acknowledgement of my team in the discovery."

"You're welcome. Your team deserves such recognition. Come with me to my office, I want to go over a couple of details with you."

Writson walked with him to his office, located on the second floor. They arrived via a dedicated elevator, where she tried to ask a question.

"Dr. Rigger, I was wondering if I could ask a favour of you regarding my team."

Before he responded, his receptionist greeted them.

"Dr. Rigger, you have several messages, including two urgent ones from the Earth Interspace Agency and one from the Alien Life Detection Board." She glanced at her monitor. "Two more messages have just arrived."

"Thank you, Ms. Griffin. It will be a busy day." He gestured for Writson to enter his office, and she was impressed with its size and the certificates hung along one wall. Several artifacts were also mounted on a wall and others were on their own stands.

He sat behind his desk, touched a control on the glass top and spoke. "Ms. Griffin, please bring in some pastries and a carafe of coffee." He looked at Writson. "Do you drink coffee? Or do you prefer tea?"

"Coffee is fine."

"Excellent. Now the reason I want to talk to you is to prepare you for what will be numerous requests for more information on the alien columns. News media will be especially aggressive. You need to work out a prepared statement. Remember to always refer to others as part of *your* team. Another point. This column in the future will be known as Rigger's Column. You need to call the area of Tharsis Vocanic Region as Writson's find. This will ensure your name will carry weight in the future. That is my advice. You need to ensure your part in history. Don't be modest about this. If you don't put your claim into this event, someone else less deserving will."

"I hadn't thought about that." She took a coffee and a pastry from the tray that Griffin had quietly brought in, suddenly discovering she was hungry.

"You need to. This has the ability to catapult your career."

Writson considered what he had said. *Being in the right place at the right time.* "I suppose you're right."

"I am. If you find yourself having trouble navigating the nuances of the interviews and news media quotes, please feel free to contact me. I don't mind helping a fellow researcher. Now I believe you wanted to ask me a favour."

"Yes. The Biblis Patera area where the columns were discovered is now off limits to everyone. However, within that region are also the lava tubes, which is why we were working in that area in the first place. Is it possible to have permission to continue to do research on the lava tubes? We would keep well away from where the columns are located."

Riggers spread his fingers apart and pressed the tips togethers. "I can't give you an answer off the top of my head. I'd have to investigate the reports first. I presume this is of some importance to you."

"Yes, it is. More so to the members of my team."

"Ah." He looked up to the ceiling. "To be honest with you, I don't know how I can facilitate your request immediately, as I need to confer with those doing work at the extrication site. Unfortunately, my calendar is rather full, especially with the news of the alien columns." Rigger leaned forward on his desk. "Here is what I can do. I'll go over the reports of the area in question and check with my team in the field. I need to discuss your request with them in greater detail. The issue here is one of time. I assume you need an answer sooner rather than later?"

"Yes, since we already have started our work on the lava tubes, I would like to continue as soon as we can."

"Very well. Now, although my days are full, I can offer an alternative. How about if we meet for dinner in two days' time? My treat, of course. We can go over your request and arrive at some sort of mutual advantageous arrangement concerning the exploration of the lava tubes."

Writson was surprised by his offer. *Dinner with Rigger? What does he want from me? If I say no, then no lava tubes research.* "Oh, that sounds very nice."

"Excellent." Riggers stood. "Ms. Griffin will contact you with the details of the time and place."

Writson nodded. *This doesn't seem right. What's going on?*

[23]

SHULTZ LOOKED UP AT MCLEOD AS HE ENTERED THE control room, studied his face for a moment and asked, "What's the matter?"

"I think I screwed up."

"How so? Is there something wrong with the ship?" He saw several heads turn in his direction.

McLeod shook his head. "No, everything with the ship is fine." He lowered his voice. "However, can we talk privately?"

"I think we better." She followed him to a meeting room just off the control room.

"I need your advice."

"On?"

"I told Tia I didn't want any personal interaction with her while on the ship."

Shultz raised her eyebrows. "And how did she take that?"

"Not well. She said something about Lisa Wagner and walked away."

"Oooh. That's not good at all. You want me to give some not so pleasant advice?"

"I sure do."

"For a moment, let's consider you're not a captain of a spaceship. Maybe you're taking a sabbatical somewhere on Earth. Tia and Lisa are both staying at the same hotel as you. Question, which one, if any, would you ask out on a romantic dinner? Or would you ask one out one night, and the other the next night?"

McLeod thought for a few seconds. "I'd ask Tia out. I don't see myself going after Lisa."

"Okay, so you like Tia enough to ask her on a romantic date. Why did you tell her any romance with her would have to wait?"

"I didn't want to jeopardize our moment in history."

Shultz frowned. "To recap, you couldn't kiss a girl and still have enough wits about you to captain this ship? I suddenly feel nervous about your capabilities as a captain."

"Perhaps I overreacted with Tia about personal relationships."

"You think? Look, if you're scared to have a personal relationship and commitment, I get it. Some people just always look for excuses to stay single. Being a couple is not in their genes. But what you told Tia was cruel. You dangled a carrot in front of her. How long has she been waiting for you to step forward now and not after the next mission?"

"I never thought of it that way. When we were mining the rocks, there was too much risk to have anything but one's full attention operating the ship."

"I say bullshit. You can be in love and still do your job. Tia has been doing just that."

"Jesus. You're right. Thanks."

"You know what to do?"

"Yeah, make amends."

24

WRITSON EXITED THE ELEVATOR, AND QUICKLY PLACED A call to Leana.

"Nellie, what do you want? You do know I worked all night, don't you?" a tired voice responded.

"Sorry, but I have a crisis."

The voice changed to being wide awake. "You called Jaret while you were drunk and now regret it?"

"No! What makes you think I would do that?"

"Because I saw something between you two. Sparks, if I'm not mistaken."

"You are blind. Have you heard the news this morning?"

"No, I was sleeping, remember?"

"Check the news conference about Alien columns on Mars, and then call me back."

Writson continued her hurried walk back to her office. *Jaret and me? What was she thinking?*

She arrived at her office, taken aback by the stares from everyone. "Good morning. I guess everyone saw the news broadcast this morning. I didn't have an opportunity to say anything, but I'll be meeting with Dr. Rigger at a later date to see if we can continue our research in the lava tubes."

Several employees started applauding and were soon joined by the others. Lindsey Smyth called out, "That's great news. How soon can we go back to the site?"

"I'm sorry, I didn't mean to get everyone's hopes up." Writson frowned. "It's not for certain we can go back to Biblis Patera, but I'll do what I can."

Writson went to her office and plopped herself in her office chair. *Shit. What happens if Rigger won't let us back to investigate the lava tubes.*

"Call from Leana Strout," the electronic female voice announced in her earpiece.

"Answer." She paused a moment. "Hi, Leana."

"Oh, my God! You were holding this from me. Shame on you. You know how much I love this stuff."

"Sorry, but I couldn't say anything."

"I understand, sort of. You know you can tell me anything, and being a bartender, I can keep a secret."

"I know, I know. But this is more along the lines of a government oath of not divulging secrets."

"Alright," said Leana. "So what's the crisis?"

"Dr. Rigger, who was doing the press conference, has invited me to dinner. He says it is to discuss the possibility of my team being allowed to work at the lava tubes." She paused. "The lava tubes fall within the area under his jurisdiction. I can't tell you the reason, but my team really, really needs to get back to that site."

"I doubt it's just dinner he wants from you."

"I know," said Wriston. "What do I do?"

"Is there any other way of getting your team on the site?"

"I doubt it."

"Then go to dinner with him. You can always walk out."

"Yeah, I suppose so. Thanks for the help." Writson attempted to focus on writing out a media statement. One longer than the other, depending on who was asking for information. She returned several calls, trying to work in the names of her team members. Her media release was sent to several organizations as well. A quick look at the news reports locally and from Earth showed Dr. Rigger's name received the most coverage, along with the image of the alien column. A few of the longer and more detailed reports mention her name, but only one included another name from her team.

She then received a message confirming her dinner date with Rigger, prompting another call to Leana.

"I have another situation."

"What is it this time?"

"The dinner is at the Olympias."

"Oh, very nice."

"Yeah, and I haven't worn a dress in three years. Can you help me pick one out?"

"Three years? And one wonders why you're still single."

———

Leana held up another dress, a dark blue green with a slit along the side. "What do you think of this?" Like most dresses in the store, there was only one copy to look at. After making a choice, the customer gave her size, preference of colour and material. The information was sent to a factory where her dress would be manufactured and be made available the next day. Or, if the customer was willing to pay extra for a rush order, in as little as an hour.

"I like it, although I'm not sure about the sleeves."

The salesclerk spoke up. "We can have the same dress made shoulder-less with spaghetti straps."

"That would look good on you." Leana pushed the dress against Writson. "That's where your assets are."

"I guess they are." Writson laughed. "I wish I had legs like yours."

"Everyone wishes they had legs like mine. But you have to flaunt what you got. Get the dress without those sleeves."

"Do I really want to entice him?"

"You want something from him, right? Then work on his eyes."

———

It had been too long since she had to dress up, Writson decided. She didn't usually wear makeup, and adding eyeshadow took longer than she remembered. She was pleased with her dress and liked the look of her shoes. She did find walking on the high heels odd after walking in boots for as long as she remembered.

"Maybe Leana is right that it's too long since I wore a dress or anything but a thermal suit." She almost forgot her purse, not used to carrying one around. "Definitely too long wearing just thermal suits."

Because of the lack of the thermal suit, she decided she better make use of the underground pedways rather than risk the cold wind on the surface streets. Like the buildings, the air was kept at a higher pressure, and she slowed her walk. Though the oxygen was also higher, her lungs weren't able to accommodate the thicker air and she knew from experience it caused her to be lightheaded if she moved too fast.

The pedways were busy and she saw there were a lot of women who wore lighter clothing rather than thermal suits. The men, she noted, may or may not have thermal suits on. It was difficult to tell what they wore under their pants and shirts.

She reached the building where the Olympias Restaurant was located on the top floor, taking the elevator that opened to a spacious restaurant. The Maître D' showed her to a window seat where Rigger stood as she approached. He held the chair for her to sit and complimented on her dress, adding, "I must say you look even lovelier than when you wear a thermal suit."

"Thank you. It's been a while since I've had the opportunity to dress up." She noticed he was wearing a dark suit, blue shirt with a red tie, looking very much like the distinguished professor the news media portrayed him to be.

Over wine and the first course he inquired about her education and what she was planning as a career.

"Right now, I'm happy where I am. There is only so much room for advancement in the Martian government."

"There are opportunities working with the government but also in the private sector. Perhaps you should consider that."

"Maybe someday. I have a lot of work to do first in my department."

"Very well. Just keep me in mind if you want to make that jump. I'm always looking for talented people who know how the government operates."

The next course arrived and Writson broached the subject on why she had accepted his dinner invitation. "Have you considered my request to continue to explore the lava tubes?"

"I did read the reports, and I can see why you would want to return there to examine the findings more closely. I can certainly see the merits of your request, but I do have to look at the complete set of circumstances." He signalled the waiter to pour more wine.

"What exactly are those circumstances?"

"As the head of the investigation of the alien columns, I have to be cognisant that there may be part of a larger set of artifacts. We need to proceed with caution, so we don't disturb vital clues as to the nature of the columns."

"Are you saying no?"

"I'm saying the decision is still to be made." He smiled. "I will discuss the details a bit later."

Writson smiled, not wanting to show him how impatient she felt. After the main meal, they ordered dessert, along with brandy.

"While we're waiting for the dessert to arrive, shall we have a turn on the dance floor?" He stood, holding out his hand.

She reluctantly accepted, wondering what he was up to with his vague answers and the desire to dance with her.

The music was slow, and Rigger used the opportunity to hold her close. After a few steps, his hand slid below her hips. Writson used a hand to grab at his wrist to pull it back to her waist. There was resistance in his arm.

"About your request." He whispered in her ear.

She released her hand on his wrist, putting her hand back on his shoulder. *So this is it. His hand on my hip so I can get an answer from him. The creep.*

"Good, we have an understanding."

"What do you want from me?"

"I want an exchange of favours. If you truly want your team to be able to work on those lava tubes, then I expect an engaging relationship from you. I don't mean bedroom activity, but I would like to have an attractive companion for my social events."

"Do you mean a dinner companion?"

"Yes, and also for some of the rather dull cocktail parties I'm required to attend. You must act like you enjoy my company and help promote my social standing. That is all I require."

"Yet you also have your hand on my ass."

"We need to play the part of a couple who enjoy each other's company."

"So, to be clear, if I agree to this arrangement, you will allow my team to investigate the lava tubes."

"Yes."

"Alright, I agree."

"Excellent. Look at it this way. You'll have the opportunity to meet some very influential people, as well as enjoy some extraordinarily good food and drink. And, if I do say so myself, you get to have the famous Dr. Rigger as your escort."

"How soon can my team return to Biblis Patera?"

"Tomorrow morning. If you decide to join your team on their exploration, keep in mind I may be requesting you join me at an event on short notice. Do *not* take my requests lightly."

25

McLeod walked down to the engine room, opened the secured door, and put on the headphones to protect his ears. The Mark Seven engines, despite their size, weren't as noisy as he expected and in fact much quieter than the engines on the McKenzie King. The sound was also a lower frequency, a sound he could feel through his boots as he made his way across the floor.

"Fish, is Tia around?"

"No, she said she had a headache and went to her room." He touched a few buttons on the console attached to a wall next to one of the engines. "Is there something wrong?"

"No. We're all good. Engines are looking great." He studied the monitor, which indicated the engine was running perfectly.

"Like the manual said they would." Fish grinned. "It's hard to believe their output even when at this low end of their capability."

McLeod went to where the officers' suites were located and paused in front of Dermott's door. He pressed the entry chime.

A few moments later the door opened, and McLeod was taken aback how sad she looked.

"Yes?"

"Permission to enter and grovel out an apology?"

She gave a ghost of a smile and stepped back.

McLeod entered and stood in the centre of the combination

living and kitchen. "I realize I've been unfair to you. We've known each other a long time, and through some stressful circumstances. We're friends, for sure, but it's more than that. You're someone I rely on and completely trust. You're a big part of my life, and I don't want to ever risk losing you." He closed the gap between them and wrapped his arms around her. He kissed her forehead as she pulled down at his neck with her hands.

"I don't want to lose you either." She breathed out the words.

The Hendrik A. Lorentz continued its journey. Midway between Mars orbit and the asteroid belt, they received a communication from the Interplanetary Enforcement Police. The IEP ship paced them five hundred metres away.

"This is Corporal Sue Regis of the IEP. May we speak with Captain Jaret McLeod?"

McLeod looked at the other surprised officers in the control room. "Ms. Wagner, it may be best they don't know you're on this ship. It may raise suspicion on why the CEO of Gibbston Space Lines is on a mining ship."

"Good point."

McLeod turned on the video communication, looking at the stern face of Sue Regis. "This is Captain McLeod. Is there a problem?"

"Perhaps. You have left port with less than a full complement of crew. That seems unusual for a new ship. We are also wondering for the need of Mark Seven engines. That is a lot of power for a mining ship."

"I can explain the lack of crew. We are just doing tests on the new ship, and don't have any plans to do any actual asteroid work yet. After our tests are completed, we are planning to return to Mars Port."

Regis looked down at something and returned her gaze to McLeod. "And the oversized engines?"

"Well, that was supposed to be a secret." McLeod gave a

sheepish smile. "Gibbston Space Lines believes they can save costs by dragging some of the rocks into closer proximity of the processing space stations and cutting them up there. More power means larger rocks. Economy of scale as they say."

"Very well." Regis frowned. "We may contact you later at Mars port for an inspection."

"That wasn't good." McLeod cut the connection. "How did she know we weren't carrying a full crew? And they know we have Mark Sevens."

"The IEP have their ways of monitoring." Wagner shrugged. "Good thing she didn't know much about mining, or she would have known that hauling larger rocks around isn't exactly an efficient way of working the asteroids."

"We just have to be aware they're watching us."

McLeod waited until the IEP ship had left the vicinity and ordered a stronger test of the engines. Gill and Dermott increased the power of the engines to forty percent of their capability, and the spaceship responded quickly to the increase.

"Tia, jump it up to sixty percent for sixty seconds and then drop it back to forty percent."

"Will do."

He heard the eagerness in her voice and checked the monitors at the captain's chair. The increase in power caused the Hendrik A. Lorentz to accelerate, but otherwise the graphs of the engine diagnostics continued to look normal. "Mr. Combs, do you detect any abnormalities?"

"No sir. Everything is right on the mark. No deviation from prime operating conditions."

"Excellent. We have one fine ship here. Tomorrow we should be close enough to the asteroid orbit to test out what we came here to do."

Lisa Wagner walked over to him. "Well, captain, are you looking forward to pushing the 'go' button tomorrow?"

He laughed. "I am, except all I get to do is actually say 'full steam ahead' or some such command. The engine room is where they'll put power into the Dowling field."

"Regardless, who gets to actually push the button, it's nice we're all going to be part of history."

"True." He stood. "If you excuse me, I'm going to the engine room and talk to the people there. I want them to know how important they are right now." *Especially our chief engineer.*

26

WRITSON GATHERED HER TEAM BY HER OFFICE, STANDING BY her door.

"We have permission to visit the lava tubes again, although we must make sure we stay away from where the columns are. I want a team of four to explore the lava tube where the trace gasses appear to originate from. I believe we need to do this as quickly as possible. The Preservation Department could change their minds at any time."

Philip Norris asked, "Will you be part of the team?"

She frowned. "I will attempt to be there. However, due to commitments, I may have to leave the site on very short notice." She saw the expressions on the faces of her staff. *I might as well tell them. They'll learn the truth when they read about me attending an event with Rigger.* "Look, the truth is I made a deal with Dr. Rigger. He is allowing us access to the lava tubes on the condition I accompany him to social events." She enunciated each word of the next sentence, "That is as much as I'll do."

"We don't need to explore the lava tubes that much. You can tell Dr. Rigger to take a hike." Norris spoke loudly, causing everyone to look at him. "I mean it. This discovery isn't worth your sacrifice."

"Thank you, Philip. But I'm fine with playing along with his ego if that allows us to accomplish what we need. Now, for our team, I want Jeremy to lead. We will also include Lindsey, but I don't want her to risk going inside the lava tube. She is our biology expert and should be included at the site. I also want Carl on the team." She heard a few murmurs from those around her. "I decided on the personnel as a balance between our geology and biology divisions, although I'm willing to consider adding anyone if Philip feels they are necessary." She looked at Smyth. "Sorry, Lindsey, you're going to have to babysit these men. I need you there because you're our expert on Martian biology and the official discoverer of the source of the lava tube gasses."

"Thanks, but you were there too." Lindsey Smyth glanced at the others, seeing if they reacted to her being acknowledged as the discoverer of the tube gasses.

"Okay, let's prepare for what we need to investigate the Smyth Lava Tube." Writson turned to enter her office, ending the meeting.

Norris approached her. "Look, I just want to say be careful with Rigger. If anything happens, *anything*, contact me right away. Please."

She stepped around her desk. "That's nice. But I do have a bite as well. Thanks for your concern." She touched his arm, preparing next to go to work in her office.

"Nellie, I know you're tough minded." He grabbed her wrist. "But if you need someone to talk to, I'm here for you."

She stuttered out her thanks and went to her office. She glanced as he walked away. *That was more than a colleague offering support. Is he indicating he's interested in me?* She took a deep breath and launched her efforts into the reports on her computer.

━━

Writson decided to go along with the team to the lava tube site. They used a cargo style of shuttle which, besides the equipment and the temporary shelters, carried a two-person transport. She decided Rigger may contact her and needed a way to quickly return to Red City.

Carl Duggan sat in the pilot's seat, although the shuttle flew on automatic. Next to him sat Smyth, and behind them, Writson sat between Norris and Tolmat.

"We should get at the site in time to set up the shelters while the sun is still up," Duggan announced.

Writson knew the shelters took only a few minutes to change from a large crate into a shelter. It was interesting to watch as the air pumps and electric motors raised the various parts in a carefully synchronized pattern. Her thoughts went over to Norris sitting next to her.

If he was interested in me, did I miss any signals? She recalled the extended handshake when she first arrived at the Tharsis Volcanic Region site. *Okay, he has made a small gesture. Maybe he's waiting to see if I show any interest. Am I interested in him? Okay, good looking. Smart, yes. Is he a multi-generation Martian? I know he was born here, but that doesn't mean much.*

She turned to look at him. "So, Philip, I understand you were born on Mars. How did you end up being a geologist?"

"There isn't much for a boy to do on Mars but play in the red dirt." He grinned. "I guess I was always interested in different kinds of rocks, so here I am."

"Were your parents born on Mars?"

"My dad was. My mother came here as a medical doctor. They met when she had to treat him for a broken arm. He had an incident using one of those man flying kites."

Writson laughed. "Those are dangerous."

"Yeah, but one has to take chances to enjoy life."

"True." *How very true.*

The shuttle landed, with the men hauling out the cargo while Writson and Smyth watched. In a quiet voice Writson asked, "Do you know if Philip is seeing anyone?"

"No, he's never mentioned any woman." Lindsey Smyth glanced at Writson. "Why do you ask? Are you interested in him?"

"I get the feeling he's hinting that he likes me. I'm trying to figure out if it was just my imagination or not."

"He's a good guy. I don't think he'd intentionally mislead you. You should get a coffee with him sometime and see where it goes."

Writson watched as Duggan initiated the power for the first

shelter, triggering a series of movements as the crate unfolded. "I'd like to be a little more certain about him first. He told me his mother was born on Earth."

"That multi-generation thing again? Are you planning to get married after you retire? Because that's how long it'll take you to find your perfect husband."

Writson sighed. "Maybe you're right."

The second shelter was set up. The first shelter contained the lab equipment, while the other provided the sleeping accommodations.

Writson held a meeting in the first shelter, going over what they needed to do to prepare the way for entering the opening to the lava tube.

"If necessary, we can enlarge the opening to the ground below. However, I think we should be able to fit through. Regardless of the readings given by your suit's indicators, wear the air masks. The sensors may not react in time to warn you of hazardous gasses. Make sure the recording equipment is working, as we may need proof of the time and place of any new life discovered. Any other concerns?"

A few comments were made, and afterward Writson suggested they break for dinner. She pulled her meal choice from the dispensary and sat at one of the worktables that also served as a, eating table and a desk. Norris joined her a minute later.

"Ready to chow down on your meal of unknown origins?"

"That doesn't make it sound appetizing." She laughed. "Now you've got me thinking about what this bowl actually contains."

"Sorry. After you've had a few of these, you question if this is supposedly good for you, then why doesn't it have any flavour."

She used her fork to poke at her meal. "For taking away my anticipation of a meal, you now owe me a decent dinner back at Red City." *There, I actually said it.*

"You're on. I promise I'll try not to ruin your appetite again."

"Not a concern." She briefly rested her hand on top of his. "I know you were only joking. But I'll still take you up on that dinner."

A few hours later, Writson closed the privacy door to her bed chambers. The sleeping shelter provided each occupant a bed, with just enough room to change their clothing. There were three small washroom facilities, with only one of them providing a small shower. With water in short supply, the shower consisted of mists of water, used after the application of waterless soap. The dry power didn't make a person feel clean, despite the assurances of the manufacturer.

She peeled off her thermal suit and climbed into bed. Her thoughts drifted to Norris and his promise of taking her to dinner. *When was the last time I actually went on a date? Gripes, I can't even remember when. Not good, girl, not good.*

In the morning, Writson received an unwelcome call from Rigger.

"I have a dinner engagement tonight and I want you to attend with me. I have taken the liberty of ordering a cocktail dress for you. Contact Truffles Dress Boutique with your measurements, and they will have your dress ready this afternoon. I will pick you up at six pm. Any questions?"

"No." Her tone was as sharp as she could make. *Bastard.*

A pause. "I see. Very well."

Writson ended the call and spoke to her team. "Unfortunately, I've been called away. However, Jeremy will now be in charge and I've full confidence that my presence here won't be needed."

"But it would be appreciated." Norris spoke up. "If we do discover something of importance, it would be great if you were here to share the moment."

"Thanks, but we won't have any moments of discovery if I don't go to this appointment."

She exited the shelter, going to where the two-person shuttle waited next to the transport shuttle. She closed the door and sat in the transparent bubble at the front of the small craft. Writson punched in the destination requirement, and moments later she was on her way back to Red City. She stared at the passing landscape, finding the series of plains, ridges and rocks relaxing.

It's not all bad. Jeremy is more than capable of handling the exploration team. I'm part of the group that discovered the columns, even though Rigger has taken over that investigation. I have to go to this dinner with him, but if he tries anything with me, he'll regret it. Her thoughts changed to the dinner and the dress he ordered for her. *It'll be interesting to see what dress he has decided is suitable for me.* She grinned. *Thanks to him I now have two new dresses. Maybe one I can wear on my date with Philip.*

The shuttle landed on the roof of the government building and she went to her office first to check on any messages or situations. There wasn't anything needing her attention. She felt like calling Gary Dorn and telling him what Rigger was requiring her to do to continue with her lava tube research, but she could hear his deep voice in head replying. *I can't tell you what to do. If those are his terms, you have to consider the merit of them. Are the terms he voiced legal? Off hand, I would say yes. Is it fair? Perhaps not. But only you can decide if they're worthwhile to you and your team. You're the head of your department, and now have reached the stage of your career where you have to face making difficult compromises. Situations are not always black and white.*

She went to Opus Bar and Grill, finding her friend Leana tending the bar.

Leana looked up in surprise. "What are you doing here? I thought you were going out to where those volcanos are."

"I was there, but his majesty called to tell me I have to go with him to a dinner tonight."

"Oh, that's not good." She placed a drink in front of her.

"No. What's more he ordered a dress for me to wear, as if I can't get my own dress to wear."

"If I recall, your closet is rather empty of such feminine garments."

Writson smiled. "Yes, but to have him pick out a dress for me? Well, let's just say I hope it isn't the kind of dress that is more sleazy than slinky."

"Take it from me, just because you're showing it, it doesn't mean you're selling it."

"Good point. Hey, I may have a real date soon. You remember me telling you about Philip?"

"Sure, the tall geologist."

"Right. He said he wants to take me out to dinner."

"Great. About time you started to notice there's more to Mars than red rock."

———

Truffles Dress Boutique was a small shop that catered to those with more expensive tastes. She still felt annoyed in being ordered to wear a dress not of her choosing. She examined the dress, a crinkled fabric burnt-red in colour. The knee length dress featured a bit of lace at the top and a bare back.

"Do you wish to try it on? We can make minor alterations on the premises."

"No, I know this will fit." *At least for the part that is covering me.*

"Excellent. Here are the matching shoes to go with it."

Great. Another pair of high heels. Okay, they do look good, but how often do I wear anything but work boots?

She went to her apartment, deciding to shower and change, not looking forward to the task of applying makeup.

By twenty minutes before six pm, she was ready, and was tempted to call Tolmat to see how they were doing on the lava tube exploration. *He might take that I was checking up on him. I know he'll contact me if he discovers anything of importance.* She was ready to check the local news when her door chime indicated she had a visitor. The door monitor showed Rigger in a dark suit.

She opened the door. "Dr. Rigger. You're a bit early."

"Yes. May I come in? I want to discuss something with you before we leave."

She nodded, careful not to turn her back on him.

He went to her small living room and seated himself in an armchair. "Perhaps we could share a drink. Do you have any wine?"

"I do." She obtained two glasses and poured white wine into them. She passed a glass to him and sat on the couch, facing him. "What do wish to talk about?"

He smiled. "Us."

[27]

McLeod found Dermott and Gill in a conversation by one of the monitors. "Is everything alright?"

"Yes, all indications are the engines are working at even higher efficiencies than expected," Fish answered. "Tia and I are very pleased with their performance so far."

"That's excellent to hear. We're nearing the point when we can test our faster than light travel theory, and I want to make sure we're ready to go."

"More than ready," Dermott answered.

"Good. You are aware the experimental ship failed to return, so there's some risk in what we are about to do."

"Yes, but we have gone over reports," Gill replied. "I believe Richard's theory is correct. The ship became lost and couldn't return to home port. I can't think of another alternative."

"I agree, but it still bothers me. Dwayne disagrees, but he has issues with Richard."

McLeod left the engine room and sought out Bentley, finding him in the lounge area next to the kitchen.

"I thought you would be in the command centre waiting for the big moment." He sat across from him. The researcher sipped water from a plastic cup.

"I might show up later. I just don't want to be around Richard. He more or less said I made a mistake with the test ship.

I didn't. I took in to account the gravity fields. That ship should have followed its course, stopped, and returned to where it was launched."

"Give me the details of the launch. Did the test ship reach faster than light travel immediately, or what was the situation?"

"No, it went at sub-light speed first. We initiated the space compression field and the diversion field and accelerated to the upper limit of our present technology. Everything appeared to be normal. Then we initiated the Dowling field. We turned off the compression field, as we didn't want it to interfere with the Dowling field."

"So, the compression field was turned off. The test ship is moving normally. No impact from rocks that might have caused a problem?"

"No. Just the usual small dust sized particles. The last communication we received was the diversion field successfully blocked them from the path of the ship."

"Is that when the Dowling field was turned on?"

"Yes. We went sub-light speed for about a half minute. Then we increased the speed to over light speed. We received confirmation that light speed was achieved, and then nothing."

"Okay, thanks." McLeod turned to walk toward the command centre. *No compression field. No rocks due to the diversion field. Light speed achieved and then...* He stopped and turned around. "After communication was lost, did you still have visual of the test rocket?"

"Yeah. Just an ultraviolet light blip from the engines before they became too weak to be seen."

"I know what happened." He ran to the command centre.

[28]

"What the hell do you mean by 'us'? If you think for one moment that you and I are going to have a romantic relationship, then you need to have your head examined."

"You need to calm down." Rigger smirked. "When I say 'us', I mean our relationship that we present to the public. A professional relationship." He took a sip of his wine and frowned. "I have studied your credentials, and you have certainly proven yourself as an excellent manager. However, I suspect your first choice is still working in the field."

"That's why I studied geology. I prefer field work, but now that I'm a manager, I have a lot of office work to do." She wondered at his choice of conversation. "What are you getting at?"

"It may surprise you to know I prefer doing field work myself. Unfortunately, I don't get to spend enough time doing so. There's a reason for that, of course. You must understand I have a passion for advancing science, and although I'd prefer to make my mark in the field, I understand I can be more effective in boardrooms and other places of influence."

Writson grunted.

"Tell me, do you feel your department has sufficient resources to do all the work you'd like to do?"

"Hardly. We have to cherry pick which areas might give us a

chance to make a discovery. I wish we had more people and equipment."

"Do you know why your department is not given a larger budget?"

She frowned. "Politics I suppose. Our Martian government depends on tax revenue from corporations and grants from Earth. In turn, a lot of our expenditures go toward maintaining the space stations and space ports. That means there isn't much left over for departments like mine that aren't considered essential services."

"I understand. I've seen that scenario play out a few times, mostly on Earth, but I can see it happens here as well. You see governments put money into what people who elect them want. If your department wants more resources, you need to convince the Martian government that's what the people want."

"How the hell can I do that?"

"Let me give you a bit of history about myself. I started my career much like yourself, working in remote areas, hoping to find the big discovery. Like you, I was willing to sacrifice my social and personal life to explore areas where no sane person wanted to live." He chuckled. "Maybe all those who love to explore the unknown are a bit anti-social."

Writson nodded. *That's me. I'd rather dig in a cave than go to a cocktail party.*

"I was fortunate. On a hunch, more so than great scientific research, I did a dig in the Antarctic on Earth just where some land was being freed of ice for the first time in tens of thousands of years. You likely know the rest, the discovery of an ancient civilization. To this day we're still doing research on the artifacts."

"I studied your discovery in university and the implications of an advanced civilization that failed to survive."

"It's good to know my initial discovery has made its way into university studies. That was a piece of luck in making that discovery. My second blessing came on a flight back to New York, where I struck up a conversation with a reporter of some merit, and he in turn wrote a well-received article on my discovery. One thing led to another and I had my claim to fame, so to speak. I appeared on talk shows and suddenly doors opened for me. I found my name was sufficient to obtain grants from government and private corporations. I know how the system works." He looked at her. "You, my dear, do not."

Writson opened her mouth to give a retort and stopped. *He's right.* "Okay, so I don't. That doesn't explain why you're dragging me to this dinner engagement. Or making me wear this dress."

"I'll go back to the fact you don't receive enough funding for your department to do enough research. You have a choice. You can go to the field and do more digging, where you may make a discovery. Or, if you're serious about advancing research on Mars, you can come with me to talk to those who do have an influence on funding. Together, we can make a very good team." He smiled. "The 'us' I refer to is the distinguished researcher with his beautiful companion. You have brains and beauty. Whether you like it or not, that dress will help influence their decisions. Now if you can be pleasant, and act like you enjoy my company, you may get the funding your department needs."

"I see. What do you get out of it?"

"Much the same as you. Funding for my projects. Plus, I do enjoy your company, even if you do have a sharp tongue."

"Alright, for an increase in funding, I'll put on my best behaviour."

"Good." He paused. "I shall tell you a little secret. Everyone likes a pretty woman. No one notices an older man in a dark suit, except when he's with the pretty woman. I have a reputation of being in the company of lovely ladies, and that helps keep me in the public eye. So that's why I'm willing to help you achieve what you want, because it gives me an opportunity to push my own agenda. Together, we have been invited to a dinner engagement with some powerful people."

"Okay, so two is better than one."

"True. That is why I didn't rely on yourself picking out your dress to wear. Appearances are very critical, and eyes will be on you."

Rigger escorted her to the street level where a shuttle car waited for them. Before they left the protection of the building, Rigger slipped off his suit jacket and placed it over her shoulders.

"I'm fine. I can take the cold," she protested.

"I have no doubt, but as a gentleman, it is my obligation to ensure your comfort comes before my own." He gently pressed her back toward the waiting shuttle.

"Thanks." She felt the cool air swirl around her as she entered the two-person shuttle. Moments later the shuttle manoeuvred down the streets. "Where are we going, by the way?"

"Some acquaintances of mine are hosting a dinner. The president of Mars will be there, as well as corporate executives. I assure you this will be one of the most important dinners you will ever attend."

"Now I'm nervous."

"Good, you should be. However, just try to be yourself. If they ask about your work, explain it as if they are students in a classroom. Not too complicated and remember their attention span for technical issues will be short. Use the three E's. Engage, enlighten and entertain."

The shuttle parked inside a garage of a ten-story building. The apartment had a decorative exterior and housed three units, with each unit having exclusive use of three floors.

"Nice place," Writson commented.

"Yes. They can afford it. They can also afford to help fund research, and in addition, have a great deal of influence on the government."

They stepped out of the shuttle and Writson handed the jacket back to Rigger. "Thanks." She smoothed down her dress and used her fingers to make sure her hair was in place.

"You look fine." He held out his arm and she hesitated before taking it as they entered the elevator. "Please, this is a formal setting we're entering. I'm aware you can walk by yourself but please indulge me."

"Okay. I'm just not used to being treated as a helpless female."

"Oh, you're far from helpless." He laughed.

The elevator doors opened, and they were greeted by a woman wearing a dark green formal dress. The woman, who identified herself as Malisa, introduced Writson to the others at the party. Writson stuttered out hellos, trying to remember names. She stayed close to Rigger, who was at ease as he chatted with others. She made a few comments but was glad a lot of questions were directed at Rigger, and not her.

"Dinner." Malisa interrupted the small talk, and Writson followed the others to the dining room.

Two servants went about with quiet efficiency, presenting the food and refreshing drinks. Writson felt more comfortable eating, which limited the conversation slightly. Rigger sat on her left, and she conversed with a blonde woman on her right, finding out the woman was the CEO of a company specializing in shuttle design and maintenance.

"That sounds interesting, although I have to admit I know nothing about spacecrafts."

"What do you do?"

"I'm the assistant director of Geology and Biology Department of the Martian Government."

"Oh, your department recently made a discovery of those alien columns. Is that how you met Dr. Rigger? Or were you friends before?"

Writson felt Rigger's knee nudge her own. *He's hinting. Why does knowing him before make a difference?* "I've known Dr. Rigger for a while now."

"That's good to know. A friend of Dr. Rigger's will have influence with us."

Dinner ended with dessert and a sweet liqueur. They carried their drinks back to the main room where the conversation grew more serious. Rigger steered Writson to where the President, his wife and another couple were talking.

Writson noted everyone was on a first name basis, and Rigger didn't hesitate to quickly include her in the conversation.

"David," Rigger spoke to the President. "I would like to formally introduce you to a dear friend of mine." He placed a hand on the small of her back and eased her forward. "Nellie Writson, David Nugent."

Writson shook his hand and stammered out a hello.

Rigger added, "Nellie is the one primarily responsible for the discovery of the alien columns. She does extraordinary work researching Mars."

Nugent replied, "That is most impressive."

Rigger continued, "That is one of the reasons why I believe she should be made head of our new Mars Museum of Natural History."

Writson was shocked at his proposition of her being head of the museum.

"Yes, I understand the implications of having a museum, and also having one of our own, born and raised Martian to oversee its operation." Nugent replied, looking at Writson.

Writson recalled the idea of a new museum being talked about for several years in the news media. The lack of funding for such a project was holding it back from being a concept to a reality. She suddenly became aware of a signal for an urgent message in her earpiece.

"Currently, there really isn't a suitable place for us to display the artifacts, and new discoveries." Rigger placed his hand on her upper arm.

"I quite agree, but I can only push projects through that have widespread support and appeal." Nugent continued to scrutinize Writson.

Writson felt Nugent was evaluating her as a possible head of the museum rather than as a woman as Rigger's companion. She met his eyes and announced, "Excuse me. I have to check a message." She turned to the side and activated the recorded message.

"Nellie, this is Jeremy. We have just returned from exploring the lava tube and have discovered life, and not just moss. Plants, insect like things and small animals! It's incredible."

Writson continued to listen to details of the message. *Complex life in the lava tubes? Mars is alive!*

[29]

WRITSON LOOKED AT NUGENT AND RIGGER. "I'M SORRY FOR the interruption. One of my teams has made an interesting discovery and sent out an urgent communication." She decided not to tell Rigger or the others until she could discuss the matter with Gary Dorn. She gave a small shrug to Rigger, hoping he would believe it was just a message from an overzealous employee.

Rigger tried to interpret her words for a moment before carrying on with his own agenda. "As we discussed before, we need to establish a museum on Mars that reflects our natural history. True, we do have the Ellie Evans museum. However, a large portion is devoted to the terraforming of Mars and there's so much more we can devote to the earlier life forms on Mars. In addition, there are tantalizing clues that Mars was visited by alien beings in its recent past."

"I have no doubt that such a museum has merit, but such a project would have substantial costs," Nugent replied. "Unfortunately, our government has limited resources for such an enterprise."

"I understand the issue of financing. The Martian government has many obligations to contend with, among them satisfying the requirements for Earth in exchange for various services. But if we delay the building of a museum too long, we will start to lose valuable artifacts." He paused, taking a sip from his glass, and aware others in the room were listening in on his conversation with the President. "I propose we ask, very nicely of course, for a contribution from corporations that have a vested interest in exploiting some of the rich minerals on Mars."

"And why would they make this donation?" Nugent asked.

"Because, if they want to have access to mineral deposits, it needs to be free of any valuable fossil remains. If they were to invest into the operation of the museum, then perhaps we can clear a specific area of their interest of any fossils and artifacts."

"That sounds like a possibility." Nugent nodded.

"A second area of revenue can come from tourist revenue. People from Earth are already making trips to Mars for pleasure and not just business. We can operate hotels to cater to that need, provide special tours around Mars and use the museum as a centre piece."

Rigger stopped speaking, knowing his suggestion for a museum would take time to take hold, and it would be best if the President was able to take credit for the idea later on. He guided Writson over to where food trays were set up. In a soft voice he asked, "Do you think the President was convinced?"

"Maybe. I can't say for sure, but I thought it sounded convincing."

"Thank you. Just understand I need you to help sell the need for a museum. A pretty woman can turn heads and people want to find a common ground with her. You need to make that common ground the need for a new museum."

"Alright, I'll try." She tried to look relaxed but kept thinking about Tolmat's message.

"Tell me more about that message you received. You looked anxious about it."

Writson considered there was little point in not telling him the truth. "There's alien life in the lava tubes. It may be Martian, or something left behind by the aliens when they made those columns."

"That's spectacular news. Does anyone else know about this discovery besides your team doing the investigation?"

Writson shook her head. "No, they would keep the information within their unit."

"Good. We will make this work to our advantage. Who's your lead on the team?"

"Jeremy Tolmat."

"Ah, I recall meeting him briefly before. Have him report to my office at eight o'clock tomorrow morning."

She looked at him questioningly.

"I'm going to make him the head of the joint exploration team from the Mars Environment Preservation Department and your Biological and Geological Department. We will shuttle down to the site the day after tomorrow, and I'll arrange to have the news media present as we announce the discovery."

"But it was Tolmat and his team that made the discovery."

"No, it was by a joint team between our departments. Don't worry, he will get enough accolades later, but for now we need to take the spotlight. This is our chance to make that museum a reality."

She sighed. *I feel this is dishonest, but what can I do about it?*

"Now let us continue to have drinks with the President and some very powerful corporate leaders."

Writson sent a message to Tolmat that he was to be at Rigger's office in the morning, adding to keep all information strictly confidential. She engaged the others in the room in small talk, occasionally explaining a bit of elementary science regarding the search for artifacts and fossils. One of the women invited her to contact her for lunch soon, making close physical contact while lightly touching Writson's bare back. She was careful to look interested in any conversation around her, recognizing she was playing a part to enhance Rigger's stature so she could benefit her team's research at the lava tube. An hour later, he took her hand, announcing they had a busy day tomorrow.

When they reached the shuttle, he informed her of his plan. "Tomorrow, we go out to the site, and inform your team that as far as they are concerned, the discovery of life in the tubes has not been verified yet. You may continue to collect data, of course, as well as specimens. However, the official discovery will not be announced until we arrive there with the news media present. Is that clear?"

"Yes, sir."

He frowned. "This has the opportunity to advance your status in the scientific community. Do not resent what I'm doing for you. That would be a mistake."

"I'm sorry. I'm not used to taking credit for something I didn't actually discover."

"But your team did, and that gives you the right to step up in front. Understand?"

"Yes, I suppose so."

Rigger escorted her to her apartment. "We'll converse more tomorrow."

━━

Writson arrived at the site where the lava tubes were being explored. She used a two-person shuttle with Tolmat, who quickly asked what Rigger wanted to speak to him about.

"He said I was being made the lead of a joint team of his and our departments to investigate the lava tubes. He's adding two members from the unit investigating the columns to the joint team."

"Are you happy with that?"

"Well, yes, I suppose so. It means that the Mars Environment Preservation department won't be completely taking over from our discoveries." He gave a shrug. "He also said I would be compensated for being in charge of the combined teams."

"That's good to hear."

"How was your dinner with Rigger?"

"Good, I met the President of Mars among other influential people. Rigger is pushing for a new museum and is using me as a way to gain their point of view."

"A new museum would be great. We have more fossils than we have room to display them."

"True, but it's all about financing. Rigger has a plan, and I'm getting pulled into it." She paused. "Jeremy, I need to tell you something on what Rigger is planning. I don't see a way to stop it, but I want you to know I don't agree with it."

"What is it?" He turned to face her, looking worried.

"He wants himself and I to take credit for the finding of life in the lava tubes. He's going to have a press conference tomorrow at the site where we'll make the official announcement. Sorry."

"Is that it?" He smiled. "You know, all of us had a role in discovering Martian life in the tubes. Someone has to make the big announcement, and I'm not one for public speaking. We're a team. You're the leader. You get the responsibility of doing the public speaking. No worries. We all know what we did to make this discovery."

"Thanks." She placed her hand on top of his.

"When we finally get back to Red City, the team can celebrate what we've done. Until then, I'll be happy to keep in the background."

The shuttle landed, and Writson quickly went to the laboratory to study the video recordings, the recording of data, and the small sample of specimens. The plant specimen, a blade of hairy looking slip of grass, was a dark purple in colour.

"The DNA is similar to Earth seaweed," Smyth commented. "The slip you see is from a cluster, all joined at a common centre." She pointed to a fragile looking insect with two pairs of large wings. It looked like a small spider with too many wings. "There're lots of those flying around. They pretty much ignored us. I'm not sure what their food source is. The DNA is a bit strange. Closer to crustaceans than anything else. The small fur covered creature has DNA close to that of a reptile."

"Are these related to Earth creatures then?"

"No, if I had to hazard a guess. Possibly a very distant ancestor. There are other creatures there as well, but we wanted to limit our invasion to the most common life forms."

"Well done."

She turned to Tolmat. "Could you call your team in here? I'd best inform them of tomorrow's events."

"Will do."

Writson informed the group around her, comprised of her

team and Rigger's, of the need to maintain absolute secrecy of the recent discoveries. She noticed Rigger's team members weren't taken aback by the news, but those who worked in her department were surprised by the stated need to keep all information within the group. "In addition, there will be an announcement made to the media tomorrow at the site by Dr. Rigger and myself. Be prepared for attention by the news media." She answered a couple of minor questions, and then asked for Tolmat to take her to the location of where they made an entrance into one of the lava tubes.

"I'll be glad to take you on a tour there. Be prepared to be amazed."

[30]

The Hallians were aware of Earth's test flight of the faster than light ship. They didn't know why it was sent on a one-way trip, wondering if it was done in error. Regardless, they began to look out for additional attempts at faster than light travel. The other space travelling species decided to resume their careful observations of Earth and keep away from direct contact until more information was known. The Hallians continued their visits to their former home world, using the trips to monitor for any more advances by Earth.

▭

THERE WERE SURPRISED LOOKS FROM THOSE IN THE command centre as the officers stared at McLeod.

"The diverter field must be turned off when we exceed light speed. That's the reason the test ship failed."

Richard Combs frowned. "How so?"

"The diverter field induces a magnetic field on nearby objects to push them out of the way. That's fine for normal travel, but when we exceed the speed of light, we will pass through the diverter field that we have generated. When that happens, the field has the possibility of affecting our own electronics."

Combs clasped his hands together across his stomach. "That

makes sense for the test ship. It didn't have much insulation as it wasn't meant to carry passengers. Our ship does have protection against electromagnetic radiation. Still, your concern is valid as our diverter field is intense. I agree we should shut it down as we approach light speed. One can't be too careful."

"I can agree with you there." McLeod smiled as he spoke louder and at the command centre at large. "Our planned attempt to break the speed of light will continue as scheduled at fourteen hundred hours." He placed a hand on Combs' shoulder. "If you have a minute, could you come with me?"

Combs touched a few keys on his console. "Sure." He stood. "What's the problem?"

"No problem." McLeod led the way down the hall. "At one time, you stated that the loss of the test ship was due to miscalculation of the gravity field. That does not appear to be the cause of the accident now."

"That's true."

"The situation is Dwayne took your criticism personally. I believe it would be prudent for you to apologize to him. We don't need to have ill feelings toward each other on the day we make history."

"I didn't know he was mad at me."

"Trust me, he is."

"All I did was to suggest a reason why we lost the test ship." Combs shrugged. "I didn't mean to say it was his fault."

McLeod pointed at the sulking Bentley. "Do your best to apologize." He watched as Combs shuffled over to Bentley and sat down. He didn't stay to listen to the conversation, but instead made his way to the engine room.

"Hi Tia, Fish." He saw them working together at a monitor.

After they acknowledged his presence, he told them of his theory of the diverter field causing the disappearance of the test ship.

Gill crossed his arms. "I can see that happening on the test ship, but I doubt that would be a concern on this ship. We have passive and active insulation from all forms of electromagnetic radiation that should prevent any damage to our own electronics."

"I trust your knowledge on this, but I'm still going to have the diverter field shut down when we approach the speed of light. If we should run into a problem, it will eliminate the diverter field as a possible cause. Also, if we're travelling faster than the speed of light, I don't see how the diverter field benefits us anyway. The field wouldn't be in front of us."

"Good point."

He looked at Dermott. "Ready to push your babies?"

She grinned. "I can hardly wait. It's going to be a beautiful sight when we open them up."

McLeod returned to the control centre, and determined all systems were still ready. "Richard, will you please send a message to Gibbston Mars' port and inform them all systems are a go. Give them our present speed, and that we will attempt FTL travel in fifteen minutes. We will report again in thirty minutes time."

———

"Thirteen-fifty, Captain," Combs announced dryly.

McLeod took a deep breath aware it was only ten minutes to their attempt at breaking the speed of light. "Inform the engine room to run up engines to seventy percent."

Although the ship was well insulated from the engine room, and the artificial gravity could make allowances for the acceleration, McLeod was sure he could feel a change on the floor from the increase in speed.

"Mr. Combs?"

"All systems normal, sir."

McLeod saw Bentley had entered the command centre, slowly inching his way forward to peer at the forward monitors. He admitted he wasn't sure what they would see as they exceeded the speed of light. Various monitors acted like windows to show what the space looked like outside of the ship. So far everything looked normal, with the slight blue shift of star light in the forward monitors too small to be easily noticed.

The command centre was quiet, as the personnel studied their monitors. Wagner walked over to him, giving him a smile as she touched his arm. "Three minutes, Captain. I don't know about you, but my stomach feels like it's tied into a knot."

"I'm trying to remember to breathe." He gave her a smile back. He glanced at the monitor that showed the performance of the engines. Every graph showed green. "Mr. Combs, prepare to engage to the Dowling field." He watched as Combs armed the electronic circuits that controlled the Dowling field. The circuits now supplied low power to the field generators, allowing for the field to be quickly ramped up when needed, without delay from capacitance power being stored.

"Sixty seconds, Captain." Combs fingers danced over several keys as he checked the ship's performance on a variety of levels.

McLeod touched his earpiece, changing it so his voice would be carried on the ship's intercom. "Attention. We will be initiating faster than light travel in thirty seconds." He watched a clock on a monitor and took a deep breath. "Mr. Combs, engage the Dowling field at my mark. Five, four, three, two, one. Engage."

Combs finger touched a square radio button on his monitor. Suddenly the monitors showing space from the front of the ship went to a rainbow of colour.

31

WRITSON USED THE LADDER TO LOWER HERSELF INTO THE lava tube. She attached a mask to cover her face to help prevent any contamination of the Martian environment, and to protect herself against any bacteria, viruses and possible toxic chemicals. Her goggles had an active optic filter, allowing her to see in the dark by adjusting the light in intensity and colour spectrum. A minute later Norris joined her.

"What do you think?"

Writson looked around in the lava tube, slightly higher than her head. Plants covered the surface, the thin stems waving in the gentle air currents. Various insects flew around her, occasionally bouncing off her. Among the plants she saw a quick movement of a small creature. "Wow, it reminds me of being underwater, the way the plants and insects float around."

"The whole lava tube is like this. We made some preliminary investigation on the neighbouring lava tubes and found the air chemical composition to be very close to this one. We sent a remote camera inside them, and it appears most of the life forms are identical, but there are few oddities as well. There's a yellow coloured plant in one tube, and we saw a snake like creature in another."

"We need to investigate lava tubes that aren't connected to these and see if they also have any life."

"True. I'm going to guess that because the lava tubes protect life forms from the harsh effects of radiation, and keep the temperature from getting too low, we will find other life forms. However, I'm going to say that these groups of lava tubes hold the most complex life. It's warmer here, and just maybe the remains of those columns have something to do with the unique life forms we found."

"Good theory." She turned in a circle, taking in the view of alien life. "Okay, I've seen it now. I guess we better get back."

"And here I thought you wanted to have a picnic here."

Writson laughed. "Sorry, too many bugs."

They returned to the shelters, where the team speculated on the Martian life forms and the DNA results. Smyth had a theory, and the others listened to what the biologist had to say. "I know some of us are wondering if the aliens that visited here in the past could have left these life forms behind. It's possible, but I doubt it. To create an ecology like we have here, we would need a lot more supporting life forms than just what we see. Bacteria, various plants, other insects, and maybe a few other more complex creatures just to keep the chain of life cycle going. It would take a lot of work to develop the interdependency of the various species. On such a small environment, one missing link could prove fatal for the group. I believe what we have here is the remains of Martian life, and that it has prospered since we began to terraform Mars."

"How about the environment centres we set up? They don't have a complex life cycle but still survive."

"True, but there's a problem with the environmental centres. They're constantly monitored, and species have to be replenished regularly. Some parts, like the plants and insects, seem to be adapting slowly over generations. But the small rodents and lizards are not doing very well. They die off, and we have to replenish the population. They are doing better as their genes are modified, but the work is slow. I can't imagine the work that would be required to do the complex life we came across in the lava tubes."

Writson announced she was ready for something to eat and

wanted to go over all the reports once more. Norris quickly offered to help her with the reports.

"I'm familiar with the reports and can help with filtering some of the data."

Smyth watched Writson and Norris leave. *Well, I'm sure that data doesn't stand a chance with those two together.*

———

Rigger arrived the following morning via a two-person shuttle, although he was the only one inside. He quickly assembled a meeting in the largest shelter. He carried a bright yellow folded garment and boots with him.

"In about an hour, a shuttle carrying various news media members will arrive to hear our announcement of confirmed advanced Martian life. This is the most important news to come from Mars since we decided to colonize and terraform it. Ms. Writson and I will be making the announcement jointly. The rest of the team will stand behind us in a semi-circle. The news media will ask questions and they will largely be directed at Ms. Writson and myself. However, some of you may be asked questions as well. If you are, try to respond as follows. One, refer to actions and discoveries as by the team, not individuals. Two, any technical questions should be directed to Ms. Writson or myself. Three, if they ask speculative questions, inform them that we are still analysing the data. Keep your responses short. I suggest everyone try to look your best. I understand that your garments here are for practical use, and the nature of exploring lava tubes will make them look less than pristine. However, do try to clean them up. Gentlemen, shave and try to look less like a Martian adventurer." He paused as he heard a few chuckles. "Ladies, it's time to dig out the makeup kits you put away for special occasions. This is one of them."

Rigger beckoned Writson over. "This is for you to wear." He passed over the garment and the boots. "You need to look like a successful, sexy, woman in charge."

She looked at the thermal suit. "Quite the colour."

"We need everyone to see you and get their attention. I'll guarantee this is the way to make sure your voice will be heard."

Writson didn't comment and made her way to her sleeping quarters. *Do I want this? I guess it's too late to say no now.*

She peeled off her old thermal suit, recognizing it did look like she had been crawling along in the Martian dirt. She pulled on the new suit and was shocked to see it was meant to show her body off more than for any practical exploring. Wide mesh strips went from her shoulders down to her legs. Two more strips went down her chest in the middle, forming a V. The suit hugged her body more than her work suit, bringing focus on her curves. She had seen other women wear something similar in Red City, and quietly smirked on how impractical the suit would be during Mars's colder seasons. Now she was wearing one of the fashionable, yet of dubious warmth, suits. *This is something Leana would wear. Can I wear this and still look like a serious researcher?* She put on the boots, noting that while they may look like work boots at first glance, the raised heel suggested more fashion appeal than for use climbing a rocky terrain. She left her room and tapped on the door of Lindsey Smyth.

Smyth slid open her door. "Hi, what's up?" She looked at what Writson was wearing. "Wow, that's some thermal suit."

"Tell me the truth. Is this over the top? Do I wear this at the media conference?"

"Why not? You've got the body to wear something like that. It will certainly gather attention. And before you say you don't want the attention, it's too late for that. Your name and pictures are already in the news."

"Okay, thanks. I guess I better make the best of it."

She entered the kitchen area of the large shelter, seeing Carl Duggan and Philip Norris. They were talking, and had already changed for the upcoming news event. They stopped speaking as soon as they saw her. Writson saw Norris take in a quick breath.

"No comments. This is what Dr. Rigger picked for me to wear."

Duggan gave her a smile. "Nice colour."

Norris added, "I think you look great."

223

"Thanks." Writson went to the kitchen and poured herself a cup of water. "I can't wait for this to be over with."

Norris went up to her, putting his hand just above her hip. "Look, don't worry about what you're wearing. I know you normally don't dress this way, but this is your moment, the team's moment, for you to draw attention to yourself and this discovery."

"Thanks." She rested a hand on his arm.

"So stand proud, and let everyone know what we've done."

"Okay, I will."

A large shuttle landed, and ten members of the media stepped out. For Mars, the day was warm, with only a few thin clouds floating in the sky. Rigger approached the group, welcoming them.

"Please, ladies and gentlemen, follow me to where we've set up an area to make a most extraordinary announcement."

"Isn't this the same area where the columns were discovered?" a reporter asked.

"It is."

"Then is this announcement related to the columns?"

"Perhaps, but I do believe you will find what we are about to reveal will absolutely astonish you." Rigger refused to say anything more, ushering the group to where the joint exploration team waited. He met with Writson, standing between the media personnel and the rest of the team.

"In a minute, we will release images to your tablets so you can see what we are about to reveal. Those images will not be released to anyone else for two hours, so everyone here will get the jump on the greatest story since we colonized Mars." He paused, watching the reporters ease forward. "Great discoveries are rarely done by one individual. In this case several people have contributed toward the steps needed here." He touched Writson on the shoulder. "Ms. Nellie Writson has done extensive work here at the lava tubes that permutate this area. I will now turn the rest of the announcement to her."

Writson felt a small wave of panic as the news media focused on her. *Why is Rigger having me make the announcement? I guess there's no point in trying to figure out his motive now.* "Thank you,

Dr. Rigger. I'll try not to keep you in suspense much longer. Several weeks ago, we noticed unusually high concentrations of gasses near the lava tubes and confirmed that those gases emanated from them. A joint team of our two departments led by Jeremy Tolmat investigated the tubes. Inside the lava tubes, which are protected from the harsh environment of the surface, they found an abundance of life. Martian life forms, which include plants, insect like creatures and small animals, are thriving inside the tubes."

"How advanced are the life forms?" a reporter shouted.

"We don't yet know the full extent of the life inside the lava tubes. From what information we have, we can speculate the highest forms would be along the lines of mice, lizards and other small creatures. But I want to stress we have not investigated much of one lava tube, let alone the neighbouring ones." Writson responded to several other questions but didn't reveal much more information.

Rigger stopped the news conference, thanked everyone for showing up, and informed the news media that as new information was obtained, they would be forwarded to the various news outlets.

He turned to Writson. "Pack your things. You will be accompanying me back to Red City."

"Now?"

"Yes, we have a few things to discuss. I've spoken to Gary Dorn. You're no longer with the Biological and Geological Department."

32

"CAPTAIN, WE HAVE JUST REACHED THE SPEED OF LIGHT," Combs announced. "Our speed is still climbing. Now at one point two."

"Hold the speed at one point five."

"Affirmative."

"Any special words for eternity, Ms. Wagner?" McLeod asked.

"I had a speech planned, but maybe I'll save that for the media. Instead, I just want to hold on to this moment. This crew, everyone on this ship, is part of this amazing accomplishment. It feels great to be truly reaching for the stars."

"Any theories on why our displays are showing a distorted view of stars?" McLeod directed his question to Combs.

"Yes. The Dowling field creates a bubble around the ship. That means there is a layer between the cosmos and our hole in the universe. When the sunlight strikes the boundary, it is distorted similar to sunlight hitting a warped piece of glass."

"Thus, the colour spectrum on the monitors."

Wagner held up a bottle of champagne. "I have glasses and a couple of bottles of bubbly. Perhaps we can all gather around and toast this incredible, special moment in human history."

"Alright, we have exceeded the speed of light in our universe. Let's drop down back to point seven-five of light speed and announce our achievement to Gibbston Mars' port."

The ship dropped to sub-light speed and Combs made the transmission, McLeod used the intercom to invite everyone to the control centre for a glass of champagne. He recognized the label from the French winery. Any wine from Earth was extremely expensive, and the thick plastic bottle for champagne made it even more so. He also understood for Wagner such costs were not an object for her.

Wagner made a speech about their special moment in human history. "To conclude, we are part of a great advance in allowing humans to be free in the universe. Congratulations to everyone here for making it possible."

McLeod drained his glass. "Okay, this ship is not supposed to fly by itself. Stations everyone."

Combs called out, "Gibbston Mars' port has offered their congratulations."

"Excellent. I believe it's time we continue our journey to Meili. Inform the engine crew to prepare for FTL travel again."

Combs relayed the message and spoke to McLeod. "They have confirmed they're ready."

"Good. Initiate the Dowling field and prepare for one point five light speed."

"Done."

He looked at Combs. "How long until we reach the vicinity of Meili?"

"At one point five light speed, we will reach there in two hours and thirty-seven minutes."

"Good. Maybe we will find something interesting there."

[33]

"WHAT DO YOU MEAN I'M NO LONGER WITH THE BIOLOGICAL and Geological Department?" Writson gasped out the words. "After we just announced this amazing discovery?"

"Yes, that is exactly what is happening. I've spoken at length to the President about the creation of a new museum, as you are aware. While there are problems with financing, he has agreed that we need to step forward in light of our latest discovery of Martian life. He understands the need for someone to promote the museum. Someone who is in the public eye, is knowledgeable about Mars in geology and biology, and is passionate about Mars as a Martian." He paused and smiled. "It also helps if that someone is attractive, and not shy about appearing in public."

"I'm to promote this new museum?"

"Yes. I can do a lot to help you, of course. However, in the end a pretty woman can gain the attention of people far beyond what a stuffy old explorer can do." He smiled. "I've put you in a place where you can make a difference. The President wants to meet you to confirm your interest in this appointment. Are you willing to grasp the opportunity?"

"Yes." Writson felt dizzy with what he just told her. *Who will take over my department? What will I do in this new role? This is overwhelming.*

The shuttle took her to Rigger's laboratory, where he escorted her to his office. "You have a meeting with the President at four o'clock."

"The President?" She looked down at her bright yellow thermal suit. "I can't see him wearing this. I need to go home and change."

He eased back into his chair behind his desk. "I suspect you don't have much in the way of office attire in meeting with the president." He smiled. "Fortunately, for you, I have taken the liberty of asking Ms. Griffin to order some clothes for you. You may change in the ladies' restroom."

"Thank you. I don't understand why you're doing this. You get me a new job overseeing the promotion of a new museum. I have to question why, and to what end."

"I have my reasons, and one of them is to help you. I do try to help those who are smart, and ambitious, to achieve goals that coincide with my own. What do I get in return for helping you? A few things. For one, you will still be obligated to accompany me to various functions. You will help me achieve something I feel is important, namely the construction of a new museum."

"Just don't expect too many return favours." She stood. "I need to change. I don't want to be late for my meeting with the President."

"Go and see Ms. Griffin. She has your new clothes."

Writson frowned at the way Rigger was manipulating her. *Not that I have much choice right now.* She took a package of clothes and shoes from Ms. Griffin.

"Dr. Rigger suggested to me that you may be of need of some other, let's say more sophisticated, clothes. I have sent additional clothes to your apartment."

"Uh, thank you." She went to the restroom and inspected the skirt and top. *Well, they look nice, but I think I better start buying my own clothes from now on. I hate these surprises Rigger keeps throwing at me.* She struggled to pull off the form fitting thermal suit and changed into the new clothes.

She checked her hair and returned to the office, where Ms. Griffin informed her a shuttle was waiting for her.

Writson tried to calm herself as the shuttle whisked her to the top of the Martian Government Building. From the rooftop she entered the security room, where she was permitted to enter the administration and reception area of the President. The receptionist was a friendly young man, who politely informed her she had to wait until President Nugent was able to see her.

Writson felt relieved she had a few more minutes to relax. She accepted a glass of water and sat in the waiting room. Fifteen minutes later she was allowed to speak to the President.

"President Nugent, it's wonderful to meet with you again."

He gestured for her to sit across from him. His office was angular in shape, with his desk near one of the full-length monitors that showed a real-time view of Red City. Away from the desk, comfortable furniture was placed around a hexagon shaped table.

"The pleasure is mine. I suppose you're wondering what the hell is going on." He chuckled.

"I am." She tried to smile.

"Dr. Rigger and I have known each other for several years. A few days ago, he mentioned you, in a most positive fashion, I may add. He brought you to our small dinner, and I have to say I was impressed as well. Ms. Writson, we have been toying with how we can build a new museum under our present funding. So much of our expenditures have strings attached to them, as Earth allocates funds with conditions to them."

"That's not right."

"Yes, well, that may be true, but it doesn't change the equation. I understand that you are a staunch supporter of Mars and have offered the opinion that Mars needs greater independence."

Writson was surprised he knew of her views. "Yes, being dependent on Earth takes away our freedom."

"I don't disagree. However, the first step is to give those who live on Mars something to take pride in. One is the uniqueness of Red City and its buildings. We have the Ellie Evans Martian Museum, and a rich heritage of our early colonization. Unfortunately, we don't have the facilities to display them."

"Does that mean we need another museum?"

"Not exactly. The Dr. Thomas Rigger Museum and Culture Centre will have artifacts, but it will be more than that. It will showcase art, have a theatre for live performances, and now an enclosed environment to showcase Martian life forms."

The Dr. Thomas Rigger Museum? I should've guessed his name would be there. "That sounds intriguing. Can we build it? Or do we need Earth's permission first?"

"The permission isn't lacking, but the funding is. That would be your job, if you were to accept the position. You see, to convince those who do have discretionary monies to spend, we need a well-known, attractive person who can move about social circles."

"I didn't know I was well known."

"After announcing the discovery of Martian life in a bright yellow thermal suit, I think it's safe to assume people will know of you."

Writson blushed.

"Your name will put you in position to ask for help in financing."

"I see."

"I have to warn you that those who have the ability to help you with the building of a new museum are also conservative in their business approaches. It would be best that you refrain from mentioning you want Mars to have greater autonomy."

Writson nodded. "I understand how that would frighten off some investors."

"Then will you accept the position? You will be suitably compensated, of course."

"Yes, I would be honoured."

"Excellent." Nugent stood. "I will have the offer officially drawn up. Someone will contact you in a few days."

Writson felt too excited to go to her apartment. She thought about calling Norris but wanted to tell him face to face about her new position. *Besides I want to talk to Gary Dorn first on who should take over my position as manager. I'd like Jeremy to have that, but it's not my decision to make. I think I'll go and see Leana.*

Leana stared at Writson as she entered the bar. She gave a whistle. "Wow, so you can dress up on occasion."

Writson laughed. "I had a big meeting. It was necessary."

"Ohhh, tell me what it was about."

"I can't." Writson sat at the bar. "In a few days you'll know."

Leana wiped down the bar before placing the drink in front of Writson. "This one is on the house. Now tell me about you holding back on me about those Martian lifeforms."

"Sorry, I guess you heard about it through the media."

"I was mad you wouldn't tell me." She gave a smile. "All forgiven. That was quite the thermal suit. You sure were the centre of attention."

"Don't remind me. Dr. Rigger picked it out for me to wear." She shook her head. "Can you imagine me wearing something like that working out in the field?"

"No." Leana giggled. "But I'll bet a bunch of men did."

"Whatever. Look, I need you to go shopping with me. So far Dr. Rigger has been picking out clothes for me to wear, and the results are something that makes me feel a little underdressed."

"I don't know about that. I thought your thermal suit looked great, despite your conservative attitude."

"Are you going to help me or not?"

"Of course, I will." She paused as she poured another drink. "Just exactly what type of clothes are we shopping for? Office? Casual? Flirty party dresses?"

Writson sighed. "Sophisticated office wear. Now stop trying to pry more information out of me."

"Me, trying to pry? Never. Would you like another drink?"

Writson laughed. "Keep this a secret. I've been offered a promotion by the President to head a new position. I won't say anything more no matter how many rums you ply me with."

"Alright. Say, have you heard from the captain, Jaret McLeod?"

"No, why?"

"He's disappeared. I know his ship, the Nevada Queen, is still at Mars. So normally he would have dropped by, but no show. I called him, and his voice message said he was unavailable."

"No, I haven't heard from him. Why do you think I would?"

"Because there's something different about you, like 'I found a guy' something different."

Writson took a drink of her rum. "I don't know what you're talking about."

34

"CAPTAIN, AT OUR CURRENT SPEED, WE'RE ONE HOUR AWAY from Meili." Combs turned slightly to speak to McLeod.

"Let's ease up on our approach. Drop our speed to point seven-five of light speed."

"Aye, sir."

"Let's do a visual of the planet. Correct for the blue shift."

McLeod and the others stared at the monitors. The monitors flickered from white to static, and to a stable image of a grey globe. "Adjust illumination. Let's put some light on the planet." The image changed, brightened to show the planet was predominately white with dark grey streaks. Brown ridges snaked along the globe from where mountains ranges sat.

Shultz studied the image in front of her. "Hello, Meili. Welcome to our Solar System."

"There looks to be a small moon circling it." McLeod pointed at a dark body on the monitor, well away from the planet.

Combs adjusted the magnification and the light in one of the monitors. "It's twelve hundred and seventy-two kilometres along the widest part, and a thousand-fifty at the narrow part. Composition of water, ice, surrounded by methane, nitrogen and some carbon monoxide."

"Richard, are there any other moons?"

Combs made adjustments to his monitor, studying the display

of images and graphs. "Negative, although there are a half-dozen rocks also orbiting Meili. They range in size from a few metres to a hundred metres." He paused as he peered at a graph. "Wait, three of these rocks appear to be artificial."

McLeod stepped behind Combs, peering at the information on the monitor. "They look to be identical in size, and equally spaced on the same orbit."

"Correct. Ninety-seven point five metres in diameter."

"We need to take a closer look at them." He approached Lisa Wagner. "I know our original plan was to send a message to Mars to announce we have arrived at Meili once we dropped below light speed. I was wondering if perhaps we should include an image of the artificial satellite in our message. I, for one, would really like to get a closer look at one of them."

"I agree with getting a closer look at the satellite. However, I don't want to delay the announcement that we have reached Meili. Mars port will be expecting a report from us, and any delay may cause them some anxious moments. This is a significant achievement, and we should do it now. As captain, you have the honour of the speech."

Once again, the entire crew gathered, this time in the engine room. Lisa Wagner stood next to McLeod, with the rest of the ship's personnel behind them. The announcement was sent to Mars, Earth and the Terra Nova space station. All three could verify the Hendrik A. Lorentz's location, and their present speed of three-quarters the speed of light. That speed alone would make the spacecraft unique, and their claim of faster than light travel would cause considerable excitement.

"This is Captain Jaret McLeod, of the spaceship Hendrik A. Lorentz. We are currently in deep space, nearing the location of the planet Meili. Our current speed is zero point seven-five the speed of light. Our mission is to visit the planet Meili, where we have spotted a small moon, and what appears to be artificial satellites. Once we have completed our preliminary investigation, we will return to Mars, and supply data and, of course, proof of exceeding the speed of light."

McLeod added the names of the crew of the ship, as well as Wagner, identifying her as the C.E.O. of Gibbston Space Lines.

"Okay, we now have sent a message to satisfy Mars port where we are and what we are going to investigate to ensure our moment in history. Now let's return to our stations. We have work to do."

McLeod spoke to Gill and Dermott as the rest of the ship's crew returned to work. "Congratulations on your part, a very big part, on reaching Meili."

"With these engines, it was child's play," Gill replied.

"I was hoping we could open them up some more," Dermott added.

"How much faster can we go with these engines?"

Gill raised his eyebrows. "I've been trying to determine that. Doubling our engine output doesn't double our speed, which is the normal situation for spacecraft. I was curious if that was also true with the Dowling field on. It turns out, as we exceed the speed of light, the Dowling field is compressed, primarily at the front, which then requires more power to sustain. The result is I believe our highest speed would be around four times the speed of light. Perhaps a bit more, but it depends more on how strong a Dowling field we can generate."

"What compresses the field?"

"I suspect dark matter, which doesn't react strongly to the Dowling field. It could also be dark energy, of course. Dwayne would have a better idea than me."

"True, he's the expert." McLeod stepped toward Dermott, and briefly squeezed her hand. "I best go up front." He made his way to the exit of the engine room.

"Hey, captain."

He turned around as Dermott put a hand on his neck and quickly kissed him.

"See you later."

The command centre was busy with images of the planet and the satellites being analysed. Shultz pointed at a monitor. "The artificial satellite is showing an unusual surface. At first it looked like a pebbled surface, but as we get a better look at it, it seems more like a textured pattern."

McLeod studied the silver coloured globe. "You're right. Any thoughts on the pattern?"

"No, other than it may be an encoding that, if we can decipher, will tell us about Meili. The other two artificial satellites have a similar pattern."

The Hendrik A. Lorentz continued its approach to Meili, establishing orbit around the planet as it closed the gap to one of the artificial satellites.

"What do you see, Richard?"

"Definitely an encoded pattern. They are using square blocks, each of which are subdivided into four triangles. Each triangle can have one of five different heights. That means each block can have a value of one to six hundred and twenty-five."

"So that would be a lot of information encoded on the satellite."

"Yeah." Combs touched a few keys on the control in front of him. I'm approximating here, but it would be two times ten to ninth power."

"Can you decipher the code?"

"I think so. I'm assuming they want the code to be read, so there should be an obvious key. I've programmed one of the computers to run a diagnostic of the pattern, and then I'll use a software program to read it. We need to circle the satellite to get a reading of the whole thing."

"We can do that." He turned to Shultz. "Lexanna, can you pilot the ship around the closest satellite?"

"Sure." Shultz whispered, "How's it going with Tia?"

"All good now. Thanks for your help."

"No worries. She looks happy, and I assumed you had patched things up."

McLeod looked on the main screen as they circled the satellite, and then again over the top and bottom.

Combs called out, "We have deciphered the code, and can read the information."

McLeod looked over at him. "What the hell does it say?"

Combs licked his lips. "We're missing a couple of details where minor rocks hit the surface of the satellite, but the record is mostly complete. It reads: We are the Hallians, and this artificial moon represents the final efforts of our species to preserve a record of all of the beauty and wonder of our world. We were casting our reach for other worlds when a large, rogue world pushed us out of our solar system. Our world is becoming cold, and soon will be frozen. We don't know the fate of our one-time beautiful world, but if you can read this message, then perhaps the memories of Hallian will be preserved. Our world was full of colourful plants, animals big and small, and us. We had great seas, mountains and valleys. Hallian was a wonder, and though it is now dead, please respect the greatness it achieved. This artificial moon is hollow inside, and the rest of code on the surface and inside the satellite is dedicated to images and sounds of our world. A final message. Do not take your own world's life for granted. What happened to us, may happen to any world."

McLeod looked at the satellite on a monitor. "So, Richard, what type of images do we have?"

"I haven't deciphered all the images yet. It's a slightly different coding system than the text, but I should have the images and sounds soon."

"There should be even more inside the satellite."

"I don't know why anyone would want to go inside that satellite. That's just too dangerous." He frowned. "There is an opening of some sort at the bottom."

"Then, let's move over there and take a closer look."

"We don't have a way to actually investigate the inside," Shultz pointed out. "We don't have a shuttle, or suits meant for anything other than emergency."

"I know, but I want to see how large the opening is, so when we return, we will be prepared."

The Hendrik A. Lorentz manoeuvred around the satellite, pausing at the bottom of the small globe.

"Into the rabbit hole?" Shultz commented. "That looks to be a three-metre wide opening."

"I wish we could look inside." McLeod peered at a monitor. "But I suppose that's for our next visit here."

"Captain, we have an incoming message." Combs looked up at McLeod. "It's from the International Space Agency and for your eyes only. It's marked private and urgent."

"Send it to my quarters." He frowned. *What the hell do they want? Nothing is ever good when they contact you.*

He entered the captain's quarters and accessed the message on a monitor. A dark-blue uniformed man looked back at him on the screen, his image frozen in front of a giant gold crest mounted on a wall behind him. McLeod didn't recognize him; the International Space Agency personnel kept their profiles to themselves. They operated the Interplanetary Enforcement Police and rarely made a public display of those ships or personnel. Still, with a large budget, it was assumed they had the ability to enforce their authority in all areas of human space. That didn't include Earth or Mars, but all other planets and asteroids fell under their jurisdiction.

McLeod pressed play, and the lantern-jawed, older man began to speak.

"Captain Jaret McLeod, I am General Steven H. Shatley of the International Space Agency forces. We have intercepted your message claiming to exceed the speed of light on the spaceship Hendrik A. Lorentz. As of this moment, we have blocked *all* further distribution of your message." Shatley paused, allowing McLeod to absorb the information. "Captain McLeod, you are hereby ordered to leave the vicinity of Meili immediately upon receipt of this message and to travel to the International Space Agency Argus port. There you will be given additional instructions and debriefed. You are also hereby instructed not to inform anyone of your new orders, nor make any attempt to send any more outgoing messages. I will now inform you, failure to comply with these orders will result in the Hendrik A. Lorentz being placed on the fugitive list. Any, including destructive force, will be used to bring your ship into port. I trust I have made myself clear what your duties are."

The message ended, with McLeod staring at the gold seal emblem of the International Space Agency forces. He took several deep breaths and went to the front of the ship. He saw Wagner looking at him with curiosity. "Is there something wrong?"

"Lisa, we have situation."

35

WRITSON WAS SMILING AS SHE MADE HER WAY TO THE secretary.

"Go right in. He's expecting you."

"Hello, Mr. Dorn."

"Come on in, Nellie, come in. I think you can call me Gary now. I'm not your boss anymore."

"Thank you, Gary." She sat in the chair in front of his desk. She couldn't help but smile.

"Congratulations on your new position. I'm very proud and happy for you."

"I feel bad about leaving on such short notice."

He waved his hand downward. "Don't give it a second thought. One of my jobs is to prepare people for promotions. Some come a bit earlier than expected." He raised his eyebrows. "In your case, it is well deserved, and I trust you will do well in your new position."

"I'll do my best." Writson found herself blushing.

"I know you will."

"I was wondering if you've given any consideration on who will be taking over as the assistant director in my place."

"There are a few names I have in mind. Due to the recent series of events, I will have to move quickly. A long posting and interview process will not necessarily be in the best interests of the department at this time." He took a drink from his coffee cup, an actual ceramic mug with a blue and orange logo on it. "Jeremy Tolmat is being promoted to a new position, one that encompasses two departments. He will assume the title of assistant director, but in two departments. That will have to do until we can figure out something else. That means we need a new manager for the Biological and Geological department. May I assume you have someone in mind?"

"Yes, I do." Writson paused. "In the matter of full disclosure, I have a personal relationship with this individual. We haven't dated, but we have plans to go to dinner together. Even with that in mind, I still believe he is the best candidate to take over as manager. His name is Paul Norris."

"Interesting. His name has come to my attention before regarding this position. Thank you for your input in this matter. Now, about you. This is quite a leap for anyone, but you have unique abilities that should serve you well."

"I'm nervous about this."

"And that's quite natural. You have the tools to succeed. My advice is don't second guess yourself. You have earned this. Continue to do what you feel is right."

"Thank you. You always make me feel better after I talk to you."

"Feel free to contact me anytime." He stood. "It doesn't have to be a problem. I would enjoy just a conversation with you over a cup of coffee."

Writson left, smiling. *He didn't say much but somehow, he made me feel good.* She made her way to her old office, wanting to say goodbye to her former staff. She knew several members of her team, including Paul Norris, were still at the Biblis Patera volcano vents.

"Hi, Jeremy."

Tolmat grinned. "What's this about you bailing out of our department?"

"Man, there aren't any secrets around here." She laughed. "It's true, I'm leaving for another position."

"Congratulations. Can you tell us what the new job is?"

She shook her head. "Not yet. How's our field crew doing?"

"Good, they're still cataloguing new species in the first vent, and it appears the other vents have life in them too. We need more people." He smiled, knowing that wasn't in the budget.

"Please let them know I'm thinking of them and wish them well."

She left, promising to stay in touch with her old department and headed to do some shopping. She sent a message to Leana, asking for her company and advice. She was surprised when Leana responded, knowing she liked to sleep in.

"Sure, I'll meet up with you. Someone has to make sure you don't pick out clothes only your mother would approve of. Besides, there's something I need your help with."

———

Leana held up blue thermal leggings. "These would look good on you."

Writson looked at the transparent patches on the front thigh and held the leggings against her. "They're low waisted."

"No, they're not. They're the right fashion height for a pretty woman. Wear a top that shows off a bit of your waist, and you have an outfit."

"So thermal pants and a bare waist. That's a bit of a contradiction."

"Since when are women's fashions practical?"

"Alright. I think I've got enough stuff now. Now tell me how you need help."

"You remember the captain, Jaret?"

"Yeah, I recall him."

"He's missing. He stopped coming to the bar, and when I contacted the hotel he was staying at, apparently he hasn't been in his room for several days."

"And you were checking up on him because…"

"Because we are friends, and Martians take care of their friends."

"Okay, so you're worried about your *friend*. What do you want to do about it?"

"I want to find out what the hell has happened to him. I know the space line he works for, Gibbston, has an office here in Red City. I want to visit them and ask if he's alright. One person going to their office might get the brush off, but two *concerned* friends might make them release a bit more information."

"Okay, I'll go and help you."

The Phobos Building was a hub for many of the space lines and related businesses. The squat building featured spheres joined together to form an odd shaped building with one side taller than the other. The soft green exterior colour made it stand out from the more metallic and sand coloured neighbouring buildings.

Writson wasn't sure exactly how she was supposed to support her friend, other than being by her side. She followed her into the elevator and to the Gibbston Space Lines administration office. After entering past a set of clear doors, they came to a counter in front of a curved blue barrier with the Gibbston Space Lines logo attached. A skinny young man greeted them nervously. He quickly stood from behind the counter and smoothed out his black hair.

"How can I help you?" His eyes gazed between the two women rapidly.

"I hope you can help us. We're looking for information on a friend of ours, Captain Jaret McLeod."

"Captain Jaret McLeod?" He repeated, his nervousness growing.

"Yes, can you tell us where he is and what's happened to him?"

Several seconds passed, and Leana was about to repeat herself when he suddenly responded.

"I'll be right back." He turned and hurried past the barrier.

"Well, I think you may have scared him." Writson laughed.

"I don't know about that. You look pretty hot in that thermal suit." She paused, "Thanks for coming here with me. I have to admit meeting these big corporate people scare me."

The nervous receptionist returned with two people, a tall blond man, and a black-haired woman almost his height. Both were heavy in a way Writson recognized. *Martians.*

The blond man announced. "I'm Derik Holman, operations manager for Gibbston on Mars. How may we be of assistance?"

Writson jumped in, "Hi, I'm Nellie Writson, and this is Leana Strout. What can you tell us as to the whereabouts of Captain Jaret McLeod? We've been unable to reach him."

He raised a finger. "Nellie Writson. I saw you during that big announcement finding Martian life." He smiled. "That was a great discovery."

"I agree. Especially for those of us who believe that Mars is our home."

He nodded. "What is your status regarding Captain McLeod? Is this an official inquiry or a personal one?"

An official inquiry? What a strange question. "Personal. But why would you think it was an official inquiry?"

"I shouldn't have said that." He sighed. "I can tell you Captain McLeod is on a special assignment and is fine. He had to leave on very short notice."

"That's good to know." She took a few steps around the counter. She smiled. "Derik, what's going on that you're worried about an official inquiry? Do you need our help? One Martian to another."

Holman took several quick breaths. "The IEP has been in contact with Gibbston Mars Port. They are limiting communication from the ship Captain McLeod is on and our port."

"Why would they do that? Has Jaret done something wrong?"

"Quite the opposite. The IEP is trying to control where his ship is heading."

"Why would they be wanting to do that?" Leana demanded.

Holman looked at Leana and made a decision. "It's because of where his ship is located right now."

"Where is that?"

"Meili."

"How the hell did he get there?" Writson asked. "Isn't that a four or five year journey?"

"It was." He sighed. "I'm going to tell you this in case the IEP tries to shut us up, too. Captain Jaret McLeod is the captain of a prototype spaceship, the Hendrik A. Lorentz. This ship is capable of faster than light travel."

"Mother of Mars. And here I thought the discovery of advanced Martian life was big. We have to get Jaret home and without the IEP blocking him."

"I agree." Holman shrugged. "I'm not sure what I can do on my end. Everything is happening on Mars port, and I no longer have access to the Gibbston office there."

[36]

"What situation?" Wagner asked.

"Watch." McLeod replayed the transmission he received. After Wagner watched the video, she responded.

"I guess they don't like anyone knowing about Meili. Well, screw them. We will stay here as long as we want, and then return to Mars port. They don't have the authority to order us around."

"They have armed ships."

"I'll call that bluff. Fire on an unarmed civilian spaceship? I doubt it."

Well, at least I know why she's head of Gibbston. Lots of guts and a must win attitude. She must also be a hell of gambler.

"Jaret, we better let the rest of the crew know what we're up against. Then we can figure out what our best strategy is."

"Agreed. I guess we stay around Meili for a while longer."

The crew listened to the message from General Shatley of the IEP. At the end, a few of them swore. McLeod quickly interrupted their complaints.

"Look, just because they demand that we report to Argus Port, doesn't mean they have the authority to do so. We can choose to go to Mars Port instead, although there is some risk in doing so."

"There's a big risk if we do report to Argus Port." Combs added his opinion. "Who knows what they'll do to us when we surrender there. I think the risk might be smaller if we go to Mars

Port. Since we can travel faster than light, they won't know exactly where we are."

"No one wants to be debriefed by the IEP," Gill added.

"You're our captain." Dermott pointed at McLeod. "What do you think we should do?"

"Mars. To hell with the IEP and the attitude that they can order everyone around."

Shultz looked around at the crew's faces. "Anyone here wanting to go to Argus Port and not Mars?" She waited a few seconds. "Okay, motion carried."

The Hendrik A. Lorentz established orbit around Meili as McLeod, Shultz and Wagner met in the captain's quarters to discuss their strategy of returning to Mars port.

Shultz was of the opinion that it would be best to return by approaching one of the polar regions of Mars. "It would be an advantage for us as there is less traffic at the poles compared to the solar plane."

"That may be good in theory, but if the IEP does spot us approaching, they could claim we looked like a USO and had to use force to contain a threat," McLeod responded. "I don't want the IEP to have any excuse to fire on us. I suggest we monitor the space near Mars and find a ship approaching Mars port. It can be a passenger ship, or a cargo ship, but in either case we follow them in close proximity. That will prevent the IEP from taking any action against us."

"That may be safer than trying to avoid detection," Wagner agreed.

"I'll check the manifests for any ships approaching Mars," Shultz added.

McLeod asked Wagner. "Are you sure you're okay with this plan?"

"I have to be." She laughed. "I've learned the captain is in charge of the spaceship in space."

The Hendrik A. Lorentz continued its orbit around Meili, gathering data from the planet using various sensors. McLeod looked at images of the planet on his monitor when Shultz reported she had found a ship heading to Mars port.

"The N. S. Halifax is due to arrive from Earth to Mars port in three days' time."

"A passenger ship. Isn't it owned by the Fredericton corporation?"

"It is," Wagner answered. "I don't believe that will be an issue. It would be nice if we could find a ship owned by Gibbston, but this one will do."

McLeod made a decision. "We will maintain orbit around Meili for another sixty hours, and then move into position close to the N. S. Halifax."

"Does that mean we just relax while we orbit Meili? Should we respond to the IEP with any message?" Shultz asked.

"No. Our receiver automatically responds with an acknowledgement that the message was received. They know we read their message, but let's not tip our hand on what we will do next. In the meantime, I'll instruct Richard to disable the auto-acknowledgement feature of the receiver. No point in giving them the satisfaction of knowing if we receive another of their threats."

Thirty-two hours passed. The Hendrik A. Lorentz continued to map the frozen surface of Meili. Radar showed where oceans and mountains used to struggle to dominate the surface.

"It's hard to believe this world used to be full of life." Dermott peered at the monitor over McLeod's shoulder. "Now this."

McLeod twisted in his chair. "Yes, but we can imagine this world as it used to be. The images decoded from the satellite shows it was a lot like Earth."

The control room was quiet as the ship maintained an orbit on automatic pilot. Wagner, Shultz and other crew members stood around in quiet conversation, occasionally looking at the world below.

"Captain! We have USO approaching." Combs usual quiet composure disappeared. "It's a big ship and its within fifty-three kilometres and closing." He gasped as McLeod looked at the readouts on the monitor. "Shouldn't we try to run away or something?"

"No, I doubt that is a solution. Let's hail them instead."

"What should we say?" Combs looked incredulous.

"Try hello. No video, just as a text message."

Combs used his console to send a message. "I texted hello. Should I add we come in peace?"

"No, let's see what their response is first." He looked at Shultz and Wagner. "Any suggestions?"

Shultz stared at him. "You sure don't get nervous easy."

"We should record images and any communications." Wagner offered her thoughts. "If we are attacked, we need to transmit everything to Earth and Mars to warn them."

"Agreed." McLeod looked at Combs. "Better start recording and transmitting data now in case we are attacked. We may not get an opportunity later."

Combs' hand shook as he pushed buttons on his console. "Captain McLeod, I'm a bit scared."

"Richard, you're in control here. One step at a time. How big is their ship?"

"Eight hundred and twenty-three metres long."

Shultz called out. "The USO is now pacing us." She checked her monitor. "It's eleven hundred and seventy-three metres away."

Combs announced. "We just received a message from the USO. It's in English."

"Show the message on the monitors." McLeod, like the rest of the crew, stared at the screens.

'We are the Hallians. Hallia used to be the world we lived on. It is well that you have discovered Hallia. Our world should not be hidden. Your species has now advanced to the next level of exploration.'

McLeod looked at Dermott. "What does this mean?"

"I think it means they aren't going to blast us out of orbit. Also, maybe they're happy we found their old world."

"Good points. Richard, ask them why they haven't contacted us before."

"Okay." Combs reluctantly sent the next message.

A few minutes passed.

"We have a reply," Combs spoke quietly.

'We have contacted your leaders. They requested that we and other species do not make contact. This has been the way for a long time.'

Shultz frowned. "That explains the secrecy of the International Space Agency. They knew what the USOs were all along but didn't feel the need to tell us."

"The right to know," McLeod agreed. "Okay, as much as this conversation is enlightening, we need to make our way to Mars port before IPE decides to do something drastic. Ask the Hallians if they would make a journey to Mars with us."

A few minutes later a message came back from the alien ship.

'We are not able to comply with your request. To proceed to one of your planets requires an invitation from one of your rulers.'

Combs looked at McLeod. "Now what?"

"Inform them we will send a message to them later. Hopefully we can get either Earth or Mars to extend an invite to them. There has to be at least one leader brave enough to face the truth."

"Alright. I'll inform them we will attempt to contact them again soon."

"Wait. Ask them if they will remain around Hallia for twenty-four hours. That should give us enough time to talk to someone from one of our governments."

Combs typed in a new message.

"We have a reply." Combs looked at Jaret. "We shall wait."

"Okay, this is going to be a bit tricky." McLeod looked at Wagner. "We have sent the recording of our communication to Mars port, Earth and Terra Nova. The IPE could still stop those messages, or claim they were a hoax."

"True. They will still be planning to intercept us."

"The message will take six hours to arrive to Earth, so we will have less than that to get to Mars port before the IPE knows we have contacted aliens. If they find out we have been in contact with the Hallians, they may get even more aggressive to stop us. Are you able to find out which ships will be out around the asteroid belt? I'm specifically thinking of the Nebula."

"Your old ship. Yes, if you can get in range of the Terra Nova, I can use the Gibbston authorization code to see the status of our ships."

"Good. The Nebula is my first choice, but any Gibbston mining ship will do. I know most of the captains of those tin cans." He knew the odds of the Nebula being in space were good. The crews usually worked eight hours or more mining, followed by a twelve-hour rest period, followed by another shift mining. Without a defined night and day, the hours working the asteroid took up the bulk of a miner's time. "Mr. Combs, let's get moving to the asteroid belt. See if we can get within ten kilometres of the Terra Nova. Ms. Wagner needs to make an inquiry of Gibbston spaceships."

"The IEP will be patrolling that area."

"That's okay. We will need only a couple of minutes to get the information we need."

The Hendrik A. Lorentz turned off the Dowling field as the ship came to a stop near the Terra Nova. Lisa Wagner quickly used the Gibbston account to locate the location of their spaceships.

"Good news, the Nebula is currently out in space. I have its approximate location."

"Mr. Combs, let's make haste to those coordinates."

"Aye, Captain."

The Hendrik A. Lorentz coasted in space. The ship still moved at a high speed, but with the engines quiet they were less likely to attract the attention of the IEP.

"Captain, we're in visual range of the Nebula."

"Set up a ship to ship messaging." McLeod looked at the monitor next to the captain's chair and saw the notification the Nebula was ready for the short-range communication. "Captain

Trevor Roy, this is Captain Jaret McLeod of the Hendrick A. Lorentz." He saw the surprised look of Roy on his monitor.

"Jaret! How did you end up on this mysterious ship that suddenly showed up on our sensors? What kind of ship is the Hendrik A. Lorentz?"

"Trevor, it's a long story. But suffice to say the Lorentz is a unique ship, and the IEP is after us. I need your help."

"Sure thing. What can I do?"

"The IEP is looking for us, and any attempt we may make to communicate with Mars port. Can you relay a message for us?"

"For you, Jaret, no problem."

McLeod gave Roy the details of his message. "Thanks, I owe you a big favour."

"You don't owe me anything. Keep clear of those IPE bastards."

[37]

WRITSON AND LEANA WAITED IN WRITSON'S APARTMENT, deciding that sitting around the Gibbston's office might cause more problems if the IPE broadened their security measures to Mars' surface. As they sat drinking tea, Leana received a recorded communication from Trevor Roy. "This is a very strange message."

"How so?" Writson asked.

"It's from a guy, Trevor Roy, that I don't recall ever meeting, but he's acting like he knows me. Something about looking for ghosts on Mars and the time I took him home after he had too many rums to drink. That's really odd because...because that's what happened to me with Jaret."

"Jaret must be sending you a message by using this Trevor person. The IPE wouldn't be monitoring any calls from him to you. What else does the message say?"

"That he'd like to meet me at Mars port if he can dock without interference."

"The IPE is after his ship."

Leana frowned. "What can we do to help him?"

"Maybe I can call in a favour."

"From whom?"

"The President of Mars." Writson directed a call to the office of the President, requesting to meet with him on an urgent matter.

The receptionist took her request and promised to relay the message. "Now we wait some more."

"Exactly how close are you to the President, and why don't I know this about you?"

"It's a recent event. The President is offering me a new position to gather support for a new museum."

"Wow, that's a big deal. Why didn't you tell me?"

"Because it's not official yet. Please don't start yapping about it until an official announcement is made."

"My lips are sealed. Congratulations. I would say this requires a toast of some sort, but I think it would be wise to refrain from alcohol right now."

Writson's mobile chirped, and she immediately answered. "Mr. President, thank you for returning my call. We have an odd, and rather urgent situation."

Leana listened to Writson's half of the conversation, picking up only the faint buzz from her earpiece. After the call ended, she stared at her. "Well?"

"Good news. The President was not pleased the IPE had taken control of a portion of Mars port. He said that was beyond their jurisdiction and was going to send the Martian Peace Services to Mars port and order the IEP to leave the Martian space territory."

"That means Gibbston can communicate directly with Jaret again."

"There's more. Because the ship Jaret is on was actually constructed at Mars port, it is considered a Martian vessel. The IEP needs the Martian Space Security permission to use any force to detain it. That permission will not be forthcoming."

"That's great. Let's go back to the Gibbston office and see if there's anything we can do there."

***

The Hendrik A. Lorentz cruised closely behind and underneath the N. S. Halifax. Captain Oliver Lucan was not pleased at their close proximity. He also challenged why Hendrik A. Lorentz's identity and locator transmitter were shut off.

McLeod apologised. "I'm sorry, Captain Lucan, but we are attempting to avoid the scrutiny of the IPE. They have made threats against our ship and this crew."

"What have you done that you decided to use my ship as a screen? Perhaps I should send a message to the IEP concerning your location."

"Please, I assure you we have not done anything illegal. We have something on this ship that they want to keep for themselves."

"Can you inform us what this is?"

"No, other than it's technology that allows this ship to outrun anything the IPE has."

"Okay, just don't get any closer to our ship."

Almost an hour passed when Combs informed McLeod they had a received a communication from Gibbston Space Lines Mars Port Authority.

"The IPE has vacated Mars Port, and you are now free to dock. The communication blockade has been lifted as well."

McLeod looked at Wagner. "Do you think it's safe to go to Mars Port, or do think this may be a trick?"

"I wouldn't bet against the IPE trying something. How can we know for sure?"

McLeod paced around the control room, staring around and seeing nothing. "Mr. Combs, set a course for Mars at the one point three the speed of light. I want to stop five hundred kilometres under the south pole."

"Aye, Captain."

Wagner gave him a questioning look.

"When we reach position at the south pole, we can do a visual for any IPE craft. If we receive any threats from them, we can quickly escape. If we don't observe any danger, I will contact Leana Strout and ask her if the IPE are still at Mars Port."

"The same woman you had Trevor Roy contact."

"Yes. She has a way of getting information."

Leana looked at Writson. "Guess who." She pointed at her earpiece.

"Jaret?"

Leana nodded. "Hello, Jaret. Coming over for a shot of rum?" She listened to his reply. "Oh, it's safe alright. The President of Mars told the IPE to scram. That, my friend, was the doing of Nellie Writson. I tell you, that girl has connections."

When Leana ended her call to McLeod, she pointed a finger at Writson. "Now you have a dinner date to get ready for. Don't bail on this one."

Writson hurried to change into her new thermal pants and top. She decided to use a touch of makeup and made her way to meet Paul Norris at Normand's Grill. Norris was already at the table waiting for her, with a half-finished glass of beer on the table. "You made it."

"Of course, I was looking forward to our dinner. I wouldn't want to stand you up, although I'm a bit late."

"You're worth waiting for."

"Thanks." She waited as the server took her order for a drink and gave her time to look over the menu. "Paul, there's something I want to tell you."

"There's something I want to tell you too. You go first."

"This is big. I want to tell you because the news should be out fairly soon. Our President had to put his foot down on the IPE, telling them they do not have any authority in Mars space."

"Really? What happened that he had to do that?"

"A spacecraft registered at Mars Port may have achieved faster than light travel."

"Seriously? That is one hell of a news story."

"It is. What did you want to tell me?"

"This isn't a news story, but what I want to tell you is I really like you and have for a long time."

"Somehow, my news doesn't seem as important right now." She smiled. "I really like you too."

"Wait until you've tried the dessert here. You'll really like me then."

━━

McLeod studied the readouts on his monitor, commenting to Combs, "It looks like the IPE is staying their distance from Mars Port."

"They are. We are receiving a message from the IPE." He glanced at the text message on the screen. "It appears they are requesting an immediate dialogue with us before proceeding to Mars Port. How should I respond?"

"Inform them we are done speaking with them."

"Yes, sir."

"Set a course for Mars Port. It's time to celebrate."

MCLEOD JOINED HANDS WITH DERMOTT. "READY TO celebrate?"

"I sure am. It was great watching those Jefferson's Sevens perform."

He laughed. "I meant being the first human spaceship that broke the speed of light."

Dermott giggled. "Okay, that too."

The crew disembarked from the Hendrik A. Lorentz, with Lisa Wagner leading the way. McLeod stayed at the back, respecting the tradition of the captain being the last to leave the ship. He heard the applause from those in Mars Port. He recognized several people from Gibbston's, and also the uniformed men and women of the Martian Peace Service. They were also applauding as he exited the spaceship with Dermott.

Lorraine Olineck, the operations manager of the Mars Port Gibbston's Space lines office, stepped forward to shake his hand.

"Congratulations, Captain McLeod, on a most extraordinary achievement. Everyone here is proud of your ship, your crew and your accomplishment." She gestured to the Martian Peace Service. "The Martian Peace Service ensured the Interplanetary Enforcement Police was not going to interfere with your docking."

"Thank you. The IEP was causing us some concern."

"The President also offers you congratulations and would like to personally meet with you tomorrow."

McLeod and the other crew members shook hands with those greeting them. Amongst those was Leana.

"Thanks for helping us out. I hoped you could figure out who was actually sending you the message for help."

"Who else do I know that drinks too much rum? I'm going to close the bar for a private party tonight for you and your crew. Tell your crew to change into casual clothes and come on down to Opus. Drinks are on me."

Lisa Wagner sipped her drink slower than most of the celebrating people in the bar. She had decided to wear one of the fashionable thermal suits, liking how they fit. She knew that as the C.E.O. of Gibbston's she would receive a few stares for wearing the bright fuchsia suit with selective cut-outs. Wagner made a point of saying hello to all the crew members of the Hendrik A. Lorentz, as well as those of Gibbston Mars Port office.

"Hello, we haven't been introduced yet. I'm Nellie Writson."

Wagner appraised the woman who had approached her, determining quickly she was a Martian. She had noticed she came in with another Martian, and the two appeared to be a couple. "Lisa Wagner. How do you fit in with our diverse group here?"

"I'm a friend of Leana's and I've met Jaret before through her."

"Are you the one who contacted the President for help?"

"Yes, fortunately I work for his office."

"May I ask in what capacity?"

"It's a new position. I am to promote the funding of a new museum. We require help from private enterprises to cover some of the costs, so my job is to speak nicely to those with the ability to provide financial assistance."

"Tell me more about this new museum."

Leana went over to McLeod and Dermott. The couple had been almost inseparable since they entered the bar.

"Well, space cowboy, it's good to know you were alright all along. I was worried about you when you disappeared."

"I'm sorry. I wasn't allowed to say anything."

"I understand," said Leana. "But do you remember my telling you on Mars we have to take care of each other?"

"I do."

"Well, your pretty friend here should not be going back to her hotel alone tonight. That would be dangerous for her. I suggest you make sure you take her to your hotel tonight for her own safety."

"I shall do that." McLeod put an arm around Dermott's waist. "I don't want anything bad to happen to her."

EPILOGUE

THE PRESIDENT OF MARS STARTED ON ANOTHER CUP OF coffee. Like the previous evening, he was prepared to work as long as he was able to stay alert. The Hallian ship was orbiting Mars, and he wanted to squeeze as much time with the Hallians before they had to depart.

One of his many things to do was to meet with the various governments of Earth, and for the first time Mars was in the superior bargaining position. Captain Jaret McLeod and his fiancée, Tia Dermott, were going to lead the delegation to visit the world the Hallians were now living on. The Hendrik A. Lorentz was not as fast as the alien spaceships, yet, but could still make the round-trip journey in a few weeks.

On his monitor another message came up concerning the Lisa A. Wagner Museum of Natural Mars. Nugent smiled at the memory of his conversation he had with Nellie Writson a few days ago.

"So many changes. We now have faster than light travel. We have met the Hallians, but there are other alien species we have not met. Tell me, Nellie, how do you think this will turn out for humans?"

"We will do just fine. We will adapt to change as we have done before."

"What makes you certain of this?"

"Mr. President, it is in our genetic make-up to succeed."

"You mean our human DNA."
"No, sir. Our Martian DNA."

THE END

Don't miss out on your next favorite book!
Join the Melange Books mailing list at
www.melange-books.com/mail.html

THANK YOU FOR READING

Did you enjoy this book?

We invite you to leave a review at the website of your choice, such as Goodreads, Amazon, Barnes & Noble, etc.

DID YOU KNOW THAT LEAVING A REVIEW...

- Helps other readers find books they may enjoy.
- Gives you a chance to let your voice be heard.
- Gives authors recognition for their hard work.
- Doesn't have to be long. A sentence or two about why you liked the book will do.

ABOUT THE AUTHOR

For a few years I wanted to try my hand at writing but too many obstacles prevented me from having the time to do so; three boys and a darling wife that loved home renovations to be more specific. Now the boys have "grown up" and left home I have time to do a bit more what I want to do, such as writing. My other interests include wine, reading, astronomy, photography and convincing my wife that our home is actually fine the way it is. I have actually lost that battle. She wants our deck replaced; apparently rotten boards isn't considered safe anymore.

www.jhwear.com

 twitter.com/JH_Wear

ALSO BY J. H. WEAR

Novels

A Taste Of Murder

Play Dead

Witches and Warriors

Shadows And Sensations

Castle Series

#1 Fall to Domum

#2 The Curse of the Dacron Gem

#3 The New King (coming soon!)